T0028963

UNCONDITIONAL REVENGE

LAURA SNIDER

SEVERN RIVER
PUBLISHING

Severn River Publishing
www.SevernRiverBooks.com

This is a work of fiction. Names, characters, businesses, places, events and incidents are either the products of the author's imagination or used in a fictitious manner. Any resemblance to actual persons, living or dead, or actual events is purely coincidental.

ISBN: 978-1-64875-447-0 (Paperback)

ALSO BY LAURA SNIDER

To find out more about Laura Snider and her books, visit

severnriverbooks.com/authors/laura-snider

PROLOGUE

Monday, August 29, 2022

Screams echoed from somewhere in the distance. Penny covered her ears and curled her knees to her chest, trying to make herself as small as possible. She was under her desk. She'd been there since Mrs. Morrison had shouted, "Active Shooter. *Hide!*"

There was silence in Penny's classroom, punctuated by the rat-a-tat-tat of gunfire somewhere else in the building. It reminded her of Black Cat Fireworks, the kind that made those sharp, bone-shattering booms without the pretty shot of sparks. But this sounded like someone had lit a whole set all at once, then another, and another, and another. Penny hated those fireworks. They hurt her ears and scared the neighborhood dogs. But she was quickly learning that she hated the sound of gunshots more.

"Nancy," a small voice came from the desk next to hers. It was Morgan, the girl who sat beside Penny.

Nancy was Penny's legal name. Penny was a nickname based on her hair color. It was a shiny, reddish brown like a copper penny. She only shared her nickname with friends. Morgan seemed like a nice girl, the type of person who could become a friend, but it was only the second week of school. There hadn't been enough time.

"Shhh," Penny said. She knew how to hide. Hiding was part of her home life. It was now, apparently, a part of her school life as well. It required two basic things. One, get behind or under something large, and two, say nothing.

"I'm scared."

"Shhh," Penny repeated. The sound of her own voice hissed in her ears, loud in the silence of the room. Shushing Morgan didn't feel good, but Penny's mother had talked to her about these situations many times. They'd even gone so far as to practice them. Penny knew what to do. She was supposed to hide. To sit still. And most importantly to never, ever, say anything. Hadn't Morgan's mother taught her the same thing?

Penny popped her thumb in her mouth. It was a bad habit, one Penny's mother had worked tirelessly to stop before Penny started Kindergarten. She was worried that the other kids would make fun of Penny. She had said it could affect Penny's social life for the remainder of her school years. Penny wasn't too concerned about that, but she'd worked hard to put an end to the habit all the same, mostly to appease her mother. She'd deprived herself of that daily comfort for a full month before school started, and she didn't even crave it anymore. Except, here she was, back at square one.

The building was once again quiet. An eerie stillness settled over the classroom. Then Penny heard something that had the hair on the back of her neck standing on end. Boots. The unmistakable *clunk, clunk, clunk* of large boots approaching Penny's classroom. The sound grew louder and louder until there was a pause. Penny held her breath.

What's happening? She had to know. This not knowing, it was the worst part so far.

From her position under her desk, she could see the bottom quarter of the doorway. She peered through the legs of her chair. She could see a pair of large, black combat boots. Man sized. They were in the center of the doorway, pointed toward her classroom. The silence stretched as the man stood silent. There was a shuffling sound and then Penny saw it. It was the tip of the gun, long and cylindrical, pointed toward the ground.

Penny's heart raced, pounding in her chest. She was trapped. It reminded her of the time a rabbit got caught in the chain link fence in her front yard. It must have been frightened by another animal and it had shoved itself through the fence, trying to get away, only to have its larger hindquarters stuck tight. It had died there.

Penny's mother had told her that the rabbit had pushed so hard while trying to get away that it had squished its insides. At the time, Penny hadn't understood how an animal could possess that kind of desperation to flee. Now she understood. She had an overwhelming urge to run, but she remained still, reminding herself that she did not want to squish her insides.

The boots and the gun lingered in the doorway for another long moment, then they started to turn away. First one foot, then the other, turning to the side slowly, ever so slowly.

Then someone within Penny's classroom issued a whine. Not the normal type of kid whine, but a keening animalistic sound, once again reminding Penny of the rabbit. It would have called for help in those last moments, wouldn't it? Asked for its mother. Penny wanted her mother, too.

The sound came again, but this time it was more of a whimper. A whine like a dog begging for food.

No, no, no, Penny thought.

That was all it took. The boots turned back and strode into Penny's classroom. Determined.

1

ASHLEY

Two Months Earlier
Friday, June 24, 2022

Ashley stared down at the decision, *Dobbs v. Jackson Women's Health Organization*, dumbfounded. It was long, but she'd read through every single page hunting for an explanation other than *we've been wrong for fifty years* but finding none. It was the Supreme Court Decision referred to as the abortion decision. It overturned *Roe v. Wade*, making fifty years of court decisions obsolete.

Ashley had printed it rather than reading it on her computer screen. It was too important, she needed to hold it in her hands, to feel its power. But now, after reading Justice Alito's savage castration of the court system, she couldn't drop it quickly enough. Words had always been powerful things. She'd never believed the whole *sticks and stones* adage she'd grown up with, because words could hurt. And these words, they would lead to oh-so-much damage.

You should have expected it, she chastised herself. She should have been prepared. The decision was leaked in April and there had been an uproar. Media outlets, social and professional, had exploded with outraged women

—and even some men—demanding that the government stay out of their bodies and their homes. While Ashley shared their concerns about the decision, her primary basis for outrage was less political, more cerebral.

Ashley saw the leaked decision and thought, *Impossible. That will not be the final decision*, but for entirely different reasons than those who had taken to social media, demanding the right to choose. Of course, she wasn't exactly surprised that politics had pushed for the overturning of *Roe v. Wade*, especially considering the politicization of the court and the political leanings of the justices. Ashley did not see herself as political, she was legal-minded. She only paid attention to politics when they got in the way of the law, which, unfortunately, was starting to happen more and more.

What surprised Ashley was that the only reason provided by Justice Alito for overturning fifty-years of precedent was, *we made a mistake and kept making it*. The Court had apparently come to the decision that they had been wrong and allowed a wrong ruling to stand for fifty years. It was like solid ground turning into quicksand while you stood there, then sucking you down without warning. It was absolutely insane. A completely foreign concept to Ashley's legal mind. If the court was wrong about that, if they were wrong for fifty straight years, then what else did they get wrong in those fifty years?

It threw the whole court system into chaos. What about *Gideon v. Wainwright*? That decision was fifty-nine years old, and it stated the Sixth Amendment required court appointed counsel for those who could not afford an attorney. That was the decision that created the basis for the public defender system. Ashley was a career public defender. She knew her job was important. She also knew her job was unpopular. Would it be the next subject of attack by the Supreme Court? Nobody knew, and that was the root of Ashley's unease with the *Dobbs* decision.

A soft rap of knuckles against Ashley's office doorframe pulled Ashley out of her thoughts. Ashley's friend, Katie, stood in her doorway. Katie was a former police officer turned private investigator. She and her father ran *Mickey and Michello Investigations*. They shared an office with Ashley, occupying two of the empty spaces in the public defender's office for their business.

"You okay?" Katie asked.

Ashley nodded. "I mean as *okay* as I can be, considering." She gestured to the opinion laying face up on her desk.

"It's a blow," Katie said. "A lot of people are upset about it. I always thought the government couldn't take rights away. I mean, if it exists, it seems like it should always exist."

"Yeah, me too," Ashley said. She dropped her hands to the side, allowing them to hang limply. It was draining. Oh, so draining.

They fell into an uncomfortable silence. Ashley didn't know what to say. The world felt full of bad news followed by worse news. There was a pandemic, tensions with China, a war in Ukraine, soaring oil prices, and sky-high inflation that only seemed to be getting worse. And now this. It didn't seem like things could get worse, even though they could. They always could.

"Do you know Vivian Ross?" Katie tactfully changed the subject.

"Umm, yeah," Ashley said, grateful for the topic reprieve. Her head hurt. She needed to focus on something more normal. Knowledge of Brine, Iowa, locals was a perfect choice. It was a small town and she'd grown up there. She knew *something* about almost everyone. "I mean I don't know her well. She's married to one of the attorneys in town."

"Do you know her husband?"

"Bruce? A little. We went to school together, but we weren't friends then, and we aren't friendly now. He's one of those political movers and shakers. You know the kind. They spend all their time at events, hobnobbing with legislative types. He's the exact type of person who was behind the scenes pulling at the strings of the *Roe v. Wade* decision, slowly unraveling it until it was overturned."

"I was trying to give you a break from the *Dobbs* decision. Aren't you tired of thinking about it?" Katie said, furrowing her brow.

"I am. Sorry. What I mean to say is that I don't know Bruce well. I know he has family money. That firm he's in was started by his great-great-great-grandfather. It's been passed down from daddy to son. Generational wealth," Ashley said with a scoff. "I've never spent much time with him, but I've heard he's not much of an attorney. I hear his partners go to one of the country clubs in Des Moines and grumble about him. He doesn't want to do the work. But that's what happens with generational wealth—they're spoiled and lack work ethic. It's a curse if you ask me."

"Do you ever talk to Bruce?"

"No. I've seen him at a function or two, but he does property work, and I'm a lowly public defender, so we don't have much in common."

"You're both attorneys."

"And that's where the similarities end. He's one of those posh private practice attorneys who makes lots of money. Or at least he *pretends* to make lots of money. He thinks he's better than me. Never mind his complete inability to practice in a courtroom in front of a jury. He's still considered the real lawyer while I'm a 'public pretender.'"

Katie rolled her eyes. "I hate that term. It's unoriginal." She was right. It was overused and overdone. People were so uninspired with their insults these days. "What's your impression of Bruce Ross's personality? You obviously don't respect him as an attorney, but what about as a person?"

Ashley shrugged.

"You have an opinion. I know you do." Katie took a few steps into Ashley's small office and plopped into one of the chairs facing her desk.

"I always have an opinion."

"So, out with it."

"He's arrogant and chauvinistic. The type of person who thinks the world revolves around him. Why are you suddenly interested in the Ross family anyway?"

"Vivian scheduled a meeting with me today."

Ashley cocked an eyebrow. "A meeting. With you. Has she lost a Birkin Bag that she wants you to track down?"

"I hope not. That would be a horrible job. Do they have the kind of money to drop $30,000 on a purse?"

"You better not call it a *purse* in front of her. It's a bag—a Birkin Bag— and who knows. He acts like they have all the money in the world, but you never can tell with people. Looking rich is not the same thing as being rich."

"True."

Katie's expression grew distant, and Ashley instantly regretted her words. Katie knew that lesson all too well. She had learned it at a young age. She had been "rich" all the way up until shortly after her sixteenth birthday when the government indicted Katie's father for financial crimes and sent him to prison. Over the years, she'd told Ashley about how her family had fractured and broken, leaving Katie to fend for herself. She'd said she went from having everything to absolutely nothing overnight.

"We're getting off track here," Ashley said, trying to pull Katie out of her thoughts. "My point is that they seem to live perfect lives. He is the high-powered, high-priced lawyer and she's the trophy wife. At least that's what they present to the world."

"She might be more of a Stepford wife."

"What gives you that impression?"

Katie shrugged. "Sometimes when a family puts the 'perfect' image out there in public, they are the ones who have the most problems."

"True." Ashley's phone started ringing. She gave Katie the *one-minute* signal and picked up the receiver. "Hi, Elena, who is it?"

Elena was Ashley's longtime office manager. She was young and bubbly, but also quite efficient and intelligent. She was the daughter of immigrant parents, fluent in both English and Spanish. She'd been only eighteen when Ashley hired her, but she had proven invaluable.

"It's the governor's office." Elena sounded out of breath with excitement. "They want to schedule your interview for the judgeship."

Judge Ahrenson, the local District Court Judge, was retiring, and Ashley had applied for the position. She hadn't planned to make a job change, but Judge Ahrenson had urged her to apply. She had thought there was no way in hell she'd get through the judicial nominating committee—not with her reputation—but she'd been wrong. Two names came through committee, and hers was one of them. The governor would choose who got the position after an interview.

"One minute," Ashley said to Elena. She lowered the receiver and turned to Katie. "Sorry. I've got to take this."

Katie stood, unperturbed by the interruption. "That's fine. Vivian should be here soon anyway."

"Let me know how it goes with her. I'm curious about Brine's golden couple."

"I'll tell you what I can," Katie said.

"Deal."

Katie strode out of Ashley's office and Ashley brought the phone back to her ear. "Alright, Elena. Patch me through."

2

KATIE

Katie wandered back down the dimly lit hallway toward the front of the office. Some of the lights had gone out, but nobody bothered to change the bulbs. It was like everyone had collectively entered into a game of chicken where each person was waiting for the other to tire of the darkness first. They were down to one lightbulb out of three. Someone would have to cave soon.

"Katie," Elena's voice drifted down the hallway. She was standing in the reception area, squinting as she peered in Katie's direction. "Is that you?"

"Yeah," Katie said, picking up her pace. "Is my appointment here?"

Elena nodded.

Katie emerged from the hallway, blinking several times. "What time is it?"

"Almost nine o'clock on the dot."

"She's punctual," Katie said.

"Is that a bad thing?"

"Depends," Katie said as she made her way to the front counter, stopping a few steps away. She could see a pregnant woman with a little girl seated in the waiting area. They were both sitting on the couch, pressed so closely together they seemed connected. Vivian Ross and a child. One was expected, but not the other.

"She brought a kid?" Katie said to Elena, keeping her voice low.

"Looks like it."

"You've got to be kidding me. What am I going to do with a child during the meeting? I can't take her back there."

Elena shrugged. "I can watch her. She seems pretty chill to me."

Neither Vivian nor the child had noticed that they had an audience, which was to Katie's advantage. It gave her an opportunity to openly observe and assess her potential client. The couch was large, which made the positioning of mother, and—Katie assumed—daughter, odd. They were scrunched together like the act of separating them would not only lead to tragedy, but it was the one catastrophe that they feared the most. This meant their fear was real, at least to them. Maybe they weren't mother and daughter after all.

Vivian held a copy of the *New Yorker* in the same way that the girl held her *Highlights* magazine, backs straight, arms up, neck slightly tilted down toward the page. When they turned pages, the girl's movements mirrored those of Vivian's in a way that reminded Katie of synchronized swimming. It felt like a performance rather than the simple task of reading.

"Vivian," Katie said, her voice echoing out into the silence of the room. Observation time was over. She needed to figure out the exact nature of this odd duo's visit. "Vivian Ross."

Vivian flinched, then lowered her magazine before looking up. The girl moved in tandem, mirroring her adult companion's movements like a tiny Vivian robot. It made Katie think of the creepy scenes with children in horror movies. Those were always the most disturbing. A shiver ran up Katie's spine.

"Yes? That's me."

"I'm Katie Mickey."

Vivian stood and the girl did the same.

"Vivian Ross," she said, striding across the room, her long legs carrying her in a way that seemed far too quick for a woman Katie guessed was at least six months into her pregnancy. "This is my daughter, Nancy. Say hello, Nancy." Vivian looked down at the little girl with such naked admiration that Katie felt uncomfortable, like she was imposing upon a private moment.

"Nice to meet you," Nancy said, grabbing the edges of her dress with the tips of her fingers and bobbing a small curtsy.

"Another red-head," Katie said, grinning at the girl.

Nancy subconsciously fingered the end of her long ponytail, the corners of her lips dipping into a faint scowl.

"There aren't enough of us if you ask me," Katie added.

Nancy looked up, her penetrating blue eyes locking onto Katie's gaze. She studied her as though trying to determine her sincerity. After a moment, she nodded and then smiled. "Mine is more copper than yours. That's why some people call me Penny."

"Can I call you Penny or should I call you Nancy?"

The girl shrugged. "I don't know yet."

"You don't know?"

"My friends call me Penny. I don't know if you are a friend yet or not."

"That's fair." Katie stood and focused her attention on Vivian. "I'm sorry, but she can't come into the meeting."

"She's coming," Vivian said. She held Katie's gaze in a challenging way as she reached over to grab the girl's hand, pulling her closer to her side, possessively.

What was it with rich people that made them think they were always running every show? This was Katie's show, not Vivian's. Katie was not asking for Vivian's help; it was the other way around. Sure, she needed business, but there was always someone in the area looking to snoop on a neighbor or ex, and it was shocking how much money they were willing to shell out to hire her to do it.

"Come on back," Katie said, forcing a smile while motioning for Vivian and Nancy to enter through the small break in the counter leading into the back part of their office. Even Katie knew Vivian couldn't leave her child alone in the front part of the office, but it was safer behind the counter. The area was controlled. A person couldn't pop in from the street and talk to the girl.

Vivian complied, but she did not release Nancy's hand or break eye contact with Katie. It felt like they were playing a hostile version of a kid's staring game. Elena seemed to sense the tension and came to Katie's side just as Vivian stopped, face to face with Katie. She was still holding Nancy by the hand.

"She's coming with us," Vivian said. "Penny is always with me. Always."

Katie shook her head and crossed her arms. "Then we aren't meeting. I have to be able to speak freely with my clients, and I can't do that in front of children. It isn't personal to you or your daughter. It's office policy."

Vivian opened her mouth to respond, but Elena dropped to her knees so she was eye level with the little girl, catching Katie and Vivian's attention.

"I've got some coloring books," Elena said. "And some colored pencils. Do you want to sit with me out here while your mother meets with this nice lady?"

Katie almost snorted when Elena described her as *nice*, but she kept her composure. She hated that word. It was almost exclusively used to describe women, and only when they were meek. Katie was not docile, and she certainly wasn't *nice*, but she did not correct Elena. It was better that the little girl considered her *nice*, even if it was a farce.

"What type of coloring books? I don't like Disney princesses." The little girl's voice was soft, but clear, enunciating every syllable like she'd spent countless hours with a speech therapist perfecting the English language.

"Princesses, pssssh," Elena waved a dismissive hand. "They are way overdone. Who wants to be a princess when you can be a warrior, right?"

The little girl nodded.

"Unfortunately, they don't make many warrior coloring books. Too violent."

Nancy nodded again.

"I do have an animal coloring book, though. One made by *National Geographic*. It's an adult coloring book, so it's got small parts to color, but you seem like you can handle higher levels of coloring."

"I can," the little girl said confidently.

Elena stood, turning back to Katie and Vivian, lifting an eyebrow as if to say *problem solved.*

"She's still coming." Vivian crossed her arms. When nobody responded, she added, "I mean, can't she come? Please." Vivian's tone had turned pleading. "I just can't leave her."

The little girl tugged at her mother's pant leg, drawing her attention. "I'm fine, Mommy. I'll stay right here."

"But..."

"I start school soon. You can't stay with me then. Let's pretend like this is a test."

It was a shockingly adult thing to say. If Katie wasn't already wondering about the relationship between these two, that would have done it. There was something off about this family. Kids were self-centered, rambunctious little beings. They didn't even seem to notice most things going on around them. Unless, of course, they'd been through some trauma.

"Pretend." A small smile crept into the corners of Vivian's mouth.

"Yes. Pretend." The little girl was smiling now, too.

"Alright," Vivian finally said.

"It's settled," Katie said, clapping her hands together. "Follow me, and we'll get started right away."

Katie waved a hand and headed toward her office. It was the first one on the left. Vivian followed, moving painfully slowly, but she eventually reached the office door, where she hesitated one last time, looking back at her daughter, before entering.

3

ASHLEY

"When I hang up, the Governor's office will be on the phone," Elena said.

"Who from the Governor's office?"

"A woman named Beatrice. That's all I know." There was a chiming noise in the background. "That's the door. Katie's appointment must be here. I've got to go. Are you ready to take the call?"

"As ready as I'll ever be." Ashley heard the click of Elena disconnecting, then waited a few beats before saying, "this is Ashley Montgomery."

"Ms. Montgomery, thank you for taking my call." The woman's voice was nasally and despite the natural meaning of the words, they came across as more of an accusation than actual appreciation.

"Umm, you're welcome. Who do I have the pleasure of speaking with?" She kept her tone icy, and she emphasized the word *pleasure* to indicate the exact opposite. Ashley could play the passive aggressive game as well as any woman. She usually gravitated toward outright verbal aggression, but today she'd decided to match this woman's energy.

"Beatrice Bunker. I'm the Governor's administrative assistant."

"Good for you."

It was a bitchy thing to say, but the haughtiness in the other woman's voice irritated Ashley. Why was she proud of her position anyway? Ashley would rather stab a pencil through her eye socket than work for the current

Iowa governor. Of course, she wouldn't publicly say that, at least not until after the Governor made her choice for Judge Ahrenson's replacement.

Two people had come through the Judicial Nominating Committee and would be presented to the Governor for final selection. Ashley, of course, was one. The other was the Brine County Magistrate, Mikala Mirko. Magistrate Court was the lowest of the courts, handling only simple misdemeanors and small claims actions. Judge Ahrenson's job handled major felonies and large lawsuits.

As a public defender, Ashley rarely appeared in magistrate court. She didn't handle simple misdemeanors. For that reason, Ashley was far more qualified for the position, but she knew as well as anyone that qualifications rarely mattered at this level. It was about politics, and that was one game Ashley had never learned how to play. But she had to try.

"I'm calling to schedule a date for your interview," Beatrice said, cutting through Ashley's thoughts. The woman's voice was high-pitched, but fierce. It reminded her of Miss Piggy, and she couldn't help picturing Beatrice as a pig with a wig.

"Okay. Let's get it scheduled." The reason for the call was obvious. Why else would someone from the governor's office call a lowly public defender like Ashley Montgomery?

"The Governor is available Wednesday, August tenth. You'll make that work." It was not a question.

"Will I now?"

"Yes. You will."

"What if I'm busy?"

"What could possibly be more important than meeting with the Governor?"

"Lots of things. My clients, for one. They depend on me. I have an ethical responsibility to them. I suppose the good Governor wouldn't know much about that."

"I'm not sure what you are implying..."

"Don't be coy," Ashley said, twisting the telephone cord around her finger, "you know exactly what I mean."

"If you are unavailable for the tenth, then how about Thursday, August eighteenth?"

"Nope. Won't work either." Ashley didn't even look at her calendar. It was more fun to fuck with this woman. Besides, she was irritated. The Governor was so presumptuous. Why did she assume that Ashley would shift everything to meet with her? Yes, she was the Governor, but she was of no more importance to Ashley than anyone else.

"This is highly irregular," Beatrice said, her tone growing impatient.

"Why? Because everyone else bends over backwards to work with Her Majesty's schedule? Well, I have other people's schedules to worry about and even though the Governor thinks she is the Queen of Iowa, she isn't. At least not to me. She may be that to most Iowans, but I'm not *most* people."

"Most people want to work with her schedule. She is making the final Judge selection."

Ashley could read between the lines. *Go with the flow or the Governor is not going to select you.* Well, it was highly doubtful that a Republican governor was going to choose a public defender, especially one with a history like Ashley's. Besides, Magistrate Mirko was already on the bench. She had more experience as a judge. She was the obvious choice.

"I'm not most people," Ashley repeated.

"Well, I'll have to speak with the Governor and get back to you. I don't have authority to offer any other dates."

"You should be more prepared next time."

"*Me?*"

"Yes, you. And the Governor, too. Listen, I really must be going. I *deeply appreciate* your phone call. We'll catch up soon, I'm sure."

"Quite."

"Ta-ta," Ashley said, then she hung up the phone, slamming it down on the receiver.

She sat there for a long moment, staring at the cradled phone. She might have completely blown what little chance she ever had to take the bench, but she couldn't help herself. That Beatrice woman had been so demanding. She'd expected Ashley to bend to her will. In that, she and the governor were sorely mistaken. She would never be a *yes-man* or *yes-woman*. Not to anyone.

What the hell was happening to the world? These days, it felt as though it was spinning out of control, and Ashley had no tools to combat it. In times like these, when there was so much turmoil, she'd always found solace in the unshakeable steadiness of the criminal justice system. It wasn't perfect, but she knew what to expect. Thanks to the *Dobbs* decision, that was even under fire. Where was she to go now? She needed to do something. She needed to fight back in some way, but how?

That was when the idea popped into her head. How does one person fight against the many? They become obstructionists. Ashley was good at that. She'd done it often, for various clients for many different reasons. But her new idea was on a far grander scale than the usual delay to avoid the imposition of a prison sentence. This plan would have major implications, both personally and professionally. Yet, she felt just desperate enough to try it.

4

KATIE

"Have a seat," Katie said, motioning to the two chairs across from her desk.

Vivian didn't move. She hovered near the doorway, casting furtive glances around Katie's small office. In that moment, this obviously wealthy potential client seemed almost pathetic. She reminded Katie of a once-beautiful, well-fed, well-kept housecat, abandoned and turned feral.

"Are you going to shut the door?" Vivian asked.

"Yes."

"I don't want that."

"Why not?"

"I just don't."

"Does this request have anything to do with your daughter?"

Vivian didn't answer.

Katie gave her a hard look, studying her features, as though somewhere in those dull, blue eyes and cold, sharp cheekbones, Vivian held a secret—one buried so deep that it would never come out in any investigation. They stood in silence for a long moment, then Katie sighed.

"Listen, I'm not trying to harass you. Closing the door is protocol. I share an office with the local public defender. She hires me for many cases, but I suspect that whatever brings you in today is not going to be one of them. Ashley's here. She could walk by at any moment." Katie paused, waiting for a response. When none came, she continued. "Our conversation is confidential, but it won't be unless I close the door."

Vivian hovered a moment longer, then she took a tentative step toward the chair closest to the door. There was a pause, then she took another step. It continued like that for an infuriating amount of time, both women remaining completely silent, until Vivian finally reached the chair and sank into it.

"Fine," Vivian said. "But Ashley Montgomery is part of the problem."

Katie closed the door, then walked around Vivian's chair to the back side of her desk, claiming her own seat. "How so?"

"I don't want her around my child. She's a public defender. She chooses to spend her time around bad people. That must mean in some sense that she, too, is a bad person."

"I disagree."

"Well, I don't want her around my child."

"Don't worry about that. Ashley doesn't want to be around your child any more than you want her to."

"What? Why not?" Vivian's perfectly sculpted eyebrows lifted, but her forehead did not wrinkle.

Botox, Katie assumed. Cosmetics like *Botox* and *Juvéderm* were becoming more and more popular, but they still hadn't completely caught on in the Midwest, especially in the rural communities. Most people weren't willing to pay the expense and take the time for the upkeep. Katie assumed they just didn't see a point in taking regular trips to Des Moines to shoot their face full of Botulism. The fact that Vivian was so invested in her appearance, especially while pregnant, meant something, and Katie made mental note of it.

"Ashley doesn't like children."

"She wouldn't," Vivian said. "But Penny is different. She's special."

"I'm sure she is."

"And I don't want Ashley around her."

"Like I said, your concern is misplaced. Ashley doesn't care for children."

"Okay," Vivian said.

"Anyway," Katie tapped the end of her pen on the empty notepad in front of her, "I understand your concern, but the sooner we get to talking, the sooner you get back to your daughter. Besides, you have no need to worry. Elena is good with children."

"Okay," Vivian said, but she didn't sound convinced. "Let's just get this over with."

"Sure. Let's get down to business. What brings you in today?" Normally, the Vivian sort of client—those with money and privilege—wanted to spend a good fifteen minutes on small talk. It was a waste of time, and Katie hated it, but that was part of the gig. Most people needed a little time discussing mundane, unimportant things before delving into the primary reason for their visit. The fact that Vivian did not choose the same route also felt significant. It could mean that she was desperate. But why?

"It's my husband."

Katie remained silent, careful to keep her features even, her expression impassive. She had heard this statement many times before, and it was almost always followed by, *I think he's cheating.* Her heart sank. She hadn't had high hopes that Vivian would bring her a more intellectually stimulating case, but there was that small part of her that had wondered. But no, this was going to be another one of those run-of-the-mill catch-a-cheater type of cases.

"What about your husband?" Katie would have liked to finish Vivian's thought for her, save them both a bit of time, but that wasn't how an investigator-potential client relationship was supposed to work. The information had to come from Vivian. None of it could be assumed.

"He's acting strangely."

Buying expensive cars, sudden interest in eating healthy and exercising, spending late nights at the office, out-of-state 'business' trips, Katie thought bitterly. It was almost always the same pattern. Cliché, but true.

"He's spending a lot of time alone."

"Alone," Katie repeated. This did not fit with the classic scenario.

"He has an office in town. He used to go there every day, but he doesn't anymore."

"Where does he go?"

"Nowhere."

"He's at home, and that's a problem?"

This was the worst part of Katie's job, listening to high-class women beat around the bush, too fancy to come out with the root of the problem. If Vivian was expecting her to read between the lines and figure out what she meant, she was wrong.

"Well, he isn't home, per se."

What that meant was anybody's guess. All Katie heard was *he's home, but he's not home.* "Is he still making money?"

Bruce was a lawyer in a firm in town. There were three partners in his firm and a couple of associates. He could have done something, unbeknownst to Vivian, that caused his partners to oust him, but it would have had to be something big. His great-great-great-grandfather started that firm. To push him out would be difficult and virtually impossible to keep quiet in a small town like Brine. Yet something like that would be embarrassing and potentially something he wouldn't want to tell his wife. Men like him almost always had an ego. That was precisely what Ashley had said about him—that he was arrogant.

It would be the simplest answer. A man's ego and a woman's exaggeration. When Katie was a police officer, she'd been taught that most of the time the simple answer was *the* answer. She'd followed that general rule until she met Ashley, who had taught her to start looking deeper. The simple answer, while sometimes the answer, was often not the whole truth. The world was far more complex than that.

"He's still making money." Vivian confirmed. "He's created an office out in the garage. In the second, detached garage. He had it built last year. I thought it was a waste of money, but he said we needed it for storage. He spends a lot of time out there."

"Define 'a lot' of time."

Vivian ran a hand through her glossy blond hair. The texture was fine, but it looked thick and healthy. If Katie had cared at all about her appearance, she'd be slightly jealous. The woman's hair was gorgeous. It was probably the baby. Katie had never been pregnant herself, but she'd heard plenty of women complaining while pregnant. Nice hair seemed to be the only positive side-effect of the affliction. Everything else sounded like a horrible disease—swollen hands and feet, vomiting, sleeplessness, weight gain, heartburn.

"He wasn't out there all that often at first," Vivian said, "but that gradually changed. At the start, it was Saturdays during the day. He said he'd created an office out there so he could keep up with overflow work without Penny disrupting him. Which was preposterous even then. Penny is not disruptive. She's a well-behaved young girl. Impeccable manners."

Katie nodded. Although limited, her experience with the little girl had been consistent with Vivian's statement. This was important because Katie needed to trust her clients. If someone came in with a request riddled with inconsistencies, however small, Katie wouldn't take their case. Although, her father would tell her *beggars can't be choosers*. She wasn't at the point of begging for business, but her father seemed to think they were.

"Like I said, the time Bruce spent out there slowly increased. It became Saturdays and Sundays. Then weeknights after work. Now, he's out there all day and nearly all night."

"But he's still making money?"

"Yes. As far as I know, he is. I'm a stay-at-home mother and Penny is in private Pre-K. We need his income. If I noticed any change in finances, I would have come much sooner, but his income seems to be stable. Better than stable, actually. Bruce acts like he is making more money than ever."

"Well, then maybe he is working out there. It sounds like he's doing something."

"That's the problem. His secretary has started calling, saying she needs to speak to Bruce. At first, she would ask for him in a normal manner. Polite *Hello's* and *can you please have Bruce ring the office*? I would have passed the messages along, but I couldn't reach him, so I'd take messages, and leave them on the counter. I don't know if he ever saw them. They just sat there, and eventually I would throw them away."

"You can't reach him?"

"He won't answer his phone, and I can't go out to his garage. That's why I've been calling it *his garage* because that's what it is. Nobody else can enter without repercussions."

"Repercussions?" Katie repeated. "Like he punishes you?"

"I tried to go inside one time and he shouted at me and slammed the door in my face. Then he locked it. I could hear the deadbolt sliding into place. Nobody else is allowed in unless specifically invited by Bruce. The door is locked and only he has the key. The shades are always drawn."

"He's secretive, but isn't that something attorneys are supposed to do— keep client confidences." Katie said this because she felt as though it was an option that must be explored. But even if this were true, she had to admit Bruce was going overboard. Ashley didn't even have that level of security with her files. This sounded almost paranoid.

"Yes, but I don't think whatever he is doing out there in that garage has anything to do with practicing law. The calls from his office have grown more insistent and frantic. One of Bruce's partners stopped by the other day, demanding to see him. All I could do was direct him to the garage. Of course, Bruce never answered the door."

"Hmm, it is an odd factual scenario. Does he suffer from depression?"

"Not to my knowledge, but he's not the same person that I married. I don't know who that man is out in that garage, holed up out there like the Unabomber."

Katie's eyes widened. Few people likened their spouse to a serial bomber. "Do you think he's dangerous?"

Vivian sighed heavily, rubbing her temples. "I don't know. That's why I'm here. I've got a child. Penny's safety is all that matters."

"A child," Katie said, looking pointedly at Vivian's swollen belly.

"This is not a child," Vivian put both hands around her belly and shook it in a way that looked like it might have been painful. "It won't be a child for a while."

"Fair enough." Katie didn't agree, but she'd learned long ago to keep personal opinions to herself. They didn't belong in business. "But why come to me? Why not go to the police?"

"Because I need someone who is subtle."

"Why?"

"One, because Bruce's income is all I've got. All Penny's got. If he is doing something illegal out there, I want to know about it so I can deter- mine how and when to intervene. The police can't just go crashing in there with search warrants."

Translation, Katie thought, *I need time to hide money so the government doesn't seize it as part of Bruce's potential criminal enterprise.* "So, it's about money."

"It's about personal and financial safety."

It was about money and control. Vivian really was a typical rich lady.

"Will you help me?" Vivian asked. Her tone was not quite pleading, but it had taken on a softer edge. But was it a manipulation or an honest portrayal of true desperation? Katie couldn't tell.

"I can help you, but I require a retainer of one thousand dollars. Do you have that?"

Katie tried to sound confident, almost demanding, but she hated asking for money. Before now, she'd never had a job that required her to do it. She'd worked at the police department, the government, then for the public defender's office, also the government, and her most recent employment had been at the mental health response team, and that was a nonprofit fully funded by a local family.

She understood that asking for money in this way was common for private practice attorneys and individuals in her private investigation profession. She'd get used to it one day, she just hadn't made it there yet. She did find it less bothersome when dealing with someone of Vivian's position, an individual who was flush with cash. She'd expected the answer to come quickly, cash exchanged, and that would be it, but to her surprise, Vivian's face crumpled.

"What is it?" Katie asked, studying the features of the other woman's face, looking for signs of deception.

"I don't have that kind of money. I expected a retainer, but I didn't realize it would be so much."

"I thought you said Bruce was making plenty of money. I think your exact words were 'he's making more than ever.' Or am I wrong on that?"

"You aren't wrong. He is, but he watches the accounts closely. If I remove a large sum of money, he'll know something is wrong."

"Are you saying you never buy expensive things?" Katie said, looking pointedly at Vivian's purse.

It was sitting on the chair next to Vivian. A soft pink, wicker looking bag with a Prada triangle in the middle. Katie had no interest in fashion, but even she knew that purse had cost at least four figures. Probably more.

Vivian followed Katie's gaze. "Oh that," she blushed. "That was a gift from him. And, yes, I can buy expensive things, but I have to use a credit card."

"I take cards."

"He also watches those statements. Probably even closer. Every month he grills me on one or two things that I've bought. He doesn't like it when I am wasteful. I can't imagine what he'd do if he saw a private investigator's fees."

"Hmm," Katie said, still staring at Vivian's purse.

"Before you say it, no, I can't sell any of my bags. They are worth a lot of money, but Bruce would know. He keeps track of everything he's bought for me. He may not realize I'd sold one right away, but he asks me about them sometimes."

"He sounds controlling."

"He's just thorough."

Katie nodded as though she understood, but privately she wondered about the truthfulness of Vivian's story. It wasn't checking out. Bruce couldn't be controlling *and* absent at the same time. It had to be one or the other. And then there was the comment Vivian made about her pregnancy. Katie understood the concept that life started at birth, but she'd never heard a pregnant woman characterize her pregnancy so negatively. It made her wonder what, exactly, was going on in that household, and that curiosity had her willing to bend the retainer rules a bit.

"Okay. So, what can you pay me today? And when will you have the remainder?"

"I can pay you five hundred today," Vivian reached into her purse and produced an envelope stuffed with green bills. "I've been saving a little at a time, stashing some when I make cash purchases."

"How long until you have the remainder?"

"Two months, maybe three."

This was the problem with potential clients, they didn't realize just how much work went into their requests. It required time, equipment, and sometimes a bit of danger. Besides, Katie was running a business. A retainer was a starting fee. Many clients went way over and had to pay more as the case progressed. One thousand rarely covered everything, and she couldn't work for free. She had a mortgage to pay and a cat to feed.

Vivian set the envelope on the desk and Katie picked it up, hating herself for caving so quickly. Vivian smiled, and Katie suspected she was being taken for a ride. But if she was, she'd find out. Vivian could count on that. Katie was bad at asking for money, but she always got to the truth.

"I can start work now, but I charge hourly. If I've billed five-hundred dollars, I'm not doing another second of work until after you've sent me the remaining cash. Got it?"

Vivian nodded. "Yes. Thank you."

"Don't thank me just yet. I can't promise a positive outcome." Whatever that may mean for someone like Vivian Ross. "All I can say is that I'll dig for evidence."

"That's all I ask."

Katie wondered if Vivian truly knew what she was asking. Katie would shake the proverbial tree, which in this case was a family tree. The problem was that nobody knew what was hidden in all the branches. They could be full of hornets' nests. It was likely that Vivian, or perhaps even Katie, would wind up regretting it.

5

ASHLEY

"Elena," Ashley called as she headed down the long hallway toward the front of the office. She needed to get a second opinion before she started wreaking havoc throughout the entire Brine County court system. "I have an idea, and I want to run it by you. On a scale of one to ten, how crazy would me filing motions to suppress in..." Ashley trailed off as she emerged into the reception area and found Elena with a small child.

"Sorry," Elena said, standing up and brushing a hand along her pants to smooth the wrinkles. She and the child had been sitting on the floor, coloring. "What's going on?"

Ashley's gaze shifted from Elena to the child, then back to Elena. "I wanted to talk to you about an idea that I had, but I didn't realize we had...company."

"Yes, sorry. Katie's client came with her daughter."

"I see."

Ashley was not good with children. She had no experience with them. She was the youngest child in her family, and she was never interested in babysitting as a teenager. Her only sister had one child, but they lived in New York State and Ashley rarely saw them. It wasn't that Ashley didn't like children; she just didn't care to connect with them. She was aloof, and kids reflected the sentiment. She couldn't—no wouldn't—raise her voice to use that chipper, annoying voice people used when talking to young children and pets.

"Is there something you need me to do?" Elena asked. "Nancy is pretty self-sufficient."

So, that's her name—Nancy. She wanted to ask, *What the hell was Vivian's reasoning for bringing a child to my office?* but she held her tongue. Cussing in front of a child was usually frowned upon. Even Ashley adhered to that rule.

"Umm, no." Ashley said.

She started to turn around without addressing the child, but the girl's small voice stopped her. She spoke quietly, but her words were clear and confident.

"Hello, there. My name is Penny," the little girl said, rising to her feet. She came toward Ashley with her hand extended like a tiny adult.

"I thought your name was Nancy," Ashley said, shaking the girl's hand. Her grip was surprisingly strong for such a small person, and she looked Ashley straight in the eye.

"It is Nancy."

"Then why did you say *Penny* just now?"

"Because my friends call me Penny."

Ashley raised an eyebrow. "We're friends?"

"Yes."

"Just like that," Ashley snapped her fingers. "We are friends."

Penny shrugged. "That's not usually how it works, but I like you. I don't know why, but I can tell I'm going to like you."

"Huh." Ashley didn't know what else to say. She was dumbstruck. No child in the history of children had ever liked Ashley. "You know, you shouldn't trust anyone that quickly. Trust is earned. It should never be given."

"See, that's why I like you. I knew you'd say something like that."

"How would you know that?"

"I just did."

"You got all that from a few seconds of interaction? I suppose you think you are psychic."

"What's a psychic?"

"Someone who knows the future."

"I didn't say anything about your future."

That was the one thing Ashley appreciated about children. They were literal, and they were honest.

"How about me?" Elena asked. "Can I call you Penny, too?"

"Umm," the little girl's freckled nose scrunched as she thought. "No."

"No?" Elena said, but she was chuckling while feigning offense. "Why not?"

"Because."

"Because?" Elena repeated.

"I mean, you're nice and all. I know that. I just don't know that we are going to be *friends*."

"Fair enough," Elena said.

"I've learned that trust shouldn't be given. It must be earned," Penny looked at Ashley through the corner of her eye.

"This one is a fast learner," Ashley said to Elena.

Ashley had never met a child like Penny. She was so small but acted so grown up. On the surface, that seemed like a positive thing, but Ashley had been in the criminal justice system too long to take anything at face value. Children were meant to be children. A grown-up child usually meant that the child had been forced to grow up for one reason or another, almost always by tragedy. A death of a sibling or parent at a young age. Cancer or other terminal illness. Ongoing physical, emotional, or sexual abuse. Something had killed their innocence. Ashley wondered what had happened to this little girl.

"My mom is here to speak to an investigator. Are you an investigator?" Penny asked.

"No," Ashley said, shaking her head. "I'm an attorney."

"Bruce is an attorney."

"Bruce?"

"People call him my dad."

"Is he your dad?"

"Biologically."

"Bruce Ross?" Katie had mentioned that she was meeting with Vivian Ross, so Ashley had known that Penny's father was Bruce Ross, but Ashley hated Bruce, the arrogant ass, and it sounded like Penny might share the same sentiment. She wanted to hear more.

"Yeah," Penny said. "He's the reason my mom is meeting with an investigator."

"Oh?" Ashley raised an eyebrow. She was torn about whether she should encourage Penny to divulge more information. It probably wasn't wise to goad a child into bad-mouthing their father, but she was curious. She also might learn something that she could relay to Katie. If Ashley knew anything, it was that clients were not always truthful.

"Mom thinks I don't know, but I pay attention. Bruce has been weird lately. Mom's been crying."

"Oh." That sounded a lot like Bruce was having an affair. Ashley hadn't seen Vivian when she came in, but she'd heard that Bruce's wife was pregnant with their second child. She'd be far along now. It should have been a reason for Bruce to dote on his wife, but some men took the exhaustion that inevitably came with pregnancy as an opportunity to find some action on the side.

"Nancy Reagan Ross," a harsh voice came from behind Ashley.

Ashley turned around to see Vivian Ross, standing with her hands on her hips. She looked almost comical with her back ramrod straight and her head held high, her belly protruding as she peered down her nose at Ashley. It was much the same way her husband had looked at Ashley in the past. Affair or not, these two had the same level of haughtiness. At least toward Ashley.

"What have I told you about talking to strangers?"

Penny nodded slowly. "I shouldn't do it. But this is Ashley. She's a friend."

"She is *not* your friend. Do you have any idea what type of people she associates with?"

"No." Penny's voice was small, growing smaller by the second.

"Bad people. That's who. Mean, horrible, people."

"Now, wait a minute." Ashley was not one to hold her punches. She had only held her tongue this long for Katie's benefit. Vivian was likely one of Katie's clients, one that would probably pay well. She didn't want to cause problems for Katie's business, but she also wasn't going to allow Vivian to speak about her or her clients in that manner. "Define 'bad.'"

"Excuse me?" Vivian said, raising her nose higher. Ashley couldn't help thinking she looked very much like a penguin.

"I said, define 'bad.' You characterized my clients as 'bad, horrible, people.' I want to know, in your holier-than-thou opinion, what is it that makes some people 'bad,' and others 'good?'"

"Criminals are bad."

"Why?"

"Because they've made poor choices. They've committed crimes."

"So, you think a person's goodness or badness lies in their choices."

"Yes."

"What about a drug dealer who deals drugs to support a family. Is that person bad?"

"Yes. He can support his family another way."

"Like what? Working at a minimum wage job? And I never said anything about *he* or *she*. Drug dealers can be male or female."

"He—*they*," she amended, "should get an education."

"With what money? Are you planning to support someone other than your own family member through college?"

"Well, no, but—"

"I didn't think so. Before you go making assumptions about others' 'goodness' or 'badness' maybe you should consider your own choices. You have far more financially than the average 'criminal.'" *Maybe* you should then consider your own 'goodness' or 'badness' since you are willing to turn a blind eye and ignore all the struggling individuals around you merely because they weren't born with a pretty face and a silver spoon in their mouth."

Vivian stared at Ashley for a long moment, her eyes blazing and her nostrils flaring. Then she turned to Penny and her tone softened a bit. "Come, Penny. It's time to leave."

Penny gave Ashley a sad smile, then she took her mother's hand and they headed toward the door.

"Did she hurt you?" Vivian was speaking to Penny, but her volume made it clear that her words were not meant for Penny's ears alone.

"No, Mommy."

Mommy, Ashley thought. Vivian didn't seem like anyone's "Mommy." She was far too self-absorbed.

Ashley watched as mother and daughter exited the office, side by side. They seemed so much alike in the way they moved, but deep down they were opposites. Ashley could see that in the short interaction she'd had with them.

"There's something off about that family," Katie muttered.

At some point during the discussion, Katie must have come out of her office and joined Elena and Ashley in the reception area. She now stood next to Ashley, side by side, watching as the two visitors left the office.

"Yeah, there is," Ashley agreed.

"I'm going to find out what it is," Katie said.

"Good," Ashley said. "Someone ought to." She would do it herself, but she didn't have the time or the patience to dwell on Vivian Ross or her arrogance. She had bigger problems. And so did all of her "criminal" clients.

6

KATIE

Katie watched Vivian leave with a heavy sense of relief. Her nonchalant delivery of insults was not bound to end well. Not with any of the women in their office. But just as Katie was turning to head back to her office, the small bell above the front door dinged. A man entered, but Katie couldn't see his face. His head was turned completely around as he shamelessly watched Vivian and Nancy walk down the front sidewalk. He stood like that for several long, uncomfortable moments. Then Ashley cleared her throat, catching his attention.

"You must be Oliver Banks," Ashley said.

The man turned to face them, and Katie got the first glimpse of his face. He was younger than she'd expected, probably in his early twenties, with mid-length, greasy black hair. He wore all black—black shorts and a black *Rancid* t-shirt. His skin was a never-seen-the-light shade of white, causing the small black teardrop tattoo below his left eye to stand out.

"Yeah," the man said.

"Then get in here and stop gawking," Ashley said.

"I wasn't—"

"Stop there," Ashley put a hand up. "We aren't going to start our attorney/client relationship with lies."

Oliver shut his mouth and closed the door, coming all the way into the office. Katie watched with interest. The conversations between Ashley and her clients never ceased to amaze her, mostly because Katie's original assumption—that Ashley excused the worst of their behaviors—was completely wrong.

"Come on back," Ashley said, motioning for Oliver to come around the partition and into the private part of the office. "We'll meet in the conference room. Katie," her eyes flicked toward Katie, "do you have a few minutes? I'd like you to join the meeting."

"Yeah, sure," Katie said.

The excitement was already building in her chest. By calling Katie into the meeting, Ashley was essentially hiring her as an investigator in Oliver's case. It would be true investigative work rather than the "catch-a-cheater" stuff that had been her bread and butter lately. The meeting with Vivian seemed to be more interesting than the run-of-the-mill private pay case, but that would probably turn out to be a dud. It would be an affair. Vivian probably already knew about it, but she wanted cold, hard evidence before she outed Bruce publicly.

Ashley led the way back to the conference room with Oliver following her and Katie at the rear. Katie took the time to study the man in front of her. Close up, she could see that his clothing was old, worn thin, and tattered in places. The garments hung off his rail-thin figure in a way that made it seem like he had recently lost a significant amount of weight. *Drugs,* she thought. He smelled of cigarettes, which was not common anymore, not with the invention and popularity of electronic cigarettes.

Oliver was too close to Ashley. He followed her at a suffocating, almost threatening distance. He was close enough for Ashley to feel his breath on her neck. What was he doing? Was he trying to intimidate her? To Ashley's credit, she didn't take the bait. She had to notice, there was no way not to notice, but she kept her cool and pretended as though nothing was out of the ordinary. Katie, on the other hand, wanted to grab his shoulders and pull him back, but she restrained herself. She was there to observe, to form impressions, and her first impression of this man was not positive.

"Have a seat," Ashley said when they reached the conference room.

The conference room was empty except for a long, skinny table surrounded by multiple roller chairs that looked to be straight out of the seventies. The upholstery on several of them had torn in places and Ashley had taped over the holes with duct tape to keep the stuffing from spilling out. Ashley didn't have the budget to buy new, so she had to make do with what she had.

Oliver sat at the far end of the table, the head, and Katie chose a chair in the middle. Ashley closed the door and sat opposite to Katie. The room was silent. Ashley had brought a stack of documents with her, and she placed them directly in front of her with a legal notepad next to it. She slid a second notepad with a pen atop it over to Katie.

Oliver didn't speak, which was atypical for Ashley's clients. They were almost always running their mouths, spilling their guts, proclaiming their innocence, and delving into the details of the events that led to their arrest. Ashley was almost always telling them to *shut up and stop talking*. Then they'd be offended. At least until Ashley explained her reasoning.

Ashley's first goal with these types of clients was to silence them because they almost always revealed some admission during their proclamation of innocence. It often tied her hands in their defense because she couldn't present evidence that she knew was untrue to the court. She was an officer of the Court, even as a defense attorney. A client who told her too much often ended up with her withdrawing as counsel. And the replacement attorneys in a rural area like Brine were not the cream of the crop.

The only way to avoid withdrawal was to remain ignorant of the assertions from Ashley's client's standpoint. She would go to great lengths to ensure that her clients did not tell her their version of events. They were not to tell her anything unless specifically asked. Ashley built her cases based on the police officer's investigation. She found the holes in the case and exploited them. Oliver's silence today meant that this was probably not his first arrest. The roughly made prison tattoo below his left eye only served to verify that sentiment.

Ashley handed a stack of stapled documents to Katie and slid an identical stack down the table to Oliver. "That's the Trial Information, the Minutes of Testimony, and the initial Police Report that was attached to the Minutes," Ashley said.

A Trial Information was a document used in Iowa in lieu of an indictment. The document had a caption that included the Defendant's name, date of birth, and picture. The document itself described each charge, ending with a list of witnesses. The Minutes of Testimony was a document drafted by the prosecutor, listing each witness individually, providing their addresses, their employment, and their expected testimony at trial.

"As you can see, you've been charged with three counts," Ashley said.

Katie studied Oliver's picture on the Trial Information. It was his booking photo, taken the night of his arrest. He looked mostly the same today as he did in the picture except he wasn't looking at the camera. His eyes were cut completely to the left as though watching something far off in that direction, but his head was still straight forward. All Katie could see was the whites of his eyes. It gave him a creepy quality, like he was only part human and there was something lurking below his skin.

"The first count is attempted murder. This is a Class B felony. You're no newcomer to felonies, but your criminal history indicates you are mostly acquainted with D's."

Iowa's felony system was rated by letters, like grades in school except they were opposite. A's were the worst. They were crimes that resulted in life imprisonment. B's were second worst with lengthy, often mandatory prison sentences, and so on down to the D felony which had a maximum of five years in prison.

"If convicted of Count I, it carries a twenty-five-year prison sentence. It is a forcible felony, which means that a prison sentence is required. You would also be required to serve seventy percent of that twenty-five-year sentence before you would become eligible for parole."

Katie's gaze cut over to Oliver, expecting some reaction, but saw nothing. He simply sat there, hands folded in front of him, watching Ashley with dull, almost disinterested eyes.

"If convicted, there is no fine associated with this charge."

Katie always thought that was odd. Fines attached to almost every offense except some of the worst offenses. It seemed like that was the opposite of what should happen, but then again, the worst crimes almost always resulted in prison sentences, and inmates didn't make much money.

"Count II is Felon in Possession of a Firearm. It's a D Felony, which typically carries a maximum of five years in prison with no mandatory minimum. It also carries a minimum fine of 1,025 dollars and a maximum fine of 10, 245 dollars."

Again, Katie looked at Oliver, but he remained impassive, wearing an almost pleasant, unperturbed expression. If Katie didn't know better, she'd think Ashley was telling him something completely benign, like describing a favorite restaurant or discussing the weather.

"*However*," Ashley said, pulling Katie out of her thoughts. "The State has added a sentencing enhancement on Count II. You've got two prior convictions for D Felonies. That means the prosecutor could enhance it under the habitual offender statute. Naturally, he did."

The prosecutor in this case was Charles Hanson. He'd been around for a while, battling Ashley at every turn. Katie wouldn't describe him as an overly zealous prosecutor, but he toed up to the line. Consequentially, Ashley and Charles did not get along.

"The enhancement turns your five-year sentence into a fifteen-year sentence with a mandatory minimum of three years before you would be eligible for parole. The enhancement removes the fine."

Oliver seemed far too young to rack up such an extensive criminal history, but he probably started young and went hard. People living his life-style—or at least what Katie assumed was his lifestyle—often did.

"Count III, the final charge, is nothing compared to the others. The charge is Driving While Barred, an aggravated misdemeanor. It carries a maximum of two years in prison with no mandatory minimum. The fine ranges from 855 dollars to 8,540 dollars."

"Okay," Oliver said, his voice quiet and even, but still strong. If he was cowed by the charges, he hid it well.

"That means your maximum prison sentence is forty-two years with a mandatory minimum of twenty and a half years. How old are you?"

"Twenty."

"That means, if convicted, you will be in prison for longer than you've been alive."

"Barely."

What an arrogant shit, Katie thought. He wasn't taking any of this seri-ously. It was a joke to him, a lark, but it wouldn't stay that way. Not if he went to prison. Ashley, though, was unperturbed by Oliver's attitude.

"You're right. The mandatory minimum is barely more years than you've been alive. However, twenty years is just the minimum. It is when you are eligible for parole. That does not mean you will make parole."

Oliver shrugged. "I know how the system works."

Katie couldn't believe it. He seemed completely unbothered by the news. Either something was wrong with this kid, which was a distinct possibility, or Katie was missing something.

Ashley slid another document over to Oliver. He lifted his index and middle finger, stopping it in front of him.

"This document is a written arraignment and plea of not guilty. I need you to sign it. Once I get that filed, the Court will schedule your trial and pretrial conference. You can choose to demand or wave a speedy trial, but I recommend that you demand."

"Okay." Oliver picked up his pen and flipped to the second page, signing at the bottom. He hardly glanced at the document.

"That's it," Ashley said, standing. "I'll make a discovery request, and I'll bring you back in when it's time to go through evidence."

Discovery was a fancy word for information. So, when Ashley said she was making a "discovery request," it meant that she was going to file a document formally asking the prosecutor to hand over everything he intended to use at Oliver's trial. Despite what Hollywood portrayed, it was a rare occurrence when there was any surprise evidence at trials. The rules of evidence did not allow for it.

"Sounds good," Oliver stood and headed for the door.

Ashley opened it and held it open for him. She followed behind him and Katie was right behind her. Oliver was a good five strides ahead of them, moving quickly toward the front door.

"Odd guy," Katie whispered to Ashley.

Ashley shrugged. "Everyone's weird."

"Not *that* weird."

Elena was at her desk. She ignored Oliver and continued typing at her computer. This wasn't rudeness on her part, she was just used to the office. She knew Oliver wouldn't need anything from her. Ashley would probably have all kinds of requests once her client was gone, but she wouldn't say those things in front of him. She probably wanted to finish whatever she was currently working on so she wouldn't have to stop in the middle of it to handle Ashley's new requests.

"We'll be in touch," Ashley said.

Oliver nodded, then disappeared out the front door.

Katie allowed a few beats of silence to pass, making sure Oliver was truly gone, then turned to Ashley and asked, "How is he out of jail?"

"He posted bond."

"How did he have the money to do that? Bond had to be astronomical, and the guy couldn't even afford a decent set of clothing."

Ashley shrugged. "That's none of my business."

This was one of the things that drove Katie crazy about Ashley's form of work. There were some things that Ashley willfully ignored. This was one of those things. If Oliver qualified for a public defender, it meant he had no money. If he had no money, then how did he post bond? Yet Ashley didn't care. She didn't even want to know. The reasoning was that Oliver likely came by that money illegally. It was something that wouldn't help in his defense. It also wouldn't hurt his defense because it wasn't admissible against him at trial. To Ashley, there was no benefit in wasting her energy learning the truth.

Katie was the opposite. It was almost painful for her to leave the question unanswered. Yet, she must. Her job was to support Ashley, and if Ashley thought they shouldn't know, Katie had to agree.

"So, what are the facts of Oliver's case?" Katie asked. She knew the charges, but she had no idea what led to them.

"Read the Minutes of Testimony. Then we'll talk."

"Okay," Katie said, but she was disappointed. "Can't you give me a basic rundown of what I'm walking into?"

"Just read. I want to know if your initial thoughts are the same as mine."

"Okay," Katie said.

Katie didn't like approaching cases this way, but it made sense. Ashley was a lawyer. She would not be able to deliver the information without putting her spin on it, focusing on some facts—usually those that were beneficial to her client—over others. She wanted to get Katie's true impression before Ashley clouded it with her lawyer talk.

"Take a look at the documents and think about it over the next few days. Then we'll talk."

"Deal," Katie said.

She spent the remainder of the day reading through the stack of documents Ashley had handed to her during their meeting with Oliver. The more she read, the more interested she became. The prosecutor seemed to have a solid case, but there were small fissures in the facts that stood out to Katie. She couldn't wait to discuss them with Ashley.

7

ASHLEY

Monday, June 27

"Oliver hit someone with his car," Katie said.

"Good morning to you, too, sunshine," Ashley said. "And allegedly. He allegedly hit someone with his car."

They were in Ashley's office. It was seven-thirty in the morning. Ashley had been there for a good hour and a half, but Katie must have just arrived and come straight back to discuss Oliver's case. It was a good thing. It meant Katie was interested. She would try harder in the investigation. Not that she didn't work her tail off in other cases. She was a work horse, better than any officer or investigator Ashley had ever met. But when Katie was fully invested in a case, she lived and breathed that investigation. It sounded like Oliver's case was about to become one of those cases, which was good because it was going to be an uphill battle.

"Don't even pretend to do the small talk thing," Katie said. "We've never wasted our time on that kind of crap."

It was true, but Ashley did have a bit of small-talk or at least small-to-her-talk that she wanted to discuss with Katie. "I heard you were out with George Thomason again this weekend."

George was one of the local Sheriff's Deputies. He and Katie had worked together as police officers before City Council defunded and scrapped the police department. They'd had a major falling-out back then, but George had worked hard over the past few years to regain Katie's confidences. If Ashley's sources were correct, he was gaining a bit more than her confidences these days.

"Don't change the subject," Katie said. "I want to talk about Oliver."

"And we will, but let's talk about George first. Get that giant elephant out of this room before moving on to the important things."

"Okay. Fine." Katie sat in one of the chairs across from Ashley's desk, crossing her legs and her arms.

"Don't pout."

"I'm not pouting."

"So, were you with George?"

Katie pursed her lips and stared at Ashley for a long moment, then threw her arms up in the air. "Fine, yes."

"Are you a thing now?"

"I don't know. We are seeing how it goes."

Ashley nodded.

Katie stared at her for a long moment, the silence stretching between them. "Alright, out with it. I know you have opinions. Tell me he's going to screw me over. That he's just using me to get a leg up on future investigations. I know you have something to say, so say it."

"Wow. I was not going to say any of that."

"You hate George."

"I *hated* George. You have noticed that I've stopped calling him Georgie and King George, right?"

"That's true. Now that I think about it, I haven't heard you say Sir George-a-lot in a long time."

"Exactly. I've buried my grudge."

"That's big of you."

"It's not *that* big. If he does anything to piss me off, I'm more than willing to dig it back up."

"Okay. I'll warn him of that."

"Good, and I'll warn you of one thing. No pillow talk about my cases.

You can discuss anyone else that hires you outside of my work, but not my stuff."

"I know," Katie said, narrowing her eyes. "I'm not a fucking moron. I realize that would be a problem."

Ashley lifted her hands in a gesture of surrender. "I had to say it. Now that it's said, I won't bring it up again."

"Okay. So, Oliver."

"Oliver," Ashley repeated.

"He hit someone with his car."

"Allegedly."

"Right, allegedly. There's only one police report attached to the Minutes of Testimony and the Minutes are pretty thin. Why did you want me to read it instead of discussing it?"

"Did you notice anything off about the case?" Ashley asked.

There was almost always something "off" about every case. Even the best of cases had loose ends that the prosecution never seemed quite able to tie up into a neat little bow. It was part of Ashley's job to find those holes and exploit them for her client's gain. Sometimes they were small things that didn't help all that much, but other times they were far larger. Ashley saw some potential holes in Oliver's case, but she wasn't sure on their size just yet.

"I noticed he was driving a BMW."

"Allegedly."

"Whatever. Can we just call this whole conversation 'alleged' events and stop adding that word to everything we say?"

"Sure. So, why did you focus on the car?"

"Because he supposedly has no money. You're representing him. How could he afford a BMW?"

"You're making assumptions."

"I'm not. I'm saying he has a hidden source of income, or the car belonged to someone else."

"Bingo," Ashley pointed Shooter McGavin style finger guns at Katie. It was so nice to have Katie back on Ashley's side. She caught these kinds of things right off. That was something that few people seemed to notice at first. "I need you to find out which one is true. If the car had a different owner, I need to know who it is."

"On it, boss," Katie said, already rising to her feet.

"One other thing."

Katie froze.

"If you do discover that Oliver owns the car, then stop there. We don't need to know any more."

Katie hesitated for a fraction of a second, then she nodded. Ashley knew Katie hated this part of the job. She was the type of investigator that wanted to follow every trail until she reached its end, but that wasn't always helpful in defense cases. It didn't matter whether Oliver was involved in something illegal outside of the present charges. They couldn't dig into how he was coming by so much money. That knowledge would not help aid in his defense. If it didn't help, it was a waste of time, and time was never worth wasting.

"I'll report back when I have some information," Katie said. Then she stood and left the office, leaving Ashley to go back to her other work.

There was a lot of it. Ashley had taken the *Dobbs* decision to mean that every prior court ruling was suspect, so she was free to file motions to suppress in every single case even if the basis of the motion was already settled law. Because what the hell, right? If one thing had been wrong for fifty years, so could everything else be. She had plenty to lose—the potential for a judgeship for one—but she also had to use every opportunity to help her clients. This was one of those rare opportunities.

She hated the *Dobbs* decision in more ways than one, but she was going to make the best of it. Her efforts could easily backfire, but she at least felt like she was fighting back in some way. It helped stave off the hopelessness of the decision. Her motions would clog up the justice system. It was like a lawyer temper tantrum, but in some ways the judicial environment made her feel like a small child. Just like a toddler, she held little power. A tantrum was all she could do, so she did it.

8

KATIE

Katie left Ashley's office, trudging down the hallway, deep in thought. If she was still a law enforcement officer, all she would have to do was call dispatch and they'd tell her the registered owner of the BMW. Of course, she would need the plate number, which she didn't have, but that would have been the only requirement. As a private investigator, she didn't have that resource at her disposal anymore. Or did she?

"Woah, there," Katie's father said, catching her attention.

She was so deep in thought that she nearly ran into him as he headed the opposite way down the hallway. Katie and her father were in business together, Mickey and Michello investigations. Katie's last name had once been Michello, but she'd changed it when she turned eighteen. Her father was in prison back then for financial crimes, and she'd wanted to be a law enforcement officer. She'd changed her name to sever any obvious connection between them. Michael had been incarcerated up until a few years ago, and he'd found her upon release, shattering her illusion of anonymity. Since then, they'd been working on rebuilding their relationship

"Sorry, Michael." She still couldn't bring herself to consistently use the word, *Dad*.

"What is on your agenda for today?" Michael said. His smile did not falter at Katie's use of his first name, but he winced ever so slightly. It was the only tell that Katie's terminology had bothered him.

"Ashley has a new attempted murder case that needs some attention. Oliver Banks. I was going to spend the day seeing what I could dig up on him."

"How did things go with Vivian Ross on Friday? Did she show for her meeting?"

He was changing the subject, which was his way of dismissing Katie's interest in Oliver's case. The Public Defender's Office only paid twenty-five dollars per hour for investigative work, and the firm charged one hundred dollars an hour for private pay clients. Naturally, Michael had little interest in Oliver. To him, the case was a waste of time.

"Yeah. She came. I was surprised you weren't here to greet her. Where were you by the way?" She lifted an eyebrow. He was the king of passive-aggressive digs, but she was learning fast.

"Did she hire you? That family has a lot of money."

"Allegedly," Katie quipped. "The Ross family allegedly has a lot of money." It was nice using Ashley's common response on someone else for a change. "And you are deflecting. You didn't answer my question. Where were you Friday when Vivian came for her meeting? You should have been here."

"I was working on some stuff," Michael said, waving his hand.

A flash of anger burst through Katie. "Did this *stuff* have to do with *our* business?"

"Yes, but it's nothing to worry—"

"Do not finish that sentence. We are in business together. This isn't some backward, antiquated business relationship where you make all the financial decisions and I remain in the dark. I'll decide what worries me."

Michael sighed and looked both directions down the hallway. Ashley was in her office and Elena was out front, but the hallway had a way of amplifying voices, even at a whisper. "Let's step into my office."

"We can go into mine." It wasn't a power play. They were right beside Katie's office and Michael's was a few doors down. There was no point in walking farther than they had to, or so she told herself.

Michael motioned in an *after you* gesture. She stepped inside her office and mimicked his motion, holding the door open as he passed and closing it behind him.

"So…" Katie said, crossing her arms, "what's the deal?"

"We are struggling a bit." He pulled at the collar of his dress shirt and loosened his tie. True to his generation—the dress like the job you want, not the one you have, generation—he wore a full suit and tie every day.

"What do you mean by 'struggling?'"

"Financially."

"Okay. How bad is it?" Katie had a mortgage to pay and a very fat orange cat to feed. She had responsibilities. "It can't be too bad, right? We aren't paying rent." Ashley was allowing them space in the Public Defender's Office free of charge.

"For now."

"What does that mean? Do you think Ashley's going to start charging us?"

"I think Ashley won't be around much longer."

"Woah," Katie put up her hands. "What, exactly, does that mean?"

"The judgeship," Michael said, leaning forward and raising an eyebrow. He didn't have a lot of facial hair, but his eyebrows were dark, bushy, and distinct. They reminded Katie of two very furry caterpillars.

"She won't get it."

"You sure are supportive, aren't you?"

"That's not what I mean. She deserves it, absolutely, but it's politics. The Governor must choose her. The Governor is a Republican. Ashley's spent the last fifteen years of her life spitting in the face of every Republican she sees."

"Literally?"

"No. Not literally. Metaphorically. But still. It's not going to play well. Plus, the other person that came through committee, Mikala Mirko, is a magistrate. She's already a quasi-judge. She's the natural choice."

"There's still only a fifty-fifty shot," Michael said. "Those odds are only marginally better than Vegas."

"Anything is better than Vegas. Those giant, opulent hotels aren't built from dreams. People lose some serious cash there."

"We are getting a little off topic here."

"Okay, okay. I see your point. If Ashley gets the judgeship, then we are out office space with no backup plan. Is that where you were on Friday?"

"Yes, but I've got bad news. Our finances aren't going to support any office space in the area and allow us to draw our salaries and remain in the black. That's why I was asking you about Vivian Ross. I know the Ross family has a lot of money. It would help if someone with some real spending power hired us."

"About that..." Katie's voice trailed off.

"What about that?" Michael placed his hands on his hips. "You offended her somehow, didn't you?"

"No." Although that was a fair assumption. Vivian and Katie's personalities were opposite. If they spent too much time together, Katie would likely say something offensive. "Vivian could only pay half the retainer."

"You allowed her to shortchange you?" Michael's tone remained even, but his words were loaded.

"She said she didn't have the cash. That husband of hers has her on a financial choke chain."

"She's not the only one that will be on a financial choke chain if our cash flow doesn't increase, and quickly."

"I get it," Katie said with a heavy sigh. "I'll do what I can to get the rest of the retainer. At least she paid me half. That's better than nothing."

"I guess. What does she want you to do?"

"Same thing as every other rich wife. Spy on her husband."

"Then you better get to spying. We need the money."

Katie harrumphed, but she knew he was right. Longshot or not, Ashley may not be around much longer. If she did ascend to the bench, there was no telling who would take her position and if that person would be amenable to their informal office-share agreement. Likely not. If that were the case, Mickey and Michello Investigations wouldn't survive the year.

9

ASHLEY

Wednesday, June 28

In Ashley's opinion, there were three types of clients. Those that never called their attorney, those that called incessantly, insisting that each new non-emergency was, in fact, an emergency, and those who relied upon their mothers to call. Oliver seemed to fall in the first category. Ashley hadn't heard anything from him since their initial meeting. Which was fine because she hadn't received discovery yet, so she didn't have anything to discuss with him.

So, the day had started out like any other. She was in the office early in the morning catching up on paperwork. She arrived early—red-eye flight early—and expected to have several hours of quiet time dedicated to the more tedious tasks of her job, but then her office phone started ringing. Ashley looked up, staring at the phone for a long, tense moment. The call had gone straight to her personal line. Few people had that number.

She debated picking up. It rang twice, then a third time, before curiosity got the better of her. She snatched the retriever and said, "This is Ashley Montgomery."

"I know who I'm calling," Judge Ahrenson said. His voice sounded scratchy, like he'd just woken up.

"Your honor," Ashley said, surprised. "How did you get this number?"

"Never mind that."

Ashley very much minded that, but his tone of voice had her holding her tongue. There was an edge to his words that felt dangerous.

"What are all these motions, Ashley? My queue is full of them."

"Oh," Ashley said with a heavy sigh.

The Judge was referring to his docket in the electronic filing system. That was what he meant by "queue." When attorneys filed documents, they went electronically to the clerk's office, who then docketed them and assigned them to specific judges. The judges called the documents waiting for their attention their "queue."

"Those are motions to suppress," Ashley said.

"Obviously. I could tell that by the captions that say *Defendant's Motion to Suppress*. I may be old, but I can read. What I don't understand is why there are so many of them. It's like you filed one for every single one of your cases."

"I did."

There was a long silence. Ashley almost asked if the Judge was still on the line, but she could hear his breathing. "Why?" He asked, and he suddenly sounded very old, tired. Every bit of his seventy-one, almost seventy-two years. "Why would you do that?"

"Because settled law is no longer settled. Precedent doesn't matter anymore. Stare decisis is dead."

Stare decisis was the legal concept that previous rulings controlled the later rulings. If the Supreme Court said, *Officers can search cars*, all the judges below them had to also decide *officers can search cars*. If a judge decided differently and an attorney appealed, that was how a decision moved up the ladder to the Court of Appeals and then to the Supreme Court.

"This is about that abortion ruling, isn't it?"

"It has nothing to do with abortion, your honor. It has to do with the change in the courts. If one thing was wrong, then everything could be wrong. As a zealous advocate for my clients, I need to challenge even what used to be considered settled law."

Judge Ahrenson sighed heavily. "Why do you insist on rocking the boat? What's in it for you? Honestly, you are so close to taking my position, yet you insist on shooting yourself in the foot. You cannot finish this marathon with a gunshot wound. The governor will never choose you. Withdraw your motions, and your chance at my position may still be possible."

It was Ashley's turn to be silent. His retribution was not unexpected, but it stung all the same. Maybe she was trying to shoot herself in the foot. Maybe she wasn't sure if she even wanted to be a judge anymore, to join the ranks of those idiots who had turned the judicial system on its head. Yet she somehow couldn't find the words to say these things. They simply didn't come. If he didn't understand now, he never would. This ruling was a tragedy, and for far more reasons than those that affected women.

"Will you withdraw your motions?" Judge Ahrenson sounded hopeful. This was one occasion Ashley was not going to regret dashing those hopes.

"No. I can't."

"You need to."

"I won't."

At first, she'd been annoyed. Now she was growing angry. He was turning this on her as though this was somehow her fault. It had nothing to do with her. She did not make the decision that changed everything. The Courts did. She would not allow him to turn this around on her. Not without saying her piece.

"You do realize that my ethical responsibility is to zealously represent each one of my clients. When, say, the officers stopped my client for a *Terry* stop, I used to counsel my clients that the seizure was legal."

A *Terry* stop was a probable cause stop that allowed officers to stop a vehicle when they had reasonable suspicion that a crime had occurred or was occurring, including traffic violations.

"That *used* to be settled law. I *used* to tell my clients that. Now, what am I supposed to tell them? Am I supposed to say, 'that's settled law, but thanks to the *Dobbs* decision, settled law is not what it used to be, so this may not be settled law, but you should trust me on this one that the Court probably wouldn't overturn it even though nobody actually thought they would overturn *Roe* but they did anyway?'"

"You are letting politics cloud your judgment."

"Politics has nothing to do with it. I have not once mentioned my political leanings through this entire discussion. This isn't about whether I believe abortion is right or wrong. It's about the castration of the criminal justice system."

"You're losing your grip on reality."

Ashley's nostrils flared. She had all kinds of things she'd like to say. Things like, *between the two of us, old man, you're the one who is on the edge of dementia*, but she held her tongue. Lashing out would do no good.

"We are going to have to agree to disagree on this one, your honor," Ashley forced herself to say.

"Fine. I just wanted you to know that you are destroying your chances at replacing me. The governor will see this as a direct attack on abortion, and you know how she feels about it."

"Yeah. I know. If she takes it personally, then she takes it personally, but it isn't personal toward her. I get she applauded the Court's decision, but she didn't make the decision. She didn't create the problem. My fight is not with her."

"I have no dog in this fight. You know that, don't you?" Judge Ahrenson said. "I won't be hearing these motions. One of the other judges from elsewhere in the district will be coming down to hear them. I'm out of here."

"I understand." She hadn't known that he was done so quickly, but she supposed his birthday was coming up. The law required that he be out of the office when he turned seventy-two. She'd lost track of dates, but she supposed that day was quickly approaching. "And I appreciate the gesture."

"Well, since you won't change your mind, good luck. I don't know who will be hearing these motions, but that person is going to be pissed off."

Ashley shrugged. "They'll forgive me."

"I doubt that," Judge Ahrenson said with a sigh. "Good luck in your next endeavors. I'll be rooting for you, but I don't think that will mean anything anymore."

"It means something to me."

Ashley and Judge Ahrenson said their goodbyes and hung up. She was happy that it ended on a positive note. He'd pushed some of her buttons, but his intentions had been good. Yet the old adage, *the road to hell is paved with good intentions*, came to mind. She had good intentions when she started filing motions to suppress. Yet she couldn't help thinking that she, too, was on the road to hell. Only time would tell.

10

KATIE

It was a rainy Wednesday morning. One of those rare summer days when the rain fell from the sky in torrents. The state desperately needed it—all the farmers said so—but the dark morning didn't help Katie get out of bed. It was nearly eight o'clock when she made it through the front door of the office.

"What the actual fuck!" Ashley's shouting was the first thing Katie heard. It was coming from her office all the way at the other end of the building, but Katie could hear her words clear as day. That's how loud she was shouting.

"What's going on?" Katie asked Elena as she made her way into the main area of the office.

Elena shrugged. "Beats me."

A long stream of obscenities came from the dark end of the hallway, Ashley's direction.

Katie leaned over and peered into the darkness. There was a small light at the end, indicating Ashley's door was at least slightly ajar. She turned back to Elena. "Has this been going on for long?"

"No. It's been quiet up until just now. I'd ask, but I don't like to get in her way when she's like this."

"Ditto," Katie said, but she didn't have the luxury of distance. Someone needed to be there for Ashley. Whatever was happening was not good. "But I'll talk to her." Katie was perhaps the only person that could.

"That mother fucker!" Ashley shouted.

"Good luck," Elena said.

"Yeah. I'll need it." Katie swallowed hard, and then started making her way toward Ashley. The screaming had stopped by the time Katie reached Ashley's door, but she could hear the attorney inside mumbling. She hesitated for only a moment, then reached up and knocked on the doorframe.

"What?" Ashley demanded.

"It's me. Can I come in?"

"Oh, good." There was a rustling sound, then Ashley pulled the door wide. "I need to talk to you." Ashley's expression was wild, almost animalistic. Her normally calm, straight brown hair, was up in a disheveled bun, tied back with a brown rubber band she'd likely pulled off a file. It looked like a rat's nest, and it was going to hurt like a bitch when Ashley tried to take it out.

"Okay," Katie said. "What's going on?" She stepped into the office and sat in one of the two chairs facing Ashley's desk.

"Charles Hanson. That's what."

Katie lifted an eyebrow, waiting for Ashley to continue. Prompting was not necessary when the attorney was like this. The story was coming, ready or not.

"He filed a motion to revoke Oliver's pretrial release."

"Why?"

Ashley slid a piece of paper across the desk. It skimmed across the desktop and Katie caught it before it fell fluttering to the floor.

"That's his motion," Ashley said.

Katie looked down at the document. It was short. Only one page, consisting of a caption and a few short paragraphs. "This doesn't say much."

"Exactly. He's trying to surprise me, the fucker."

That was a tactic Ashley regularly used against Charles—the element of surprise—but it wouldn't be wise for Katie to point that out, at least not for a good hour or two. In that moment, Ashley was incapable of anything but rage.

"This is about my motions to suppress. I know it. He's punishing me through Oliver."

"I don't follow…"

"And the Court is letting him get away with it because they want to punish me, too."

"Now you've really lost me." Katie was starting to grow concerned. Ashley looked deranged with those wild eyes and quick words.

"I filed motions to suppress in all my cases."

"Surely not *all* of them." Ashley had a massive caseload; Katie knew that from years of watching her in practice. Sometimes it waned a bit, but it never dropped down below eighty.

"Every. Single. One."

"Why?" It was all Katie could think to ask.

Ashley had always been an extra zealous defense attorney, but the number of cases with potentially winnable motions to suppress was somewhere between ten and fifteen percent. The officers didn't screw up that often, and certainly not in every case. George was going to lose his shit when he heard, and so were all the other deputies.

"*Dobbs.*"

"Okay." Katie didn't understand, but she wasn't going to push for clarification. The sooner this conversation ended, the better. Ashley's entire face and neck were red with rage and her eyes were wide and shifty. Her heart rate had to be sky high. If this kept up much longer, the attorney was bound to suffer a stroke.

"Charles is mad and he's going to take it out on Oliver. The Court set the hearing for Monday. *This Monday*. And I don't even know what the issues are." She tapped Charles's motion with the tip of her index finger. "He's so vague. It could be anything. How do I defend against that?"

"Honestly, I don't know. I'd start with Oliver. Maybe he has some idea."

"That's the cop in you talking. You know my clients are never honest with me."

Katie shrugged. "That's all I've got. Otherwise, you're on your own." She was trying not to feel offended by Ashley's comments about her previous employment, but it was hard. She'd been working outside the police department for nearly as long as she'd been an officer, yet her law enforcement past was still Ashley's go-to when they disagreed on anything case related.

Ashley's phone starting ringing and Katie took that as her cue to leave. Ashley picked it up as she was nearing the door.

"You've got a visitor." Katie could hear Elena's voice echoing down the hall as she spoke to Ashley on the phone. "Nancy's here."

Nancy Ross, Katie thought, *that's curious*. She was just a small girl. Vivian did not seem at all happy when she left her and Katie's appointment to find her daughter talking to Ashley Montgomery. It was unlikely she would approve a return visit. That meant Nancy was either alone or she was with her father. Either way, it could be an ideal opportunity to get some honest background information on the Ross family.

11

ASHLEY

The rage was all consuming. Even Katie couldn't calm her down. There were so many problems in the world, so many ways in which things were going wrong, and this—the application to revoke Oliver's bond and put him back in jail—was the icing on a very shitty cake.

Anger was not new to Ashley. It was one of her more common emotions. Yet, what she was feeling now was something foreign. So overwhelming that it controlled her rather than the other way around. Then her phone started ringing. She snatched it off the receiver as Katie rose and scurried out the door. Even she had been frightened off by the monster inside Ashley.

"What?" Ashley barked.

"You have a visitor. Nancy's here." Elena pronounced the words in her usual, upbeat manner. A sound that was almost as recognizable to Ashley as her own voice. But still, it sounded odd to her as it burst through her fury.

"Penny?" The anger was slowly starting to seep away. "What is she doing here?"

"I don't know. I'd guess it has something to do with the box of donuts she's brought along with her."

"Who is with her?" Miraculously, the anger seemed to seep right out of

Ashley, draining down from her head, through her body, and out through the soles of her feet.

There was a short pause. "I think she's alone. Do you want me to tell her to leave?"

"No. I'll be out in a few minutes."

Ashley hung up and took a few calming breaths before smoothing her jacket and heading out to the front of the office. When she emerged into the reception area, Elena and Katie stood to the side, watching Ashley in the same way they might eye a wild animal—quiet, cautious, with a touch of wariness.

Penny did not wear the same expression. Her face was open, innocent, and her eyes lit up when they settled on Ashley. She hadn't witnessed Ashley's meltdown. If she had, she'd be out the door in a heartbeat.

"Ashley!" Penny said excitedly. "I brought donuts from Genie's Diner. Genie said you like blueberry frosted. There are others if she was wrong..."

"No, that's wonderful. Thank you, Penny," Ashley said as she gave Penny a genuine smile. She reached into the donut box and removed a blueberry frosted o-shaped mound of sugar and dough. She ripped off a piece and placed it in her mouth and feigned delight in its flavor.

Ashley never ate donuts. That kind of sugar in the morning would cause her blood sugar to spike. But Genie was right that Ashley would choose blueberry if forced to eat one. Yet this didn't feel like force. She wanted to make Penny happy. It was a visceral desire, one she could not ignore, even if she tried. Not that she did.

"Good?" Penny asked.

"Very good," Ashley agreed.

"So, Penny," Katie said, stepping up beside Ashley. She seemed tentative and stood a bit away from Ashley, like she was afraid Ashley might bite.

"Nancy."

Katie grimaced. "Right. Nancy."

It bothered Katie that Ashley was the only one allowed to use Penny's nickname, of that Ashley felt sure. Yet she relished the idea that someone had selected her over everyone else. She'd never been a popular person. Not in childhood and certainly not as an adult. It was nice to feel chosen.

"Do your parents know you are here?" Katie asked.

"Yes and no."

Ashley smiled and took another bite of the sickly-sweet donut. That was the kind of answer Ashley might give.

"Can you elaborate?" Katie said.

"Mom knows that I'm out. I told her I was leaving to go downtown. She knew I was going to Genie's diner, but I didn't tell her I was coming here. It's not a lie because I am still downtown."

"It's an omission and most people consider those lies."

"Well, most people are wrong."

Ashley barked a laugh. She couldn't help herself. This little girl was hilarious.

Penny smiled in return. "Mom sleeps almost all the time now. She's seeing a therapist once a week through the computer. I heard them one day. The therapist says mom is depressed. Mom wanted medicine, but the doctor wouldn't prescribe anything since she's pregnant with my little brother."

"A boy, huh?" Elena said. "You must be excited about that."

Penny shrugged. "Mom says nothing about him, and Bruce is always gone. I don't know what to feel about him. He's part of the reason mom is in therapy. They talk about the baby a lot in therapy. The therapist calls him a 'baby' and mom calls him a 'fetus.' There's a lot of talk around those words."

"How do you feel he should be described?" Katie asked.

Penny shrugged. "A burden."

Another laugh burst from Ashley. This time Elena and Katie both gave her a hard look. "Sorry," she said, casting a sheepish look at all three. She knew she shouldn't be encouraging Penny, but it was hilarious. Babies were burdens.

"How did you get here?" Katie asked. "You didn't walk all the way over here from the other side of town, did you?"

"No." Penny shook her head. "I rode my bike."

"Well, it's probably time we get you home, don't you think?" Katie said. "We can get your bike home later. Your mother is probably worried about you. I can take you. I need to talk to your mother anyway."

"Okay," Penny said with a nod. "I'm fine with that." Her gaze shifted to Ashley. "I'm glad I was able to see you again. I like our talks."

"Me, too," Ashley said, a smile stretching across her face. She couldn't remember the last time she'd grinned so much. There was something about this girl. She ignited something deep within Ashley. A feeling that had been buried for what felt like centuries. Joy.

They said their goodbyes and Ashley watched as Katie and Penny left through the front door of the Public Defender's Office. She'd never thought she'd feel anything more than a passing interest for any child. Yet Penny was different. She was really starting to grow on Ashley. If she wasn't careful, she was going to get attached. But with Vivian's dislike of Ashley, that didn't seem like it would be good for anyone.

12

KATIE

Nancy lived on the far western side of town, by the golf course. It was the newest and most expensive area of Brine. Katie had already done some research into her new client, Vivian Ross, so she knew where to go without asking directions.

"Are you supposed to be in a car seat?" Katie asked.

Nancy was in the backseat, buckled up. When Katie looked back at her in the rear-view mirror, she seemed so small all alone in the back. She didn't have any children, so she didn't know the current law on car seats. They weren't required for Katie when she was five, but that was the thing about laws—they changed every legislative session.

"Yes."

Katie wasn't one to break laws, not even minor traffic offenses, but she couldn't see any other way to get the child home unless she called her parents. "Is your mother going to be upset when she sees that you rode in my car without a car seat?"

Nancy shrugged. "I rode in the Uber without one. She knew about that. I don't see how this is different."

Katie did. Despite the child's astonishing maturity, she still didn't fully understand the nature of people. Vivian might be angry about something entirely different—unwanted pregnancy, absent husband, financial troubles—and still take those frustrations out on Katie when she pulled up with Nancy in the backseat improperly restrained.

"Let's hope you're right."

They got into Katie's old Impala, and she started driving west. They were silent for the first minute, then Katie forced herself to start questioning Nancy about her home life. She didn't feel good about it, but it might be her only opportunity to get the information.

"So, your dad has been gone a lot? That's what your mom tells me."

"Bruce isn't *gone*. He's always in the garage, but we never see him."

"Has he always been like that?"

Nancy shook her head. "No. It's only been the last few months."

"Is he happy about your mom's pregnancy?"

"I think so. Maybe not at first, but he wants a boy."

"How do you know he wants a boy?"

"He said so."

"Does that make you feel bad?"

"Him saying he wants a boy? No. He's acting weird, so that makes me feel bad, but that's only because I don't understand. Mom doesn't understand either."

"Does she talk about those things with you?"

"She talks to me about everything."

"What other things does she tell you?"

"That she doesn't like the 'little burden' inside her. She doesn't want him."

"Oh," Katie said, lifting her eyebrows. "Why?"

"I'm all she needs."

"That must be nice to hear."

"It is, but it's also a lot of pressure. I'm not perfect, but Mom seems to think I am."

"Most mothers are like that. They love their daughters unconditionally."

"Do you have kids?"

"No. But I did have a mother, and she was that way as well." At least she'd seemed that way until Katie's father went to prison, and she ran off with another man. Katie kept this little bit to herself. It sounded like Nancy was starting to experience those same abandonment feelings with her father. It would do no good to place doubts in Nancy's mind about her mother.

"Will you have kids?"

"Maybe someday. I'm not in a place in my life to make decisions like that."

"Because you aren't married?"

"Something like that."

"Don't marry someone like Bruce."

"Why not?" Katie met Nancy's gaze in the rearview mirror. The little girl's expression was intense.

"He's a bad guy."

"What do you mean by that?"

"I don't know," Nancy said with a shrug. "He's changed. He wasn't always bad, but he is now. I can feel it."

The statement was tinged with melancholy so strong it was infectious. Katie couldn't imagine feeling that way about her father. Yes, he'd violated some major laws, cost them everything financially, was tried, convicted, and sent to prison, but she still never thought of him as *bad*. Flawed, yes, but never bad.

"Has he done something bad?"

"No. I don't know," she shrugged. "Maybe."

"What bad things has he done?"

Nancy crossed her arms. "I don't know."

"Why do you call your father 'Bruce,' and not 'Dad' or 'Daddy?'"

"Nicknames are earned, not given."

"And he hasn't earned it yet?"

"Nope. And he probably never will."

"Okay, well, we're here." Katie put the car in park.

Nancy hopped out, bouncing on the balls of her feet like she hadn't just participated in a heavy conversation about her home life. "Thanks for driving me."

"Thanks for the donuts, Nancy."

"You can call me Penny."

Katie smiled. It gave her a surprising sense of joy, this invitation into the

Penny club. Nicknames were earned, not given, and she'd somehow earned it. "Okay, Penny."

"Bye." Penny closed the car door and walked up to the enormous front door. It was double wide with a wreath of peonies, roses, and lush greenery —live flowers and quite expensive, no doubt—hanging centered on each door. Penny waved one last time, then pulled the right door open and disappeared inside.

The house was three stories with large picture windows that would allow copious amounts of natural lighting inside. The windows also allowed Katie to see a lot more than she'd expected. Vivian was home, and somewhere on the second floor in a room that looked like it was dedicated to exercise. From her vantage point, Katie could see a few pieces of lifting equipment, an elliptical and a tread mill. Vivian was running on the tread-mill. She looked ridiculous with sweat running down her face and her belly protruding out in front of her.

Katie grabbed her phone, opened the camera application, and snapped a few pictures. She added them to a text to Ashley and typed, "She was such an ass to you the other day, I thought you might want to see her looking a fool. The stars sweat just like *US*."

This was a joke between Ashley and Katie. They had some old gossip magazines out on the office table and some of them were *US Weekly* magazines. Each edition featured a picture of a famous person doing some mundane task like getting coffee or tying their shoes with a caption claiming they were "just like us." They weren't, nobody believed that, and that was why it was funny.

Ashley responded within seconds. "Thanks," her message said. "I needed that. It's been a shitty day."

"I know," Katie typed. "We'll get the Oliver stuff sorted, though."

"I hope so."

Katie lowered her phone and put her car in reverse, ready to back out. As she did, she saw a black BMW pull up to the detached garage behind Vivian's house, where Bruce had been spending all his time. She pulled to the side of the road and stopped her car. A thin man hopped out of the car and ran up to the door. He looked around, then began knocking incessantly until the door finally swung open.

Katie threw her car in park and grabbed her phone, snapping picture after picture. She wished she had her professional camera with better zoom, but she hadn't been prepared for an investigation. Which was stupid, stupid, stupid. Rule number one in investigations—you never know when you'll come across a clue—required constant readiness. But she could berate herself about that later. Right now, she needed to take pictures.

For the driver of the BMW was none other than Ashley's client, Oliver Banks.

13

ASHLEY

Katie burst through the front door, breathing heavily. Ashley was in the front reception area with Elena going over witnesses to subpoena for the upcoming court hearings. They'd been at it for a while. There were quite a few, considering the number of motions to suppress.

Elena had five separate notepads strewn across her desk, each with a separate set of witnesses, addresses, and phone numbers. Ashley was still listing off times and dates when Katie interrupted them.

"Thank God," Elena said, appearing to welcome the interruption.

"What is it? What's wrong?" Ashley turned toward the door. Katie was rarely like this, frazzled with excitement radiating off her. Ashley's first thought was that some emergency had come up with a client. Officers were executing a warrant at a client's house, or a client was picked up on a new charge and undergoing active questioning.

"I think I know who owns the BMW," Katie said, rushing to the counter. She stood there for a moment, panting like she'd just finished sprints, then came around it into the employee area with Elena and Ashley.

"BMW?" Ashley asked. Her brain couldn't switch gears that quickly.

"The one Oliver was driving."

"Allegedly."

"Right, right, allegedly," Katie said, waving her hand. "Bruce Ross. See, look at these." Katie grabbed her phone out of her bag. She lifted it to her face and her fingers flew across the touch screen, pressing buttons. Then she turned it and handed it to Ashley. "See, look," she said.

Ashley accepted the phone and peered down at the little screen. There was no license plate number, but it was a black BMW sedan with front end damage. She continued scrolling through pictures. Katie had taken one after the other at rapid speed, so it was almost like looking at a modern version of those old flip books, where it felt like the drawings were moving when flipping through the pages quickly.

A man was knocking at a garage door, hood pulled low over his dark, scraggly hair. The man looked away, then straight at the camera. It was Oliver, no doubt. There was that stupid teardrop tattoo, the idiot. *He should really start covering that with makeup*, Ashley thought. That was the least he could do if he was going to continue driving the attempted murder weapon around town.

Oliver knocked again and again. Several pictures depicted him with his fist banging against the door. Then it opened, and there was Bruce Ross, Mr. High and Mighty himself, but Ashley could barely recognize him.

"Bruce looks like shit," Ashley said, her voice upbeat.

He looked like he'd aged ten years since the last time Ashley saw him, and that was only six months earlier at a Brine County Bar Association meeting. He was the president of the local bar, but he seemed to think the position made him God or king, not president.

The association had been spending a lot on lavish events, and Ashley had tried to ask a question about it. He'd told her, *Finances are fine, but I wouldn't expect money to be your thing. You focus on criminals. I'll worry about the money.* She'd wanted to make him worry about her fist in his face, but she'd restrained herself.

"I think you are missing the point," Katie said.

"No, no. I know that's not the *point*, but it's what I'm focusing on right now. Just give me this tiny moment. It's at least a little validating that someone who always thought he was so much better than me now looks like he could easily be one of my clients while he is also caught fraternizing with one of my clients. It feels like poetic justice."

"Okay. Have your moment," Katie said, crossing her arms.

Ashley looked down at the picture for another few seconds, taking in Bruce's sunken cheeks and messy hair. His skin was a sallow color, untouched by sunshine for some time. What the hell had happened to him? Was he sick or something? She'd heard nothing about him around town, and Brine was a typical small town. People loved to gossip. After staring at Bruce's altered image for another moment, Ashley sighed and flipped to the next picture. Back to business.

"See there," Katie pointed at the picture. "He's got something in his hands, and he gives it to Bruce."

Ashley couldn't tell what it was. She zoomed in on Oliver's hands, but she still couldn't tell. "What do you think it is?"

"Something small, but aside from that, it could be anything. Drugs. Money. Keys. Jewelry. You name it."

"Did Oliver leave in the BMW?"

"Yes."

"Well, it can't be the keys to the car then."

Katie shrugged. "Maybe it was a spare key, and they were making arrangements for Oliver to drop it off somewhere."

"Seems like that could have been handled by phone."

"But phones leave records. If they are doing something illegal, they won't want record of it."

She had a point. But then she had another thought. "Why isn't that car impounded? I thought the government would be holding it as evidence."

The State almost always held onto anything that could have some potential value, at least through the trial date. Especially cars, which was something that had always bothered Ashley. They couldn't carry it into the courtroom. So, why keep it in storage once the investigation was complete? The only answer was that they wanted to show Ashley's clients that they had power. They didn't want to release items, and they didn't have to, so they wouldn't.

"I called George about that on the way here. He said they don't have space in the impound lot, so they had to let it go. Oliver was one of the few who could pay the impound fee, so his was one of those that was released."

"Weird," Ashley said. "There's that money thing again." Impounding a vehicle, especially for police reasons, was not cheap. It would have cost

Oliver hundreds and possibly thousands to get the car released. Who was footing that bill? It wasn't Oliver. He was a twenty-year-old, unemployed, high school dropout.

"I can see what I can dig up about Oliver's finances."

"No, don't," Ashley said.

She doubted Oliver had filed a single tax return since he'd turned eighteen. That meant he was earning money illegally, ignoring the tax laws, also illegal, or he was receiving money as a gift, which wasn't likely. No good would come out of investigating the source of his income. They weren't Oliver's mothers. Ashley had no responsibility to him outside his current pending case.

"Okay," Katie said. "Then how do we follow the money trail? It feels like there is something there."

"Yeah, but it probably won't lead to a defense for Oliver in the hit and run case. We can't get sidetracked here."

Katie groaned.

"I get it. I'm curious, too, but we just can't expend our resources that way. Oliver and Bruce's side project is not our focus unless we can tie it to the hit and run, *and* that would somehow lead to a defense."

"Okay. So, what do we do, then?"

"I will talk to him, though. I'm not going to ask any questions, but I'll tell him to knock off any illegal activity. We are already risking the loss of his pretrial release. We'll fight that in court, but we will have no dog in that fight if he gets picked up on additional charges. That includes driving on a barred driver's license. What the hell is he doing driving around at all?"

"Beats me."

"I'm going to rip him a new asshole for that one. I'm trying to douse the fire and he tosses another handful of gasoline onto it."

Ashley shook her head and started making her way back toward her office. She would be calling her client, and it wouldn't be a pleasant conversation. At least she now knew—or potentially knew—the basis of Charles Hanson's motion to revoke Oliver's pretrial release. He was still out there driving. He needed to knock that shit off, and now.

14

KATIE

Monday, August 1

Oliver fidgeted in his chair, but Ashley sat perfectly still. They were at defense table, waiting for the Court to appear and address the State's motion to revoke Oliver's pretrial release. Charles Hanson, the prosecutor, was alone at his table, and Katie was the only onlooker seated in the gallery.

Oliver's case hadn't caught much traction in the news. The alleged victim of his hit and run was a loner drug addict who was still in the hospital, struggling to survive, and she either had no family or none that cared enough to show up on her behalf.

"All rise," a small, sharp voice called, and everyone stood. The court reporter scurried into the room, seating herself at the steno machine positioned in front of the Judge's bench. "The Honorable Judge Ahrenson presiding," she announced as the judge entered the courtroom.

The judge trudged up the steps and sat behind the bench, surveying the courtroom with a tired expression. Now that he was on the verge of retirement, he seemed to be visibly aging by the day.

"We are convened today in State of Iowa versus Oliver Banks, Brine County Case Number FECR001983, on the State's motion to modify the

Defendant's bond. Are the parties ready to proceed?" His gaze shifted to Ashley.

"Yes, your honor," Ashley said.

Beside her, Oliver looked down, unable to meet the Judge's gaze. He'd tried to improve his appearance that morning. He'd combed his long hair and pulled it back into a ponytail, gathered at the nape of his neck. He'd also changed into more appropriate clothing—black slacks, and a dark red, button-down shirt. He wore no tie, but few clients did anymore.

"Is the State ready to proceed?" Judge Ahrenson asked.

"Yes," Charles said.

"It's the State's motion. You have the burden of proof. Call your first witness, Mr. Hanson."

"The State calls Vivian Ross."

Katie slapped a hand over her mouth to keep herself from gasping. Vivian hadn't seen Oliver stop at the garage that day Katie had taken the photographs, she felt sure of that. Vivian had been exercising on a treadmill that faced away from the garage. Katie had seen her clearly through the windows of the house.

Katie had thought that she was the only one who saw the short exchange between Oliver and Bruce, but maybe she'd been wrong. She could have missed something. Ashley hadn't wanted to look into it, but maybe Katie would end up getting some answers into the Bruce and Oliver thing. She grabbed her phone to search for the picture she'd taken of Vivian. A text came through as she was opening her phone. It was from Ashley.

Katie looked up to see Ashley turned all the way around in her seat motioning to her phone and mouthing the words, "I texted you." Katie clicked on the text. *Email that picture of Vivian to Elena and ask her to print it off and mark it as Defense's Exhibit A.*

Okay. Katie typed back.

She did as Ashley requested, opening a text to Elena and typing Ashley's request. Elena said she'd be over with the printed picture in a "jiff." Katie thanked her and put the phone away. She wasn't sure if there was much evidentiary value to the photograph, but it did show that Vivian was facing away from the garage. Vivian wouldn't have been able to see Oliver pull up unless she'd stopped running and turned completely around. Katie never saw her do that. Maybe that was where Ashley intended to go with the evidence. That, or she simply wanted to embarrass Vivian, which was also possible.

When Katie focused back on the proceeding, Vivian had already been sworn in and was taking the witness stand. She gingerly lowered herself into the seat, keeping her back ramrod straight and her nose high. She sat with her knees to the side to allow room for her protruding belly.

"Good morning, Mrs. Ross," Charles said, a genial smile spreading across his full face.

"Yes, well, it is a morning, that's for sure."

"That much is for sure," Charles said with a chuckle. "Do you recognize the Defendant here, Oliver Banks?" He gestured toward defense table.

Vivian's gaze cut toward Oliver and Ashley, but only for a moment. "Yes. I don't know him by name, but I do recognize his face."

"How do you recognize him?"

"He's been hanging around the elementary school."

"The elementary school you say?"

Katie watched the questioning with rapt attention. Where was the prosecutor going with this? Oliver wasn't charged with a sex crime, so there was nothing preventing him from going near a school.

"Yes. My daughter, Nancy, will be attending the school this fall. I have been taking her to the school playground every day to get her accustomed to the surroundings. I want her to feel comfortable when she starts in the fall."

"Why does the Defendant's presence bother you, Mrs. Ross?" The prosecutor had asked the question in a kindly way. A way that made it sound as though he believed her testimony and found her concerns entirely reasonable.

"He doesn't have a child with him. He's always alone, watching the playground, the school. It's like he's scoping the place out. With all the school shootings these days, it has made me extremely uncomfortable."

"Was there anything else that made you uncomfortable?"

"Yes. I thought he was carrying a gun."

Katie expected Ashley to jump up and object, but she didn't. She remained seated, scribbling notes on a notepad.

"Why did you think that?" Charles asked.

"I could see a dark object hanging from his pants where a belt would be. I didn't look closely, so I can't be sure. I didn't want to draw attention to myself. I was frightened. That school needs better security."

"How many times have you seen the Defendant at the elementary school playground?"

"Four or five."

"Four or five," Charles Hanson repeated, turning to give Oliver a hard look.

Oliver squirmed in his seat, but Ashley didn't react.

Nothing Vivian had said so far seemed like a solid basis for revoking Oliver's pretrial release, but it was odd. Why would a twenty-year-old man hang around a school playground when he had no children of his own?

"I don't have any further questions for this witness," Charles said.

"Cross," Judge Ahrenson said, turning his attention to Ashley.

"Thank you, your honor," Ashley said. "If I could have a moment to speak with—"

Just then, Elena stepped into the courtroom, holding an enlarged version of Katie's picture, printed and marked as an exhibit.

"One moment." Ashley stood and approached Elena, meeting her halfway down the aisle. She leaned forward, whispered something into Elena's ear, then turned and headed back up to defense table. She sat down and pulled the microphone on her table closer to her. "Good morning, Mrs. Ross."

"It was," Vivian said, raising her head higher, so she could look down upon Ashley.

"I can call you Mrs. Ross, right? That's how the prosecutor referred to you."

"Yes."

"This next question is a question that propriety says I'm not supposed to ask, but I'm not much for propriety."

"That's obvious," Vivian said with a snort.

If Ashley was bothered by Vivian's haughtiness, she didn't show it. "Are you pregnant?"

"Yes."

"How far along?"

"Five, six months."

"Which is it. Five or six?"

"Does it matter?"

"It matters to me."

"I'm not sure."

Katie cocked her head to the side. Who didn't know how far along they were in their pregnancy? Most pregnant women knew the exact week and they'd already read up on how the baby had grown and changed in the past week, comparing it to a fruit size. *This week my baby is the size of a pear. An orange. A tangerine.* The conversations always ended with Katie feeling hungry.

"Do you have any complications with your pregnancy?"

"Objection, relevance," Charles Hanson shouted.

Judge Ahrenson's gaze swung to Ashley, and he raised his eyebrow.

"Let me rephrase," Ashley said. "Do you have any complications with your pregnancy that would prevent you from walking to the park?"

Katie had learned that this line of questioning was what attorneys called a "fishing expedition." Ashley had no argument, so she was casting a line out and hoping she would catch a fish. Katie wasn't so sure she actually needed it, though. The prosecutor's argument *I think I saw a gun* was not very persuasive. At least not to Katie.

"Overruled," Judge Ahrenson said. "This question is clearly relevant." He turned to Vivian. "You may answer.'

"I'm not sure why that matters."

Ashley's head turned to look directly at Charles, and it was her turn to raise an eyebrow. She sat there for a long moment, making her point that Vivian was potentially an untrustworthy witness, then turned her attention back to the witness stand. "The Judge has said that it matters, so you need to answer."

Vivian shifted her weight. "What was the question again?"

"Do you have any complications with your pregnancy that would prevent you from walking to the park?"

"I'm supposed to be on bedrest."

"Bedrest, you say?" Ashley repeated the words as though shocked. "Then what are you doing walking to the park every single day?"

"I'm taking care of the child that actually exists. My pregnancy doesn't end my duties in caring for Nancy. You'd know that if you bothered to have children yourself."

It was meant to be a dig, but it wouldn't bother Ashley. Katie knew that without even seeing her expression. Ashley didn't desire motherhood. It was a choice, and she hadn't spent a day regretting it. She had told Katie several times.

"May I approach, your honor," Ashley asked.

"You may," Judge Ahrenson said.

"What I'm showing you has been marked as 'Defendant's Exhibit A,'" Ashley stopped by the prosecution bench, allowing Charles to look at the photo before bringing it up to the witness stand and handing it to Vivian. "Who is that in 'Exhibit A?'"

Vivian narrowed her eyes, staring at the picture. "That's my house. How did you get this picture?"

"Never mind *how*, we were discussing *who*. Now, who is it in that picture?"

"That's me, I guess."

"You guess?"

"It's me."

"What are you doing?"

"I'm on the treadmill."

"Running on the treadmill, right?"

"Yes."

"Your belly in this picture looks similar in size to your belly today. Would you agree with that statement?"

"Yes."

"So, it's a recent picture?"

"It appears to be recent."

"How long have you known you were supposed to be on bedrest?"

"A few weeks."

"Yet, you've been running."

"It appears so," Vivian said, her tone dark.

"You are endangering your unborn child, wouldn't you agree?"

"No. I would not agree. It isn't a *child*. It's a *fetus*."

"If you say so," Ashley said with a shrug. "You never saw Oliver with a gun, did you?"

"I said I thought it was a gun, but I didn't get a good look."

"It could have been a cell phone."

"Nobody clips cell phones to their belts anymore."

"Nobody?" Ashley cocked an eyebrow.

"Well, not 'nobody.' There is probably someone out there still holding fast to that ridiculous fashion disaster."

"It could have been a chain, right?"

"People don't hang chains from their belts anymore either."

"They don't? How do you know?"

"If they do, they shouldn't."

"So, you are amending your answer to 'if they do, they shouldn't?'"

"Yes."

"I don't have any further questions for this witness."

Ashley was quitting while she was ahead. Her cross had cast Vivian's credibility into question. She'd made her point. She didn't need to go any farther. Katie had found it a little surprising that Ashley was challenging Vivian on her behaviors surrounding her pregnancy considering her position on the *Dobbs* decision. Yet, Katie was also unsurprised. It was the best way to discredit Vivian as a witness, and Ashley needed to discredit her if she wanted to keep Oliver out of jail. Ashley's job was to zealously represent her clients, personal opinions be damned, and that's what she was doing.

"Re-direct?" Judge Ahrenson asked Charles.

"No, your honor."

"Any further evidence?"

"No, your honor," Charles sank a little lower in his seat.

"Evidence on the Defense's behalf?"

"No, your honor," Ashley said, but her tone was upbeat, almost chipper.

"Very well. The State's motion is denied. There is no term of the Defendant's pretrial release requiring him to stay away from schools. He is precluded from violating the law, and possessing a firearm as a felon would be a law violation, but Mrs. Ross's evidence is extremely weak. She testified she *thought* it was a gun. On cross, she admitted it could have been a cell phone or a chain, she didn't look that closely. There is no violation of pretrial release here, so I am denying the State's Motion." With that, Judge Ahrenson stood and walked out of the courtroom.

Katie was not shocked, not after hearing the evidence. Judges didn't rule from the bench often, but Charles's evidence was thin, and Ashley had torn it to pieces. The result would have been different had Charles had access to the pictures Katie had taken of Oliver driving. That was a violation of the law since his license was barred, but he didn't have access to those pictures, and he didn't have the right to access them. So, that little secret would remain safe with her.

The evidence was thin, the ruling correct, yet something didn't sit right with Katie about the hearing. Vivian had been telling the truth about Oliver, Katie could feel it in her bones. He had been hanging around the school, and that made Katie both curious and filled her with foreboding. What did he want with those children?

15

ASHLEY

Relief.

That was Ashley's primary emotion when Judge Ahrenson ruled against the State's motion to revoke Oliver's bond. The motion had been retaliatory, she felt certain of that, based on Ashley's motions to suppress in almost all of her cases. Every hearing where a client might lose their liberty was fraught with stress and uncertainty, but this hearing had been worse because at least some of the blame, Ashley felt, was squarely on her shoulders.

"Ms. Montgomery," Judge Ahrenson said, catching her attention. "A word, please." He was standing in the doorway that led from chambers back into the courtroom, holding the door open. He'd already removed his robe, which meant he wanted to talk to her as a person, not a judge. Normally, that was a cause to relax, but not today. His stiff demeanor and sharp tone indicated that this was not going to be a pleasant meeting.

"Yes, your honor." Ashley shoved her laptop into its bag, talking to Oliver as she retrieved the notepads and pens from the table. "Call my office in the next couple days. We need to meet soon. We have to strategize on next steps. I would normally try to do that now, but I've got to talk to the judge."

"Okay."

"And whatever you do," she paused meeting her client's gaze. "Don't drive. Not any car, but definitely not that BMW."

"How did you—"

"Don't say anything. I don't need your admissions. I need you to stop playing with fire. We won this hearing, but that's only because the prosecutor did not know. If he comes armed with that evidence the next time, you're screwed. Do you understand me?"

"Umm, yes."

"Take my advice. That's why I'm here."

It seemed obvious that a client should listen to their attorney, but Ashley had learned over the years that this was not strictly true. With many clients, it seemed like information went in one ear and out the other, like they hadn't even heard it at all. Most people did what they wanted, that was the nature of adulthood, and Ashley was powerless to stop it. All she could do was issue the warning. It was up to them at that point.

"Okay."

"Talk soon," Ashley said as she slung her laptop bag over her shoulder and strode toward judge's chambers.

Judge Ahrenson was in his small office; she could see him when she passed from the courtroom into the back area. This was not the Judge's personal office, that was on the next floor of the courthouse. This was where he stayed during court service days, like today. She stepped into a hallway that ran the length of the courtroom. Behind that were three offices, one straight ahead reserved for the court reporter, one to the right where Judge Ahrenson currently sat, and one to the left where the magistrate officed on her court service days.

The court reporter was out, but Judge Ahrenson must have heard Ashley come in because he looked up and motioned for her to enter. "Come on back, Ashley. Come on back."

"Hello, judge," she said, stepping into his office and dropping into one of the chairs. "You wanted to speak with me?"

"Yeah. I did. I've been hearing some things about you."

"All good, I hope," Ashley forced a smile. By his stern expression, she knew it was the opposite.

"Not exactly."

"Lay it on me." She made a *bring it on* gesture with her hand. "You've already chewed my ass about the motions to suppress, and I'm not withdrawing those by the way, so let's not get bogged down on that topic."

"It's not that."

"Okay..."

"I heard you were rude to the Governor's Office."

"Who told you that?"

"Is it true?"

"They were rude first."

Judge Ahrenson sighed and rubbed his temples. "Ashley, Ashley, Ashley. What am I going to do with you?"

"I told you I suck at politics."

"That's not politics. It's common sense. Don't you realize it's down to two people, you and Makala." He gestured to the right, toward the magistrate office.

"I do understand that, but I also know that the Governor is never going to choose me."

"Maybe not as it stands, but this is still salvageable."

"Oh?" Ashley lifted an eyebrow. She didn't believe him, but she'd hear him out.

"You think you've burned all your bridges with your bombastic reactions, but you have done one thing right. You haven't been openly political. You haven't publicly chosen a political party."

"Why would I do that? I'm a defense attorney. I can't afford to alienate most of the jury with my personal politics straight out of the gates."

"Exactly. But Mikala hasn't been so careful. She's a staunch supporter of the Democratic party. She always has been. That's going to cut against her."

"So, you're saying I have a chance."

"Yeah. If you start playing the game instead of setting the field on fire, you do have a chance."

Ashley sighed. "Why?" She was suddenly exhausted.

"Why what?"

"Why should I even want to become a judge? You are supporting me." She gave him a hard, assessing look. "But you've never told me why."

"Because you're the best person for the job. I want my replacement to be a woman. We need more women on the bench. You don't care about politics, which is one of the major reasons you are appropriate. Law and politics are separate. People keep forgetting that these days. I know you won't be persuaded by political star power. You're going to do what's right. Always. No matter who is touting which side."

He was right about that. No politician had her ear, and none ever would. "Okay. I'll call the Governor's Office and schedule the meeting."

"And apologize."

"That's too far."

"It's just far enough." A small smile had crept into the corners of his mouth. He'd gotten his way, and he knew it.

"Alright." Ashley rose to her feet. "I guess I better get out of here. I have a call to make."

"You do."

Ashley strode out of Judge's chambers and into the courtroom. The space was empty. Oliver was long gone by now, but Ashley wondered where Katie had gone. She hadn't expected her to stick around while Ashley chatted with the judge, but most of the time she did. Ashley continued out into the hallway.

"Hi," said a small voice to Ashley's right.

She jumped and swung toward the voice, her hand gripping her chest. "Penny," she said. The little girl was seated on a bench right outside the courtroom doors. "What are you doing here?"

"I came with Mom."

Ashley paused, looking around. She didn't see Vivian anywhere. "Where is your mother?"

"Meeting with Katie."

"Oh..."

That explained Katie's absence. Ashley hoped she was ripping Vivian a new asshole for coming into the courtroom with that kind of bullshit evidence. She hadn't seen Oliver do anything wrong. It was all speculation and nonsense. Vivian should be ashamed of herself, but Ashley doubted that was the case. People like Vivian—beautiful, rich, polished people—didn't have to bother themselves with a moral compass. Society would always give them a pass.

"She told me to wait here."

"Okay, well, I'm sure she will be along soon," Ashley said, readjusting the shoulder strap on her laptop bag and glancing around.

"Can you, um, wait with me?" Penny looked down at her hands, intertwined in her lap. "I mean, do you mind?"

"Oh, I don't mind, Penny. It's just, well," she sighed heavily. "I'm not sure your mother is my biggest fan."

"She just doesn't know you."

"True, but you don't know me all that well either."

"I know you well enough."

"Oh? And what do you think you know about me?"

"I know you say what you mean, and you mean what you say."

"How do you know that?"

Ashley didn't deny it. There was no point. Her years as a public defender had molded her. Her job in the courtroom was to manipulate others to her way of thinking, but that was more of an act. A show. One reserved only for juries. Which only occurred a few times a year. Most of her job was counseling clients, and in these one-on-one meetings, she never held anything back. They deserved to know what they were up against. She didn't sugar coat bad facts or dismal chances.

"I just do."

"Nancy Reagan Ross," Vivian's sharp voice echoed through the high-ceilinged hallway.

Ashley froze, listening to the click of heels approaching her from behind. Only Vivian Ross would wear heels while majorly pregnant.

"What did I tell you about talking to strangers?"

"Ashley isn't a stranger, Mama," Penny said, her voice small.

"If she isn't, then she should be."

"Wow," Ashley said, with a snort. "Tell me how you really feel."

Vivian gave her a hard look. "This is between me and my daughter. Mind your own business."

For Penny's sake, Ashley swallowed back her next words. If not for the child's presence, Ashley would have enjoyed asking Vivian where she purchased the pole rammed up her ass, because it's past its expiration date and it's time she removed it.

"Well, it's been *lovely* speaking with you Vivian. Truly a gift. But I must be going. I need to make a call to the Governor's office."

"The Governor." Vivian narrowed her eyes. "Sure."

"Believe me or don't," Ashley said with a shrug. "I'm a finalist for Judge Ahrenson's position. Haven't you heard?" By Vivian's shocked expression, the answer to that was a resounding *no*. "There's a fifty-percent chance I'll be the one on that bench swearing you in as a witness and listening to your lies. Maybe then you'll think twice about manipulating evidence in a court-room. I'd love to hold you in contempt of court. That truly would be a wonderful day for me."

Vivian's mouth opened and then closed, her eyes wide.

"Sorry, Penny." Ashley's gaze shifted to the little girl. "I hope you can forgive me." And she did. This little girl was growing on her. She didn't want to lose her new little friend.

Penny shrugged. "Honesty."

"You can always count on me for that," Ashley said with a chuckle. Then she turned on her heel and marched out of the courthouse. She had a call to make.

16

KATIE

"Have you learned anything about Bruce?" Vivian asked, her voice low.

They were in one of the meeting rooms inside the courthouse. The rooms intended for attorneys and their clients. Oliver's hearing had ended moments earlier, and Ashley had gone to meet with Judge Ahrenson. Katie decided to wait for her in the hallway. That's what she was doing when Vivian had accosted her, demanding that they speak.

"Not much yet."

"Not much?" Vivian began pacing back and forth inside the small room, taking several steps one direction, then turning sharply and returning along the same path.

"Should you be doing that?"

"Doing what?" The look Vivian gave Katie was one of almost rabid intensity. She was daring Katie to challenge her.

"I was just thinking it might be better if we both sit down."

She'd never seen Vivian like this. She doubted anyone else in the Brine community had either. She was always so polished and perfect. All that was gone now, replaced by something fierce, almost animalistic. If this was how Vivian behaved around Bruce, case closed. He moved out because he was afraid of her. Katie wouldn't blame him either.

"Is that what you were thinking? Or was it about the *baby*?" She said baby with a sarcastic lilt while punctuating it with air quotes.

"Umm, both."

"It's a fetus. Not a baby. It won't be a baby until it is born."

Katie wasn't pro-life or pro-choice. She was pro-people. The abortion topic was front and center after the Supreme Court had overturned *Roe v. Wade*, but Katie had never gotten too far entrenched in either position. She didn't understand why it had to be an all or nothing concept. There was a point when an unborn child could live outside the womb if the mother went into early labor. Surely that was too late. There was also a time when doctors wouldn't even attempt to provide medical attention because there was no chance of living. It seemed like any time before then was too early for a ban.

Either way, Vivian's pregnancy was past the point of viability in Katie's eyes. She was at least six or seven months along. "We are going to have to agree to disagree on that one."

Vivian scoffed.

The room had one small table and two chairs. Katie lowered herself into the chair nearest to her, trying to keep her movements slow and non-threatening. "Just out of curiosity, did you have these kinds of conversations with Bruce before he moved out to the garage?"

"Yes."

"Do you think that could be the reason he moved out there?"

"Partially, but that doesn't explain why he hasn't gone to the office in months."

"You're sure he hasn't left the garage?"

"Pretty sure."

"Okay," Katie said slowly.

The case was starting to seem clearer and clearer to Katie. This wasn't about infidelity. Bruce merely wanted to get away from his wife, and Katie didn't blame him. And now Vivian wasn't sure if he was going to work or not. She could easily be as mistaken about that as she was about Oliver and the playground. That reminded her of Vivian's testimony and Oliver's presence at Bruce's garage.

"What is the connection between your husband and Oliver Banks?"

"Connection? There's no connection." Vivian finally sat down, her temper seeming to cool slightly.

"He brought something to Bruce the other day." Katie was mindful of her words. She didn't want Vivian using anything she said to harm Ashley's case.

"You're sure of that?"

"Pretty sure."

"I don't know."

"Surely you know something," Katie pressed. "That's why you wanted Oliver back in jail."

Vivian sighed. "I want him back in jail because he is a creeper hanging around school grounds. He shouldn't be there. He doesn't have children with him."

"It's a public place."

"Still, it's creepy. I'm trying to protect Penny. The child that exists. I need to keep her safe, and that man makes me uncomfortable. He pops up everywhere. The park. The grocery store. Even outside your office. Everywhere I go with Penny."

"Maybe Bruce has hired him to do the same thing I'm doing for you," Katie suggested.

"Yeah, well he's a criminal. He tried to kill someone by hitting them with his car. He's a psychopath. If Bruce hired that kind of person to investigate me, then we've got real problems."

Katie thought their problems were *real* one way or another. They were essentially separated. It was possible that the healthy birth of the baby Vivian carried would mend that, but the way she seemed to flout doctor's orders, it didn't seem like she even wanted that.

"Let me ask you this," Katie said. "Do you even *want* a second child?"

"I want Penny. That's my focus right now. I'm sure it will shift after birth, but for now, I'm worried about the child currently in my life."

That was a non-answer if Katie had ever heard one. "Okay, well, we aren't getting anywhere with this. We know there is some connection between Bruce and Oliver. Maybe it's nothing sinister. Maybe Oliver took a side job with Uber Eats and he was delivering food." She knew this wasn't true. No company with driving as the basis of employment would hire a barred driver as an employee. But she felt it was time to end the conversation, and this was one way out.

"Maybe," Vivian said chewing on her bottom lip. "I'll let you know if I learn anything."

"Same," Katie said, rising to her feet. "I better get going. Ashley's probably waiting for me."

"Ashley? Ashley Montgomery?"

"Umm, yeah. Of course."

Vivian pushed past Katie and marched out into the hallway. "Nancy Reagan Ross. What did I tell you about talking to strangers?" Vivian said before Katie could even get out of the small room they'd been sharing.

A muffled, sarcastic-sounding answer followed, but Katie couldn't make out the words. No doubt it was Ashley. She hurried out of the room and into the hallway, heading straight for the two adults and one small girl at the other end of the hallway. The exchange ended quickly, and Ashley was on her way out of the building before Katie even reached the group. By the stiffness in her shoulders and the length of her stride, Katie guessed Ashley was furious.

"Why do you have to set her off?" Katie said when she finally reached Vivian.

"Why does she talk to my daughter?"

"Why do you care?"

"I don't like attorneys."

"You made a poor choice in spouse, then."

"Yeah, well. I didn't feel the same way back then."

For the second time that day, Katie was starting to understand Bruce's decision to move to the garage. It also potentially explained his choice to stay away from the office. If Bruce wanted to mend his relationship with his wife, he might be keeping away from the office to distance himself from his profession.

"Alright, well, I need to get going," Katie said.

Ashley would need her help. There was still so much to do in preparation for Oliver's defense, and so much to learn about his case. He'd hit someone with a car—seemingly intentionally—but why? That was one of the questions Ashley might not want answered, but Katie felt like it was important to understand. Without the *why*, they might be able to convince a jury it was an accident. With it, well, that could be a real problem.

Vivian was crouched down in front of Penny, and they were murmuring in low, private voices, their heads leaned close, foreheads grazing. In that moment, Katie could see the emotional bond between this mother and daughter. Whatever Vivian's flaws, she loved her daughter deeply, and that was something. Just before Katie turned to leave, Vivian grimaced and clutched her swollen belly. Her face contorted in pain, then smoothed back out. The expression was gone as quickly as it had come.

The love for Penny was clear, but Vivian's disinterest for her pregnancy was equally clear. She felt certain that this was at least part of Vivian's marital problems. The only question was whether it would become the source of even more, far more serious problems.

17

ASHLEY

Ashley fumed as she stormed out of the courthouse. Vivian had some nerve. Ashley wasn't a saint, but she also wasn't a villain. She posed no danger to Penny, and deep down Vivian knew it.

She burst out of the front door and into the sticky summer air. Sweat instantly beaded along her brow. By the time she reached her office across the street, a thin line of perspiration had made its way down her back, soaking into her shirt.

"Great, just great," Ashley mumbled when she opened the door to her office. The cool air-conditioned air was a relief for the moment, but it would only be a matter of time before she started shivering in her damp clothing.

Elena heard the bell and came to the counter. "Oh, hello, Ashley. How did the hearing go?"

Ashley stormed past the reception desk and into the back portion of the office.

'That bad, huh?" Elena said, her voice dropping low.

"It wasn't bad," Ashley said, stopping and slowly turning toward her office manager. She was furious, but she couldn't take it out on Elena. That wasn't fair. "We actually won the hearing."

"Oh, good."

"I just happened to run into Penny in the hallway."

"Vivian Ross's daughter? What was she doing there alone?"

"She wasn't alone. That was the problem. Vivian was with her. She's a snake. Always prancing around judging other people. Yet she's the one running on a treadmill while she's supposed to be on bedrest. She's probably trying to force an abortion. She doesn't want that child. It's obvious to anyone with eyes."

"That's not good. Is there a way to stop her?"

"No." People had the right to freedom of movement. Despite her dislike for Vivian, she wasn't for changing that concept. Not for any reason.

"Oh, well, I hope everything turns out okay."

"For Penny's sake, I do, too." Ashley paused, then switched the subject. There was no point in discussing that family any further. "I need to make a phone call to the Governor's office. It should only take a few minutes. Can you hold any other calls until I tell you otherwise?"

"Yeah. Sure." Elena nodded enthusiastically.

Ashley headed back to her office with a heavy knot twisting its way into her stomach. She was dreading this call. Not because of the cold reception she would likely receive from the Governor's office, but because she was going to have to hold her tongue, which was distinctly unlike her. She'd have to pretend to be someone else over the next few minutes, but that felt manipulative and wrong. It felt like politics.

Once in her personal office, she settled into her battered, but comfortable chair and lifted the phone receiver. The number was on a letter she'd received the month before. It had come in the mail shortly after the Judicial Nominating Committee had selected her as one of the two finalists. It was from the Governor's office. There was nothing personal about the letter. It was stock, the same thing sent to every attorney who'd made it through committee. It outlined the process and provided the number to call and schedule an interview. Ashley had set the letter next to her phone, and she used it now to dial.

The phone rang twice. Then someone picked up.

"Governor Ingram's office," a high-pitched voice chirped into her ear. "How may I direct your call?"

"Yes. This is Ashley Montgomery. I'm one of the judicial nominees. I was told to—"

"Yes. Ashley Montgomery." The voice had cooled. "The honorable Governor Ingram is available on Thursday, August eighteenth, at two o'clock in the afternoon. Will you make yourself available?"

It probably wouldn't work for her. She'd have to move meetings and continue hearings to make Thursday work. She was a public defender. Every second counted. Yet the Governor seemed to think she had all the time in the world to mold her schedule around whatever worked for "her honor."

"I'll make it work," Ashley said through clenched teeth.

She had a voodoo doll shaped stress ball with "prosecutor" stitched across its chest sitting on her desk. She grabbed it and started squishing its round head in her hand, pressing and crushing, releasing and watching it expand. It was all she could do to keep her temper in check.

"I've put you on her schedule. You should arrive thirty minutes early for your appointment."

"In Des Moines?"

"Yes." What the woman didn't say was *obviously*, but that was clearly conveyed in her tone.

Ashley squished the prosecutor voodoo doll harder in her hand. *Keep your cool. Keep your cool*, she reminded herself. Ashley was going to have to completely block the day off for this interview. Clients would be placed on the backburner, and she hated the thought of that.

"Thank you." Ashley forced the words. There was no reason to thank this person.

"You're welcome. We'll see you on the eighteenth."

Then the receiver went dead. Ashley sighed heavily and cradled her phone. At least that was over. Now she needed to focus on work. Oliver's case. She wondered if Katie had learned anything more about the owner of the vehicle Oliver had been driving at the time of the incident. That was what Ashley considered charges prior to convictions. Incidents. They weren't crimes. Not until conviction. But where was Katie, anyway? She hadn't seen her since Oliver's hearing.

Ashley started heading down the long hallway to the reception area when her cell phone started buzzing. She pulled it out of her back pocket. The screen read *Katie Mickey*. She picked up.

"Speak of the devi—" Ashley froze mid-word.

"Get over here. *Now*."

"Over where?" There was screaming in the background. Blood curdling screams. "What's going on?"

"It's...I...Oh, God."

There were more screams.

"Where are you, Katie?"

But the phone went dead. Ashley called her back, but the line was busy. *Fuck. Fuck. Fuck.* Whatever was happening sounded bad. She wanted to help, but where was Katie? The last time Ashley had seen her investigator was at the courthouse. She pocketed her phone and started running that direction. She didn't know if Katie was still there, but at least she was doing something. She couldn't stand there twiddling her thumbs. Katie was in trouble.

18

KATIE

"Wait," Vivian called out. Her voice was twisted with pain between bouts of heavy breathing. "Please."

Katie was on her way out of the courthouse. She'd only made it a few steps before Vivian's strangled cries had her turning and rushing back.

Vivian was on her knees in the middle of the hallway, one hand clutching her belly with Penny at her side, holding her other hand. Aside from the three of them, the hallway was empty. This was typical of small courthouses. The hallways were busy when a hearing was going on, but people scattered afterward, like roaches disappearing into woodwork. It was the lunch hour, too, so the place was exceptionally empty.

"What happened?" Katie said, rushing to Vivian's side. It had been years since she'd been employed as a police officer, but at times like these, her past experience and training as a first responder resurfaced.

"I. Don't. Know," Vivian said between heavy breaths. "My stomach hurts."

Penny leaned toward Katie and whispered, "I think she had an accident." Her eyes were wide, frightened. She'd probably never seen her mother unglued like this.

Katie looked below Vivian to see a puddle of liquid slowly spreading out around her. "It's her water," Katie said. "It's broken. She's having the baby."

"I can't have this baby. It's too early."

There were a lot of things Katie could have said in that moment. Mainly that Vivian had brought this on herself. She'd disregarded doctor's orders that she remain on bedrest. The doctor had given those orders for a reason —to avoid early labor. The inevitable had happened, and Vivian's reaction was *this can't be happening*. It irritated Katie, but she held her tongue. It was not the time or the place to lecture Vivian.

"I'm going to call an ambulance," Katie said, pulling out her phone and dialing as she spoke. Her voice sounded so calm, the opposite of how she felt. Inside, she was all jitters and nervous energy.

Vivian had dropped forward so she was on her hands and her knees. She moaned and rocked forward and backward. Penny was backing away slowly.

"9-1-1 what's your emergency?"

"This is Katie Mickey. I'm on the second floor of the courthouse. I need an ambulance. A woman is in preterm labor."

"Someone will be there shortly."

Seconds later, Katie heard sirens. Then George Thomanson came running up the stairs in his full deputy uniform. "What's happening here?"

"She's having her baby," Katie said.

"It isn't a baby yet," Vivian said through gritted teeth.

A moment later, three EMT's came rushing up the stairs, crowding around Vivian.

Katie's eyes drifted to Penny. She was in a corner, scrunched behind a chair, seemingly hiding from her mother's pain. Katie instantly felt sorry for the girl. She was not meant to see any of this. It was too much.

"Vivian," Katie said, coming closer to the woman in labor. The EMT's were loading her onto a stretcher. "What do you want me to do with Penny? Bring her to the hospital?"

"No. Keep her with you. Penny," Vivian shouted, looking around her. Penny came out of hiding and to her mother's side. "I'm going to the hospital for a bit. Can you stay with Miss Katie here?" She was trying to keep her voice upbeat, a failed attempt to ease Penny's worry, and it made her sound unhinged rather than positive.

Penny nodded.

"I'll come get you as soon as I can. Okay?"

Penny nodded again, a tear sliding down her cheek.

"I love you, baby."

"I love you too, Mommy," Penny said with a sob.

Katie grabbed her phone and dialed Ashley's number.

"Speak of the devi—"

Katie cut her off. "Get over here, *now*."

"Over where?"

Vivian screamed. A blood-curdling cry that settled into a whimper.

"What's going on?" Ashley sounded scared.

"It's...I..." Blood started pooling beneath Vivian, and she whined like a dying animal. Katie was no medical expert, but it didn't take an expert to realize this was not a good sign. "Oh, God."

"Mommy," Penny shouted, reaching a hand toward her mother.

Katie pulled the little girl into her arms. "It's going to be okay," she said, her voice soft. "Your mom is going to be fine." She had no idea if there was any truth to her words. Vivian was losing a lot of blood. There was a hospital in Brine County, but it was at the edge of the county. It would take even an ambulance crew ten or fifteen minutes to get there.

The EMTs carried Vivian out. Ashley came rushing up the stairs shouting, "*Katie! Katie! Where are you?*"

"I'm here," Katie said, pulling Penny closer to her side.

"What happened?" Ashley said when she finally reached Katie. She was short of breath but for an entirely different reason than Vivian had been. "Are you okay?"

"A little shaken up, but we are fine. Vivian's in labor."

Ashley's eyes traveled down to Penny and her expression softened. "Oh, Penny. That must have been hard to see."

Penny nodded and wiped her tears with the back of her hand.

"Do you want to come back to our office? We can send Elena to get some ice cream. Would you like that?" Katie asked.

Penny's head slowly bobbed in a nod. Her head was pressed up against Katie's thigh, so she felt the motion more than she saw it.

A janitor appeared and began mopping up the mess on the floor with a grimace on his face. George Thomanson stepped around him and came up to Ashley and Katie.

"You two, always rushing to one another's rescue. I have to say it warms my heart."

Ashley narrowed her eyes. "We don't need a knight in shining armor when we have each other."

"Yet, here I am," he gestured to himself with open arms, chuckling to himself.

Ashley rolled her eyes. "Yet here you are."

Katie and George's friendship had blossomed over the past year, and that friendship had translated into a few casual dates. It was too soon to know if it was going anywhere, but it was nice to see that Ashley and George could be in the same room without ripping at one another's throats. There was a time when that wasn't possible. This banter between them now wasn't exactly kind, but it was more playful than it was vicious.

"Well, I better get going."

"Where?" Katie asked. She had thought he would come have lunch with them. It was nearing one o'clock and her stomach was growling.

"Sheriff St. James wants me out at the hospital."

"Why?" Ashley's tone had grown incredulous.

"Don't know. He just said he wanted someone there in case things go bad."

"Things," Ashley repeated. "What kinds of things?"

"I don't know. I'm not him. I'm just a peon deputy. I do as I'm told."

"Will you keep us updated?" Katie asked.

"Yeah."

It was odd that the sheriff would request a deputy's presence for the birth of a baby, but it was also a bit fortuitous, or so Katie thought. This way they'd get live updates. Penny was going to be worried about her mother. There was nothing they could do about that. She'd worry until her mother was back home and on her feet. What they could do was give her regular updates so she knew that Vivian and the baby were going to be okay.

"Thank you," Katie said.

They all made their way out of the courthouse. George in front and the two women flanking the sniffling little girl. It felt ominous, walking out like that behind a fully clothed deputy, like they were being escorted to jail.

19

VIVIAN

The pain was excruciating. Vivian's body was betraying her. There was fire everywhere, burning her from the inside, stretching to every inch of her body. She was being ripped in half by wave after wave of body-shattering contractions, earthquakes that shook her to her core. It wasn't this way with Penny. It couldn't have been. She would have remembered.

Am I dying? Vivian wondered. Did people still die in childbirth. She didn't know. The news covered the criminals and the murders, but she couldn't think of a time any media outlet had mentioned a woman who had died in childbirth. Did that mean it didn't happen or they didn't care to discuss it?

"Keep breathing, Ms. Ross," a kind-eyed, female paramedic said as they loaded Vivian's stretcher into the ambulance. "You've done this before. You can do it again."

Breathing was not easy. Her body and mind were panicking. Vivian gritted her teeth as another soul splitting wave passed, then she looked at the paramedic. She was in her early twenties. Vivian studied her features and saw nothing recognizable.

"Do I know you?" She asked. Bruce had wanted Vivian to become a local socialite, to know everyone in town. He thought it was good for business, but Vivian wasn't socialite material. She may look like one, but she was an introvert. She preferred solitude over the company of others.

"No. But your husband handled my grandparents' estate after they died. He's a great guy."

"Everyone seems to think so," Vivian said. This was the most honest answer she could give, the one she often handed out to the public. Bruce was well liked, just not by his family.

"Have you called him?"

Vivian gritted her teeth as another wave of pain started building within her.

"I can call him." The paramedic removed a cell phone from her back pocket. "I have his number." The paramedic looked up and must have seen the rage in Vivian's eyes, because she quickly added, "Not for personal reasons, of course. I called him a lot when he was working on the estate. He would never..." Her voice trailed off.

If Vivian wasn't in so much pain, she would have laughed at that statement. She didn't give two shits if Bruce cheated on her, and she'd welcome it if he'd leave. That would be a relief. It would make the whole process of getting away from him far easier. But that wasn't the case. Bruce owned her. He owned Penny. He had put a good deal of effort into selling the perfect family scenario to the Brine public. Their fictitious love was another thing he owned, and he did not leave his belongings behind.

"I'll just give him a heads up—" The young paramedic unlocked her phone and started pressing buttons.

"No!" Vivian shouted. It was a grunt and a shout. She was at war with her body, and she didn't need to get into a separate battle with this well-meaning, but naïve paramedic. Yet, she couldn't just allow her to call Bruce like he was a regular husband.

"You don't want him to know?"

"Not. Right. Now," Vivian said, heaving several breaths. "It may be nothing."

The paramedic's eyes shifted from Vivian's sweating face to her protruding belly, then back up to her face.

"Your water broke. That isn't good. Not when you are just seven months along with the baby."

"Fetus," Vivian corrected. "It's a baby when it's born."

The paramedic narrowed her eyes, then turned back to her phone. "Bruce should be a part of this, Mrs. Ross."

Just great, Vivian thought, *I'm "Mrs. Ross" and he's "Bruce."*

This girl was infatuated with her husband. Another person loyal to him while demoting Vivian to his last name with a *Mrs.* in front of it. It was like she wasn't a real person before Bruce came into her life. She was disappointed, but really, she shouldn't be. Brine was full of people like this. That was why she'd hired Katie Mickey to investigate Bruce. Vivian wanted Katie to dig up dirt on her husband, gather some definitive evidence that would remove him from the pedestal where Brine had placed him.

"This is *my* medical emergency," Vivian screeched, trying in vain to get through to the girl. "Not Bruce's. *I* will decide when to call him."

The paramedic pocketed her phone, but she wore a mutinous expression. She would call Bruce the moment she was out of Vivian's line of sight, Vivian felt sure of it. Thankfully, that was the last of their conversation. The paramedic did not speak to Vivian, and she did not respond. The only sound was the whirring of the siren atop the ambulance, and Vivian's grunts and groans in pain.

After what felt like an eternity, the siren cut off, and the ambulance slowed. They were at the hospital. It was a relief. She couldn't wait to get out of this judgmental paramedic's presence. A back door flung open, revealing another paramedic. Together, the paramedics wheeled her out of the ambulance and through the emergency entrance. Once inside, her relief dissipated, instantly replaced by dread.

"Hello, sweetheart," Bruce said, baring what everyone else would see as a kind smile. To Vivian, it was twisted, and it held cruelty beneath those lips. "I came as soon as I heard."

Vivian didn't doubt that. There was no other way he could have beaten the ambulance to the hospital. Why had she dared to hope that he wouldn't be there? Nobody knew the real *him*. They still saw him as that polished attorney from a high-powered family. They didn't know the monster lurking beneath or his downward spiral over the past month. His law partners knew or suspected, but they'd kept quiet about the changes in Bruce. It was strictly business. Their firm bore Bruce's father, grandfather, great-grandfather, and great-great-grandfather's names. They attracted clients based on that name. They wouldn't want it sullied.

But Bruce did look better today than he had in quite some time. He seemed sober, but then again, he was good at acting. Prescription pills were his poison of choice, so there would be no smell like alcohol or marijuana. It was easier to fake sobriety that way. All he needed to do was pretend around people who hardly knew him. She could catch the telltale signs of using, like enlarged pupils, and fidgeting hands, but nobody aside from her would look at him that closely. Bruce's clothes were clean and pressed, his hair brushed. He looked like a regular husband there to support his wife. Yet, to Vivian, he couldn't cover up the sallowness of his skin or the crazy in his eyes.

A doctor and a nurse took over for the paramedics, wheeling her into a room, barking questions about her due date and medical conditions. Vivian ignored them all. They weren't talking to her; their questions were aimed at Bruce. As always, when Bruce was around, her input wasn't necessary. Even though the discussion involved her body, not his.

"Get her in a hospital gown, and then I'll take a look," the doctor said to the nurse.

The doctor was in complete medical gear with a mask over his face, but the voice was distinctly male, and the eyes crinkled in the corners as he spoke. She'd guess he was a man somewhere between forty and sixty.

"Yes, sir." The nurse was dressed similarly, with blonde hair pulled tightly into a bun behind her head. Her voice was high pitched, and her eyes were an aqua green with no crow's feet. She was young.

Bruce stood back in a corner with his arms crossed, watching as the nurse helped Vivian out of her clothes and into the loose-fitting hospital gown. He wore an expression of disgust that could only mean that he was angry, too angry to touch her. At least not in front of medical professionals.

"Lie down," the nurse said once Vivian was dressed. "I'll be right back with the doctor."

Vivian did as instructed, and another wave of pain washed over her, causing her to whimper.

Bruce pushed off the wall, coming to her bedside, his arms still crossed. "That's right. Whimper like the little bitch that you are."

Vivian clamped her lips together, but she couldn't stop the keening sound from escaping.

"It hurts, doesn't it?" He said, his voice low and cruel. "You deserve it, you little bitch. Do you know who called me to tell me you were in labor?"

Vivian shook her head, unable to speak. This was so much like an incident in her bedroom a few weeks earlier. He'd assaulted her then and he would again now. Soon she would feel his hands in her hair, gripping it at its base and pulling, ripping, tugging at the only place in her body that wasn't already burning with pain.

"Lucy Green, in the Clerk's office." He stopped talking, giving her a hard look. One that said, *I expect an answer, and I expect it now.* But she didn't know what to answer. He hadn't asked a question.

"Okay," Vivian forced out.

"Do you know what she also told me?"

Vivian shook her head. This was a game he liked to play. Guess the answer. It was fun for him because he always won and she was the perpetual loser. Which was par for the course in their marriage. Bruce would always win.

"Lucy said that you were in Court today, testifying against Oliver Banks. Is that true?"

Another contraction ripped through her, taking her breath away.

He shook his head. "I don't know why I even bother to ask you these kinds of questions. You can't be trusted to tell the truth."

"Why do you care?" Vivian asked when the pain started to recede. "You don't even know Oliver."

"You have no idea who I know and who I don't know. That's why you are supposed to *ask* before you do dumb shit like testifying against someone in open court."

Just then, the doctor returned. Bruce took a step back, smiling at him. "The good doctor is back," he said, his tone suddenly cheery. Mr. Hyde had disappeared, at least for the moment.

The doctor took his place between Vivian's legs without saying a word to her first. It felt like a violation for him to be moving around down there without explaining to her what he planned to do. He remained down there for a few minutes that would have seemed long and awkward if Vivian hadn't spent the past six months with doctors between her legs inspecting "the baby."

Then he wheeled his chair back and stood, turning to Bruce. "The baby's coming. We can't stop it at this point."

It was asinine that this kind of thing was happening in 2022. She was the patient, not her husband. She was a whole person, not simply a vessel for Bruce's precious "baby." Why did everyone insist on treating her like she didn't matter? The answer was Bruce, of course. He treated her like a second-class citizen, and others followed his lead. He was an important man, after all.

"Would you like an epidural?" Again, this question was addressed to Bruce.

It made Vivian want to scream. They could put an epidural in Bruce's head if they wanted. That would solve a whole lot of problems for her.

"If you want one," the doctor continued, "now is the time. If this progresses much further, it'll be too late."

"No. We are going about it naturally, aren't we honey?" Bruce said, a smile on his face and a warning in his eyes. "She wants to experience every second of pain so she can remember all that she went through to bring this beautiful baby boy into the world."

This was his punishment for her testimony at Oliver's hearing. Even though she had no idea at the time there was some connection between her husband and that violent man. Now, as the doctor and Bruce chatted on, discussing the chances of the baby and for Vivian, pieces started clicking together. The news had reported that Oliver had struck his victim with a BMW. Their BMW was missing. And now all this about her testifying against Oliver. It meant only one thing. *He knew*. He knew her connection to Oliver's victim. How? She had no idea, but Bruce always seemed to have his ways.

"Preeclampsia!" Bruce shouted, pulling Vivian out of her thoughts. His face was red with rage.

"Yes, sir," the doctor said, his tone remaining even, calm. Parents shouting at him was obviously not a new thing. "She's on bedrest. That's what her chart says. I would have reacted sooner, but–"

"Why didn't I know about this?"

Both men's gazes shifted to Vivian. Now they wanted to talk to her. She forced her expression to remain firm, unwavering, despite the pain that continually ripped through her body. She had kept something from Bruce. A secret that he could not force her to reveal. And that was a win of sorts.

"What does that mean?" Bruce said, turning back to the doctor, his tone growing higher pitched, more desperate.

"It means this will be a dangerous delivery for the baby and the mother."

Vivian's ears perked up at this news. That meant they'd put her out or give her an epidural at the very least. Either way, Bruce's "punishment" would be thwarted.

"The baby and his mother are in grave danger."

"But the baby will live." Of course Bruce didn't give two shits if Vivian lived, at least not at this point.

"I can't make any promises," the doctor said.

Several nurses bustled into the room, running around Vivian with shocking speed. As they moved faster, her head seemed to move slower.

"We are going to have to put her under and wheel her to surgery," the doctor said.

"Can I come?"

"I'm sorry, but no. If this was a normal cesarean, I would say yes. It's common for fathers to sit behind the mother while the baby is extracted. But that's when the procedure can be done with an epidural. We have to put Mrs. Ross completely under. This is a complicated surgical procedure. We cannot have any guests present."

"You're kidding."

A nurse came to her side, and murmured something about an IV, but Vivian wasn't listening. She couldn't help but feel as though she had won. At least for now. The nurse must have given her the medicine to put her under because her pain quickly receded and the voices around her started fuzzing. Her eyes grew heavy, and she laid her head back. She had won. Even if she died during the surgery, she'd done so on her terms. She'd escaped Bruce's dominion. He had no control over her or this thing living inside of her. At least not for now.

20

ASHLEY

Penny was distraught. That was expected. Her whole world had changed in a matter of minutes. Her mother could be dead or dying in childbirth. The baby inside her mother was most certainly dead, dying or barely hanging on. Penny could lose everyone she loves. They could already be gone.

"Would anyone like some hot chocolate?" Elena said, breaking through Ashley's thoughts. They were all in the conference room at the public defender's office—Penny, Elena, Ashley, and Katie—but Ashley didn't know quite what to say. Penny had been sitting silently, staring at the wall, since they'd arrived.

Nobody answered. Penny didn't move.

"I'll go ahead and fetch some anyway." Elena dashed out of the room, probably thankful to get out of the tense environment.

"What do we do now?" Katie said, her gaze resting on Penny's frozen features. "We can't just sit here twiddling our thumbs. There's got to be *something* we can do."

Ashley was about to answer. To tell Katie that there wasn't anything else they could do. At least not until they had some updates from George out at the hospital. But she was interrupted by the sound of raised voices. It sounded like a man and a woman, but the woman was not Elena.

"I'm going to go check on that," Ashley said. She glanced at Penny, who hadn't moved a muscle. Her entire body was still taut, rigid, and frozen into position. "You stay here with Penny."

The voices grew louder.

"Are you sure?"

There was a loud banging sound and Ashley stood. "Yes. Whatever this is, Penny doesn't need to see it."

Ashley stepped out of the conference room and strode down the hallway, her hands balled into fists and her head held high. When she reached the main reception area, she saw Elena was cowering in a corner, trying to make herself small. Elena was never good with conflict, and Michael Michello, Katie's father, was at the reception desk. A woman stood at the other side, banging a fist on the desk.

"She's here. I know it! Why are you lying to me?" the woman shouted.

"No! She's not. This is a place of business, not a daycare," Michael shouted back. He didn't lose his cool often. He wasn't young anymore, but it was almost frightening to see him rising to his full height, face red with rage.

"You have her."

"By God woman, are you hard of hearing?"

It seemed like this conversation was going round and round in circles. Ashley figured now was as good a time as any to interrupt. "Who?" Ashley said, coming to Michael's side.

"Oh, good. Ashley's here. A voice of reason." The woman's gaze cut to Ashley, her nostril's flaring.

"Hello, Miranda," Ashley said.

At first Ashley did not recognize the woman, but now that she saw her face straight on, she recognized her as Miranda Birch. They'd gone to high school together. They'd run around with different crowds, but the class size wasn't large, so everyone knew everyone back then. But Miranda had moved away after graduation and Ashley hadn't seen her for at least twenty years, maybe more.

"I didn't realize you were back in town," Ashley said.

"Yeah, well, I am."

Miranda was tall and whip thin with dark brown hair and bright, piercing blue eyes. She'd always been pretty, but in a hard way. She'd grown up in the trailer park at the outskirts of town. Her parents had been drug dealers, in and out of prison until both their lives ended prematurely. Overdoses and hard living did not make for longevity in life.

"So, you are. What is the problem here?"

"This man," Miranda pointed a finger at Michael, her long, fake nail merely inches from his nose, "is lying to me."

"What is the *alleged* lie?" Ashley liked Michael. He'd been in trouble before, but he had straightened his life out. Or at least he was trying to stay straight. That was more than Ashley could say about most of her clients.

"He says that Nancy Reagan Ross is not here."

"Why are you looking for her?"

"So, she is here."

"I didn't say that. I asked why you, an adult individual who is not a mother or a relative of any kind, is looking for a child. Naturally, that raises some red flags in my mind."

"Whatever, Ashley. You sound like a prosecutor."

Ashley's face reddened. She was instantly reminded of why she and Miranda had never been friends. Miranda always knew how to cut to the quick. Her words had a bite, and she almost always used them against other girls or women. She was one of those people who described herself as a "guy's girl." Which only meant that all connections formed with women were superficial, and she'd throw another woman under the bus any day without a second thought so long as it suited her.

"I sound like a human being," Ashley growled. "One with sense. And if you had any sense, you'd answer my questions before I call the cops and have you removed from my building." High school classmate or not, Ashley was not going to tolerate bullying. Not here, not anywhere.

"Bruce wants her."

"Bruce? Are you two still friends?"

"Yes."

Bruce Ross had also been in Ashley's high school class. Back then neither of them had been lawyers, but Bruce still thought of himself as far higher on the social ladder than Ashley. He'd been the football player who dated cheerleaders, Vivian and her kind. Ashley had been nerdy. An introvert reader who kept to herself. She did not run around with their crowd.

Miranda had not been part of Bruce's crowd, either. She'd hung around the hard partiers, the drug users, and juvenile delinquents. Yet somehow, she and Bruce had formed a friendship. A one-sided friendship in Ashley's opinion. Miranda would do anything for Bruce, but Bruce couldn't be bothered to return the favor. Ashley hadn't understood it. They'd been close by the time they all graduated, but Ashley hadn't seen Miranda since. She assumed Bruce hadn't either. Apparently, she'd been wrong about that.

"Well, you aren't Bruce, and you aren't her parent, so I'm not going to disclose the whereabouts of Nancy Reagan Ross. If Bruce wants to stop by and ask the same question, I'm more than willing to provide whatever knowledge I do or do not have about Ms. Ross."

"That sounds like a bullshit lawyer answer."

"It is a bullshit lawyer answer. That's all you're going to get. I'm a lawyer, remember?"

"I thought you were my friend."

"Oh, Miranda. We aren't friends. I haven't seen you for two decades. We aren't even acquaintances." It was Ashley's turn to use her words as a weapon.

"Whatever," Miranda said, turning on her heel and marching toward the door, opening it wide to let in a burst of hot, summer air. "You haven't heard the end of this," she called over her shoulder before slamming the door behind her.

"That was lovely," Ashley mumbled.

"That woman is a snake," Michael hissed.

"Yeah. One with a bizarre reappearing act. I haven't thought of her in years. What the hell is she doing back here?"

"Hopefully, she's back for a short visit," Michael said. "A very short visit."

Somehow, Ashley knew he was wrong. She felt certain that Miranda would be back for Penny, but why? Why was a woman that Penny didn't even know showing up to collect her? Something was happening out at that hospital, and Ashley needed to know what it was. Penny's future depended on it.

21

KATIE

"Go to the hospital," Ashley said as she walked back into the conference room. Outwardly, she appeared calm, but Katie knew better. The slight flush to her cheeks and the tight set of her jaw revealed the rage hidden beneath.

"Who was that?" Katie asked.

Ashley's gaze cut to Penny—she hadn't moved the entire time Ashley was gone—then cut back to Katie. "It doesn't matter."

"What do you mean it –"

Ashley cut her off. "Just go," she said, her eyes pleading.

Katie didn't know what was happening, but it seemed bad. "Shouldn't I wait for George to call?"

"No. George might have a muzzle."

That caught Katie's attention. George's metaphoric muzzling would only happen if the Sheriff's Department was actively investigating a crime. He couldn't talk to someone outside the agency about an ongoing investigation. But what crime? There was only one way to find out. She had to go to the hospital.

"Okay," Katie rose to her feet. "I'm on my way." She grabbed her keys and rushed out the door.

It took her fifteen minutes to reach the hospital, five to find a parking spot, and another five to get inside the building. It didn't take her long to find Vivian. Hers was the room with all the deputies standing around outside. George was with the group. When he saw her, he made a quick jerk of his head, indicating she should head further down the hallway, away from the other deputies' line of sight. It was not a good sign. At least not for Vivian.

Katie retreated to a far corner near an exit door and waited for George. He showed up a few minutes later.

"What's going on?" Katie said, careful to keep her voice low.

"Sorry I didn't call," George looked sheepish. "I couldn't."

"You're muzzled. I get it. But why?"

George looked left and then right, checking to see if anyone was nearby. Then he leaned forward and whispered, "The baby died."

"How sad for Vivian," Katie said. Although, her words were half-hearted. She doubted Vivian cared at all about the child. She'd made it clear that she had no bond with the baby, and she didn't intend to bond with him until after birth.

"And Bruce."

"Bruce? Did he want the baby?"

"Judging by the number of calls our office has received from him, yeah, yeah, he did."

Katie scoffed. Actions spoke louder than words, and Bruce's behaviors —hiding out in that garage, spending time with people like Oliver Banks— did not translate into "loving Dad."

"That's not all."

"What do you mean?" Katie asked, alarm electrifying every inch of her body. Childbirth was common, but it wasn't safe. If Vivian was on bedrest, that directive could have been more for her safety than the safety of the baby. If something happened to Vivian, there was no telling what would happen to Penny.

"Is Vivian okay?"

George opened his mouth to speak, but no words followed.

"She's not," Katie swallowed hard, "dead, is she?" It wasn't common for women to die in childbirth anymore, but that didn't mean it never happened.

"Vivian's fine. She's recovering in the room over there. The hospital staff won't let the deputies take her until after she's fully recovered."

"Take her," Katie repeated. "Take her where?"

This was not a necessary question. Katie knew the answer. But the words had come from her as a filler, allowing time for her emotions to unfurl. To catch up with the idea that the Government was criminally charging a mother who had just lost her child.

"To jail."

"For what?" It was more of a demand rather than a question.

"The death of the child. The County Attorney instructed us to charge her with Child Endangerment Causing Death."

Katie's nostrils flared. Child Endangerment Causing Death was a Class B Felony in the state of Iowa. It was not as serious as a murder charge, but it was pretty close. B Felonies commonly carried a twenty-five-year prison sentence, which was bad enough, but Child Endangerment Causing Death was a special sort of B Felony. It carried a fifty-year prison sentence. If Charles Hanson, the local prosecutor, got a conviction, Vivian would spend the remainder of her life behind bars.

"I don't understand. How can the prosecutor do that?"

Society seemed to be trending toward awarding personhood to fetuses, but the law had not reached that point. If the baby was stillborn, that meant that he died inside Vivian's body, and wasn't technically a "child." Without a child, there could be no child endangerment. There was no "fetus endangerment" code section in Iowa. At least not yet.

"The baby was alive at birth, but he only lived for a few minutes."

Through her career investigating crimes, first as a police officer, and later as a private investigator, Katie had realized the importance of minutes. A back turned for a few minutes made the difference between a drowned child and a wet kid. Delaying a trip to the bank by five minutes could be the difference between becoming a hostage or a spectator to a hostage situation. So many crimes were this way. A game of minutes. A package of seconds that forever changed lives.

"Okay, but I don't see what Vivian had to do with that. Isn't that more of a doctor problem than a mother issue?" Katie's mind whirred and her nerves grated. Logically, the charges made sense, but it didn't feel fair.

Mothers were not solely responsible for the wellbeing of their unborn children.

"In this case, no, but I'll tell you the doctors and nurses around here seem awfully nervous about this turn of events."

"Yeah, well they should be."

Any misdiagnosis or a mistake during delivery in the future could result in incarceration. Katie imagined it was stressful enough facing malpractice lawsuits. The possibility of criminal charges would cause that stress to skyrocket. If this trend continued, it wouldn't be long before these medical professionals found a new area of expertise outside labor and delivery. That would make things less safe for the mother and child, not more safe.

"There was apparently a hearing earlier today," George said, turning the conversation back to Vivian. "Maybe you were there. One for Oliver Banks. Ashley was representing him. Charles said that Ashley presented some evidence indicating that Vivian was on bedrest, and she'd been running on a treadmill."

"Yeah, and..." Katie's anger grew. She knew what he would say, but she wanted to make him say it. They were going to blame the charges on Ashley and Vivian.

"And the doctors are prepared to testify that Vivian's disregarding of the order for bedrest was the reason she went into early labor. The early labor caused the baby to die. Ergo, Vivian's actions endangered a living child and caused him to die."

"But he wasn't a child when she was doing those things. He was a fetus. He wasn't a child until he was born. And when he was born, he was born in a hospital. What was Vivian doing to endanger him at that point? Only what every other mother does, rely on medical staff."

George shrugged. "That kind of analysis is above my pay grade. Sheriff St. James and the County Attorney want her charged. It's a political thing and an election year for both of them. There's nothing I can do about it." He paused, then looked around furtively. "Listen, I got to go. If I'm caught talking to you, I'm going to get a boot up my ass."

Katie nodded. The deputies all knew Katie's relationship with Ashley. They'd consider George a traitor if they saw him talking to her now. Battle lines had been drawn, and Katie was not on George's team anymore.

"Go ahead. I've got to call Ashley anyway. Penny is at the office. We'll have to find somewhere for her to go." Although Katie had no idea where that would be. Penny did not have a relationship with her father. She didn't seem to even like him. Yet he was the only parent left.

"Penny?"

"Vivian's daughter, Nancy. She goes by Penny, at least to her friends."

"Oh. Okay. I'll call you tonight," George said. Then he saluted and flashed her a sad grin before heading down the hallway and disappearing around the corner, undoubtedly to join his fellow deputies as they acted as sentries outside Vivian's door.

"Fuck," Katie said as she let out a long breath.

This was a mess. One partially of Ashley and her own making. Katie had taken that picture of Vivian on the treadmill. Ashley had introduced it into the public record. Now Charles was using it to charge Vivian criminally. Katie was not eager to share any of this information with Ashley, but there was no point in delaying the inevitable. It was time to return to the office, face the music, then do what Ashley did best—find a way to get Vivian out of this mess. Katie hoped it wouldn't be an impossible task.

22

ASHLEY

"They are charging Vivian," Katie said. Ashley could hear the strain in her voice through the phone. "And it's our fault."

"Give me a minute," Ashley said, rising to her feet, every nerve in her body tense.

She was still in the conference room with Penny. The little girl was finally starting to come out of her shock, sitting quietly and coloring. It was a good sign that she was moving again, but not so good that she'd chosen to color her page in all blacks and grays. Ashley would normally describe a songbird as chipper, but a gray songbird with black wings didn't look all that different from a crow.

"I'll be right back," she said to Penny. She stepped out of the room and closed the door behind her. "Now, what's going on? Of course, the hospital is charging her. Babies are expensive. Vivian is not trying to say that we need to pay her medical bills, is she? Aren't we doing enough by watching her kid?" It was just like Vivian to say they somehow caused her early labor. She was the type of woman who thought the world revolved around her.

"They are charging her criminally."

It took a few beats of silence for that statement to sink in, then Ashley's heartrate doubled. "With what?"

"Child Endangerment Causing Death."

"The fetus died?"

"Yup."

"Shit."

"Exactly."

"But Penny..." Ashley said, her voice trailing off.

How was she was going to explain any of this to poor Penny? *Hey, Penny, your mother, she's going to jail for a very long time, and that baby, well, he's dead. Now you have to live with your dad. What's that? You have no relationship with him. Well, the law doesn't differentiate between good dads and shit dads. All dads get their children over non-blood-related friends.* Then a thought struck her.

"How can they charge that? The hospital staff oversaw the baby's care after birth. Wouldn't they be the ones responsible for the health and safety of the child?"

"I thought the same thing. I asked George about it. He said the baby lived a few minutes. The deputies found some doctors that are saying that Vivian's avoidance of bedrest caused early labor and that caused the death of the baby. The prosecutor has the picture of Vivian running on the treadmill. The one we used during Oliver's hearing. That's why they are charging her."

"That's bullshit."

"I get the sense that George feels the same way, but the Sheriff and the County Attorney made the charging decision together. It's over his head."

Ashley could guess there was one other person in that decision-making process and that was the alleged "victim," Bruce Ross.

"Have you left the hospital?"

"Yes."

"Go back."

"Why?"

"I want you to talk to Vivian. Tell her not to talk to the cops."

"That won't work. They won't let me in to see her. There are at least five deputies outside her room at all times. They would have taken her to jail already, but the hospital staff won't allow it. They want her to recover first. It'll be a few days before they can take her."

"They can't prevent you from talking to her."

"Well, they have."

"Shit. Shit. Shit." Ashley paused, biting a nail, and ripping the corner off painfully. "Call her then. They can't prevent her from talking on the phone."

"Okay."

"Do it when you get back here. I want to talk to Vivian myself. Penny can hang out with Elena while we do that."

"Alright. I'll be back in a few minutes."

Ashley hung up and paced up and down the long hallway a few times, taking long, even breaths, trying to calm her racing heart. Katie was right. They'd given the County Attorney the ammunition to charge Vivian. Ashley had introduced the exhibit and elicited the information about bedrest on cross examination. She'd done it out of spite. There was little to no evidentiary value in the use of the photograph, but still she'd used it. Now it was backfiring.

But still, the charges were problematic. No matter the change in the United States Supreme Court's protection of abortion, the Iowa Code defined a child as after birth until the age of thirteen, at least that was the definition in the code sections dedicated to child endangerment. That meant a minor thirteen years or older was not a "child," and neither was a fetus.

After a few more calming breaths, she mustered the energy to return to the conference room with Penny.

"Was that my mom?" Penny said, without looking away from her gray bird. She was in the process of shading the sky a thick, inky black.

"It was Katie."

"Was she calling about my mom?"

"Yes."

"She's alive?"

"Yes," Ashley felt a surge of gratefulness that she could provide at least this small morsel of good news to the little girl.

"But..."

"But she won't be coming home for a while."

"Because..."

There was no easy way to say this, but jail was better than serious medical issues, and honesty was often the best policy. Especially with children. "Because she's going to jail. The baby, umm, didn't make it."

"Why would my mom be in trouble for that?"

"Honestly," Ashley dropped into the chair beside the little girl. "I don't know. That shouldn't be the case, but sometimes adults make bad decisions."

"Adults make bad decisions a lot."

"Yeah, I guess we do."

They settled into silence, the only sound the scrape of the crayon against paper as Penny continued darkening the sky, enclosing the tiny bird in bleakness. She couldn't help thinking that Penny must feel very much like that little bird. Like the world was closing in around her, and there was nothing she could do to stop it.

"Ashley," Katie burst into the room, Elena trailing behind her. "Are you ready to do this?"

Ashley stood and turned to Penny, who still hadn't looked away from her coloring. "I'm going to go with Katie to call your mom."

"I want to talk to her."

Ashley should have expected this, but for some reason, the thought hadn't even crossed her mind. "For now, are you okay with waiting with Elena? We have some serious adult stuff to tell your mom, but then you can speak to her. Does that work?" She was phrasing it as a question, an option that the child could choose. Penny had no control over this situation, and Ashley wanted to give her a little freedom over her life.

It wasn't much, but it seemed to have a positive effect on the child. For the first time, Penny paused in coloring and met Ashley's gaze. "That's acceptable."

Ashley smiled and stood, allowing Elena to claim her seat, then she disappeared out of the conference room, motioning for Katie to join her in her office so they could make the call. This was not going to be an easy conversation. Vivian already hated her. She was going to blow a gasket when she found out that Penny had been with Ashley since she'd left for the hospital, *and* she was facing serious criminal charges.

Yet it had to be done.

"Are you ready?" Katie said once they were inside Ashley's office with the door closed.

"As I'll ever be."

Then Katie started dialing.

23

VIVIAN

Vivian didn't dream during the procedure. There was no pain from the surgery, so she knew she was well and truly asleep, but it was more suffocating than regular sleep. Darkness pressed upon her like a tomb. Maybe she was dead, and this was her eternity. She hadn't lived all that great of a life. She could be a better person; she could be a worse person. An eternity of nothingness would be as fitting a punishment as any.

Then she started hearing faint noises. Far away at first but growing steadily louder. A rhythmic beep—beep—beep, and a whirring sound. They sounded mechanical, but she couldn't pinpoint the machines or why she'd be anywhere near machines. As the haze of anesthesia continued to subside, she forced her heavy eyelids to flutter open. It took her a moment to register her surroundings. Beige walls. Sterile smell. Beige furniture. No knickknacks. No pictures. She was in a hospital.

"How are you feeling?" A soft voice asked.

Vivian turned her head to see a middle-aged black woman, looking toward Vivian with a soft, almost sad gaze.

"I, um, I don't know," Vivian's voice was scratchy with disuse.

"I'm Nurse Jackie," the nurse said. "I'll be taking care of you this afternoon."

Jackie brought a mug that said *Brine County Hospital* on the side toward

Vivian. It was large and plastic with a lid and a bending straw. Hash marks ticked across the side, indicating different measurements. Nurse Jackie brought the straw to Vivian's lips, and she drank deeply.

"Thank you," Vivian said.

Nurse Jackie wheeled a table to her bedside and placed the mug of water on top of it, the ice rattling against its sides.

"I'll give you a few moments for your head to clear, but then we'll need to get you up and moving around."

"Get me up?" Vivian asked. "Didn't I just have surgery?"

Nurse Jackie nodded. "But a cesarean is a different type of surgery. It is typical to get you up and moving within hours of the procedure. We find it best that patients get up right away, otherwise it gets harder and harder to cross that bridge."

That was when it hit her. She'd had a cesarean, which meant the baby was here. She looked around the room, left, then right, then left again. "The baby." Vivian said, surprised to hear the panic in her voice. "Where is he?"

She'd tried so hard not to love him, to distance herself from even the idea of a child. He was one more thing to tie her to Bruce. A person he could wield against her, hold over her, use to force her into submission. But now that he was here, she had to have him, to hold him, to smell the soft baby smell of his head.

Nurse Jackie pursed her full lips.

"Where is Bruce?" Vivian said, panic building within her chest. He took her baby. He had followed through with the threat he'd made over and over again, *you will have him and he will be mine. Not yours. Mine.* "Where did he take my baby? He can't have him. I made him. He's my baby."

"Oh, child," Nurse Jackie said, clasping her hands in front of her. "That man didn't take the baby."

Relief flooded through Vivian, and she released a sigh of relief. "Is he in the NICU?"

"We don't have a NICU. This hospital is too small."

That made sense. "So, then, someone has taken my baby to Des Moines?" She pushed herself up on her elbows. "Let's get going then. I need to get to him. He needs his mother."

Nurse Jackie slowly shook her head. "I'm sorry. I don't want to be the one to tell you this, but the baby didn't make it."

"What?" Vivian said, shaking her head. "I don't understand..."

"He was too young. We couldn't save him. I'm truly sorry."

Vivian shook her head, staring at the nurse, waiting for her to burst out laughing and say, "just kidding, he's right here," but her expression didn't change. It would have been a cruel joke, something no nurse would do, but still she would have welcomed it over this loss.

"We have a grief counselor on staff." Nurse Jackie's soft, melodic voice felt wrong in the sterile, cruel environment surrounding Vivian. "I have already notified her. She'll be up here within the next few hours. For now, we need to focus on your health."

"I...I...I need some time," Vivian said, unable to wrap her head around what was happening.

Everything was changing so quickly. She hadn't wanted the baby. There was no room in her head for him. She'd done everything she could to avoid bonding with him. But somehow it had still happened. The news felt like someone had ripped her heart out of her chest. This was why she didn't want to have the baby. It was why she wanted to terminate the pregnancy. This agony, this terror, could have been avoided.

"It won't be easy," Nurse Jackie said. "The grieving process never is. I lost one of my own. It's been twenty years and I still ache with her loss. That's a pain that never leaves you, but it will get better. One day—far off in the future, mind—you'll realize that you have more good days than bad days, and that's healing. You will always miss him, even though you never met him."

Hot tears tracked their way down Vivian's face. She would never meet her son. She'd fought so hard to keep barriers between them, but none of them were real. They'd shared a body. There was nothing more intimate than that. No love deeper.

"Would you like me to try and track down your husband? I know he was very worried during the procedure. I'm sure he'd like to see that you, at least, have pulled through. It isn't everything, but it's not nothing. One life is better than none."

How could Vivian begin to explain the nature of her relationship with her husband to this kind woman? She didn't want to see Bruce. She never wanted to see him again. That was the only silver lining from this tragedy. He lost his ability to control her. He knew she'd love the baby once he was born, and he knew he could control her by taking him from her. Now there was nothing for him to take. Except...

"Penny," Vivian said, her heart beating wildly in her chest.

"Excuse me?" Nurse Jackie's eyes grew concerned.

"My daughter, Penny. She's five-years-old. Copper colored hair. Like a penny. Have you seen her?"

Nurse Jackie shook her head. "No, honey. I haven't. Would she be with her father?"

"No." Or, at least, she'd better not be with him.

He knew about the loss of the baby—he would have been the first to know—and he would be furious. She could imagine how his face looked, screwed up with anger and frustration, castrated by the lack of control over the situation. He'd want to take it out on someone. He'd want to punish Vivian, but she was in the hospital, surrounded by doctors and nurses. But Penny wasn't. She was—oh no, where was she? The last time Vivian had seen her precious daughter, she was at the courthouse. What had happened to her?

"Is there anything I can do for you, Vivian? Anything to make you feel more comfortable?" Nurse Jackie asked, bringing Vivian out of her spiraling thoughts.

"Do you know where my things are? My cell phone. I need it."

The nurse nodded and moved toward a chair in the corner. She lifted Vivian's cell phone and brought it to her bedside, but she paused before handing it to her. "I caution you. Please don't check the news. You need to talk to the grief counselor first."

A burst of irritation flashed through Vivian. "I don't want to check the news. I want to check on my daughter. I need to know she is with someone safe."

At that moment, the phone started buzzing. Nurse Jackie handed it to Vivian. The screen read, *Katie Mickey, PI.* "Oh, thank God," Vivian said. Katie was the last person to see Penny. She'd know where Vivian's daughter had gone. She would have answers.

She pressed the green button on the screen, accepting the call.

24

KATIE

"Katie?" Vivian's voice sounded weak, brittle. It was like the birthing process had leeched every ounce of strength within her.

"Hello, Vivian." Katie said. The words sounded awkward. Too common for the dire situation, but still the only proper way to open a conversation.

Katie had the phone on speaker, placed in the middle of Ashley's desk. Ashley was in her regular seat, behind the desk, and Katie was in one of the chairs across from her. She leaned forward, moving closer to the phone as she spoke. "How are you?"

"I could be better."

Ashley and Katie exchanged a look. What could they say in response? Vivian's statement was like a minefield, any step could be wrong. Every step was dangerous. The stakes were high, and disaster awaited at the end of any utterance.

"Is Penny still with you?"

"Yes," Katie said, relieved to be on a safe topic. "She's with Elena in the conference room, coloring." Transforming a yellow canary into a grey version of a blackbird, but Katie left that little tidbit out.

"Can I speak to her?"

"There are a couple things we want to discuss first," Ashley said.

"Who is that?" Vivian's tone cut an edge, some of the brittleness chipping away to form a sharp point.

"It's Ashley Montgomery," Ashley said. "And before you start coming at me like I'm the worst person, keep in mind that I'm participating in this call out of concern for you. That's all."

"Concern," Vivian repeated. "For. Me." She was incredulous.

"I was at the hospital earlier," Katie said. She felt it was best that she took the lead. Ashley and Vivian were not friends, and that wasn't likely to change with the information they needed to relay. Bearers of bad news often got blowback.

"You were? Why didn't you say hi? I'm going to be here for days with nothing to do, nobody to talk to. Was Penny with you? I want to see her."

"Because your room is surrounded by deputies."

Vivian was silent for a long moment. "Deputies? Why?"

"They are going to arrest you when hospital staff clears you for release."

"Why?"

"Child Endangerment Causing Death."

Vivian was silent for a long moment. Katie and Ashley followed suit, allowing Vivian time to process the knowledge. "Can they do that?"

"Can they do it?" Ashley repeated. "Yes, yes, they can. Should they do it? No. That's my opinion, at least, but it seems like they are hellbent on war, so it's best that we start digging our trenches."

"We?"

"You do want help out of this mess, don't you?" Ashley said, her tone matter of fact.

"Yes."

"We're the best ones to ensure that."

Ashley wasn't blustering. She was the best defense attorney in the entire district, and possibly the state. If Vivian had any hope of beating these charges, Ashley's expertise and Katie's investigative skills were a must-have.

"Okay," Vivian said in a slow, tentative way that also said *I-don't-like-it-but-I'll-accept-it.*

"First things first," Ashley said. "Do not speak with law enforcement. Do not speak with the nursing staff. Say nothing to anyone."

"Nothing?"

"Unless you need to discuss medical issues, of course," Katie added. "Don't let your silence be the death of you."

"But don't allow your speech to be the incarceration of you either," Ashley added. "It's a thin line. When in doubt, say nothing at all. They can't use your silence against you."

"Okay."

"Have the doctors indicated when you will be released?"

"Probably tomorrow sometime. I'm still bleeding. They want to make sure it slows to a trickle before they let me out."

"Try to delay as much as possible. Hospitals aren't comfortable, but they are far more relaxing than a jail cell. Believe me, I know from experience."

Again, Ashley was not blustering. Years earlier she had been charged with a crime and incarcerated in the Brine County jail pending trial.

"I'll try. Can I speak with Penny now?"

Katie's gaze flicked to Ashley. She nodded. There was a lot more that they needed to discuss, but they had touched on the most important points —charges are coming and keep your mouth shut—everything else could wait.

"I'll go get her," Katie said, rising from her seat.

She walked down the hallway and opened the door to the conference room to see Penny standing directly at the other side, eyes wide with anticipation.

"Woah," Katie said, surprised to see Penny so close to the door.

"Can I talk to her now?" Penny asked.

"Yes. That's why I'm here."

Katie gestured for Penny to follow her and led the little girl into Ashley's office. Ashley turned off the speaker function and handed the phone to Penny.

"Mommy?" Penny asked, her voice shaking. "Are you okay?"

Katie couldn't hear Vivian's response, but it caused Penny to burst into tears. She was probably telling her about the baby, her soon-to-be long absence from home, or both. Regardless, it was a private conversation. One for family alone. Katie took that as her cue and stepped out of the office. Ashley followed, closing the door behind her with a soft click.

"Poor girl," Katie said.

They meandered down the hallway, not wanting to get too far away but also wanting Penny to have the space she needed. The office was silent, almost peaceful, for a few beats, then a voice sliced through the moment.

"I want to see your supervisor!" A male voice bellowed from the front of the office.

Elena's soft voice followed, but Katie couldn't hear the words.

"Whoever that is better have a good reason for shouting at Elena," Ashley hissed as she picked up her pace, jogging down the hallway toward the front of the office.

Katie didn't run. She'd get there soon enough. She needed the few moments to decompress from the last battle before entering a new war. Ashley, on the other hand, switched gears on a dime. She was primed and ready for a fight. Katie almost felt sorry for the man. Almost.

25

VIVIAN

Vivian wasn't winning; she hadn't won at all. How could she have allowed herself to think that she could beat Bruce? While she'd been in a medically induced slumber—giving birth to his baby—he'd been out pulling strings, finding a new way to punish her.

"I'm going to jail," Vivian said to Penny.

They were the hardest four words she'd ever had to utter to her child. How was she going to explain the situation? She'd spent Penny's entire life telling her daughter that criminals were *bad*, and now she might become a convicted felon herself.

"I thought you were at the hospital."

"I am at the hospital, but Ashley says there are deputies outside my door ready to arrest me when the medical staff clears me to leave."

"Why?"

"Because," Vivian sighed heavily, "your brother wasn't healthy."

"That's not your fault."

"It is a little. Honey, these things are so complicated. I didn't follow all the doctor's orders."

"Nobody does."

Once again, Vivian's bright, young child was surprising her with her ability to observe.

"Doesn't Bruce have diabetes?"

"Diabetes. Yes, he does."

"And he isn't supposed to have sugar, right?"

"That's true."

"But he used to eat sugar all the time. I remember. He ate all my Easter candy one year. He eats so much more sugar than us. He's not following doctors' orders. He should go to jail."

"Oh, honey, it isn't that simple."

"Why not?"

"It just isn't."

"It isn't because adults always complicate things. If you can go to jail for ignoring a doctor, then so should he. That's not complicated. That's fairness."

"Unfortunately, the world isn't fair."

"Well, it should be."

Vivian smiled, but it was a sad one that wobbled in the corners as a tear trickled down her cheek. "You are such a good girl. Do you know that?"

"Yes." There was an intensity in Penny's voice that Vivian had not noticed in the past.

"One day, when you grow up, you'll make a big difference. You can be a congresswoman, or maybe even President. You can be anything you want to be."

"Why are you talking like you won't see me for a long time?"

Vivian swallowed hard. "Because I'm going to jail, and I don't think Bruce will bring you to visit me there."

"Bruce? I'm not going with Bruce."

"My sweet, strong, intelligent girl. You won't have a choice."

"I'm going to stay with Ashley and Katie. They won't let Bruce take me."

"They can't stop it. He's your father in the eyes of the law."

"Then I'll run away. I can come back here, to the public defender's office."

"You'll only get Ashley and Katie into trouble, and they've decided to help me out. Isn't that nice of them?" She was trying to keep her voice upbeat, but it was growing more difficult by the second.

The song *Isn't it Ironic* popped into her head. Because it was ironic that she'd considered herself so much better than Ashley and her clients only days earlier, and now, after the worst experience in her life, she was going to have to depend on Ashley. Bruce wouldn't allow her to hire an attorney. This was her only option, and she'd heard that Ashley was good at her job, so it was also probably the best option.

"Ashley and Katie are going to get you out of jail?"

"Maybe. They're going to try."

"I told you I liked them."

"You've always been smarter than me, sweetheart. I've never denied that."

"You're smart, too, Mommy."

Vivian looked around the sparsely furnished hospital room, decorated in dull, unexciting colors. It was cold, impersonal, and uninviting, but it would be hand-over-fist better than her next accommodations. She'd thought she had outsmarted Bruce. It turned out that she wasn't as intelligent as she'd thought.

"What happened to the baby?" Penny asked.

That was the next, more difficult discussion. Vivian knew her daughter needed to know that he'd died, that he too was gone, but how could she explain it?

"He didn't make it, honey. The doctors tried, but he was too young to live outside of my belly."

"Then he wasn't a baby," Penny's response was automatic, unwavering. "You said so yourself many times."

"He was breathing when he came out of my stomach, but he didn't last long."

"Is that why you are going to jail? They are blaming you for that?"

"In part."

"This is Bruce's fault, isn't it? He did this. He's punishing you."

Vivian sighed, pinching the bridge of her nose to keep the tears at bay. "It is probably both of our fault. We were too busy fighting with one another to think about you. We were selfish."

"Don't say 'we' when you talk about *him*. You are not the same."

"Oh, Penny, you are such a lovely girl."

"Ashley is going to get you out of jail. I'm going to help her."

"If Ashley wants your help, I'd be happy to have you as a part of my defense team."

"I'll draw you pictures every day."

"I would like that."

"And I'll color them."

"I'd like that, too." She couldn't stop the tears from flowing from her eyes. How had Penny turned out so well? At such a young age, she was so selfless, despite the fact that she had a narcissist for a mother and a psychopath for a father.

"I'll call you every day."

"Okay. But I'll understand if you can't. Bruce might not allow it."

"I'll find a way."

Vivian smiled again, forcing the edges of her lips to push through the tears. There were so many emotions warring within her—fear, sadness, anger, loss—that she couldn't begin to understand how she would heal from the trauma of the situation. But she knew she had one light, and that was her daughter, Penny. If anyone could motivate her to stay positive, it was Penny. But Penny was also in danger. Bruce would come for her, and Vivian needed her daughter to be prepared.

"I want you to try to stay with Ashley and Katie as long as you can, okay?" Vivian said.

"I will."

"Are you in the front or the back of their office?"

"I'm in the back. In Ashley's office. It's tiny in here, littler than my closet."

Vivian doubted the office was quite as small as Penny had described, but Penny had a large, walk-in closet in her bedroom. Their entire house was spacious. And that was the only point of reference for the little girl.

"So, people who come into the office can't see you?"

"No."

"Stay back there as long as you can. Ashley and Katie will keep you safe."

"I know."

"But he will come for you, sweetheart, and you will have to be strong."

"Why now? He's never come for me before."

Vivian swallowed hard. This was another delicate conversation. The third in a phone call that had already been wrought with pain and loss. "He's mad at me."

"Because of the baby." It was a statement, not a question. "He's always mad at you about that baby. I hate that baby."

"No, you don't. It isn't his fault. This is Bruce's fault." Vivian had to put a stop to this kind of statement. Penny couldn't talk like that around her father, there was no telling what Bruce would do to her. She was in danger, grave danger, and she had no idea.

"So, what do I do?"

"You need to be careful around him. You know how he can get. Keep your voice soft, and don't get excited. Try to stay out of his way."

"He won't move back into the house, will he?"

"I don't know what he will do. I hope he stays in the garage, but I don't know for sure."

"I hope he stays in the garage."

"Me, too."

They fell silent for a moment, then Vivian heard a rustling noise, like Penny had set the phone down.

"Penny?" Vivian said. There was no answer. She waited a few seconds then repeated her daughter's name. Still, nothing.

A rustling sound returned. "Are you still there, Mommy?"

"Yes. I'm still here."

"I can hear yelling. I think it's Bruce."

He was already there for her. She had thought she'd have more time. Although, she should have expected it. The town of Brine kept no secrets from its golden boy, Bruce Ross. That person in the Clerk's Office had called Bruce to tell him that Vivian was giving birth, she'd probably also told him that Ashley and Katie had taken Penny.

"Okay. Go with him. Let him think that it's voluntary, okay? Make him think you want to be with him. Appease him. That's the best way to deal with his anger."

Vivian hated that she was having to say these things to her daughter. Women appeasing men was not how the world was supposed to work anymore, but that was how their world worked. Vivian had kept Penny safe from Bruce's wrath, but she couldn't anymore.

"Okay, Mommy."

"I love you. Remember that, always."

"I love you, too, Mommy."

"Keep yourself safe. That's your number one priority."

"Okay."

"Goodbye, sweetheart," Vivian said, biting her lip to stifle a sob. "I'll talk to you real soon, okay?"

"Okay."

Then Vivian did the hardest thing she'd ever had to do; she hung up the phone. She didn't know if she'd ever speak to Penny again. She didn't know if she'd see the smattering of freckles across her nose or her copper red hair again, either. After the things she'd already been through, she'd thought it was impossible for her heart to break any further. But she'd been wrong. The conversation with Penny had left her shattered. Bruce had won. He'd taken everything away from her. Her daughter, her home, her freedom.

26

ASHLEY

When Ashley emerged into the front of the office, Elena was at the reception desk, her arms crossed protectively across her chest, but she was holding her ground. A man stood across from Elena, face red with rage. Ashley knew the man, even with his uncommonly disheveled appearance and features twisted in anger. At the sight of him, she froze, wheeling around and hurrying back toward Katie.

"Go sit with Penny," Ashley whispered.

"I thought we were giving her privacy."

"Then stand outside the door."

"But why?"

"That's Bruce Ross out there. He's probably here for her. I don't want her to be alone right now."

"Okay," Katie said. She looked almost relieved.

That handled, Ashley turned back around and marched into the front of the office, moving to Elena's side.

"What's going on here?"

"Oh, good, you're here," Elena said. "Mr. Ross is looking for his daughter."

"Nancy. Nancy Reagan Ross," Bruce said. His voice was scratchy.

Ashley studied the other lawyer for a long moment, weighing her options for the conversation. There was nothing she could do to prevent him from taking Penny. She was his daughter, after all. The law was firmly on his side on that one. But there was also something very wrong with him. She'd known him all her life. He was a clean-shaven type, always impeccably dressed and well-groomed. Not today. He looked like the alcoholic version of himself. Maybe that was the problem.

"What's going on with you Bruce?" Ashley said, choosing to focus on him rather than answering his question as to Penny's whereabouts.

"What do you mean?"

"I mean you look like shit."

"Gee, thanks," he said sarcastically.

"No, seriously. Drugs?"

"No."

"Booze?"

"No."

"Gambling?"

"Will you stop asking questions. I'm fine."

"You don't look fine."

"Yeah, well, my wife just forced an abortion, killed our baby boy, and is going to jail for probably the rest of her life. And I can't find my daughter. Forgive me if my appearance doesn't shape up to expectations."

It was none of those things. This was not an instant change based on his new circumstances. He had the sallow, sour appearance of someone who had long been abusing something. Ashley knew the signs. She'd been working with drug users for years.

"Are you still friends with Miranda Birch?"

"What does that matter?"

"She stopped by here earlier today."

"I know. She told me."

"So, you are still friends. You aren't dabbling in her family business, are you?"

Miranda's parents, long dead now, had been well-known drug distributors. Ashley hadn't seen Miranda for years, but it wouldn't surprise her if Miranda had picked up where her parents left off. The drug business was hard to escape. Easy money and all.

"I've had enough of this conversation," Bruce growled. "I'm here for my daughter, not an interrogation."

"It seems you are getting both."

"So, she is here."

"I never said she wasn't."

"Well, then, go and get her and I'll be on my way."

"Are you sober?"

"Yes," he said, but his gaze cut to the floor.

"What is it? Pills?"

"Will you stop with all this? I'm not answering your questions. You, of all people, should understand the right to remain silent."

"Touché," Ashley said, scowling. "Although," she tapped her index finger against her chin, "I don't think the right to remain silent transfers from criminal court to juvenile court."

"I never said anything about juvenile court."

"Something is going on with you, and you want me to hand over a minor child. One that is quite small and unable to protect herself. I may be a defense attorney, but I'm also an officer of the court, and duty bound to report incidents of child abuse. If I give her to you, you'd better not hurt her."

A flush crept up Bruce's neck, coloring it a red so deep it looked purple. "I'm a lawyer too, Ashley. I'm also an officer of the court."

"Are you though, Bruce? You don't seem to be practicing these days."

"I won't harm Nancy," he said through clenched teeth. "Is that what you want to hear?"

"You'd better not. If you do, I'll find out."

"Miranda will oversee Nancy, okay? Is that what you wanted to hear? A woman will be supervising. I don't have time for little girls."

Ashley shook her head, slowly, sadly. It wasn't what she wanted to hear. She wanted Bruce to show up there fighting for his daughter. Not this, him demanding his daughter out of some sense of ownership. Penny's father should love her as fiercely as Vivian did. But for the foreseeable future, Penny was going to be without her mother. That shouldn't mean that she was alone, but in Penny's case, it did. At least the little girl had Ashley and Katie. Ashley wasn't kidding, they'd be watching Bruce.

"I don't have time for any of this," he gestured around him. "I should be working, but instead, I'm standing in this hellhole bickering while you act as a gatekeeper between my daughter and me."

"Working," Ashley said, ignoring his insults, "What kind of work are you doing these days, Bruce?"

"That's none of your business."

"I've heard rumors."

"Yeah, well, there are plenty of rumors out there about you, too."

He had a point.

"Why are you here?" A small, but firm voice came from behind Ashley.

Ashley turned to see Penny and Katie emerging from the hallway. Penny was first with Katie scuttling close behind her. Katie mouthed "I'm sorry" to Ashley, but she bore no blame. Ashley and Bruce had been discussing Penny. However small, Penny had a high level of emotional intelligence, so it was unsurprising that she wanted her voice heard.

"I'm taking you home."

"Which home?" Penny crossed her arms. "The house or the garage?"

"You aren't allowed in the garage."

"Why not?"

"Yeah," Ashley chimed in. "Why not?"

"We've been over this," Bruce ran a hand through his hair, disheveling it further. "That's where Daddy works."

Penny scoffed.

"We've been over this," Ashley said, "but you wouldn't answer it. What kind of work are you doing out there?"

"Law," Bruce said with a snort.

"Weird place to practice law."

Bruce looked around him, staring pointedly at the old furniture and 70's style wood paneling. "I'd say the same goes for you."

"This is an actual office."

"What makes you think *that* isn't?" Bruce paused for a second, then raised a hand. "You know what, don't answer that. I don't care what you think. I'm here for my daughter. You have no legal right to keep her, now give her over."

Nobody moved.

"If you don't, I'll call the cops and they can sort this out." Bruce removed his phone from his pocket, holding it out menacingly.

Ashley knew she couldn't block a father from taking his daughter home, even though her whole body screamed that this was *wrong, wrong, wrong*. The law was settled on the issue. Unless there was clear and convincing evidence of child abuse, nobody could interfere with a person's parental rights. Ashley had no such evidence, only suspicions.

"I'll go," Penny said, her voice breaking.

Ashley's heart broke along with it. Penny had been through so much that day. She had lost her mother and a potential brother and now a stranger was taking her away from a safe, trusting environment, and there was nothing anyone could do to stop it. Because that's exactly who her father was to her—a stranger—and everyone in the room knew it. The problem was that nobody else did. The world saw Bruce through rose-colored glasses. But Katie and Ashley could fix that problem. They could right the wrongs of the past day. Ashley would get Vivian out of jail and expose Bruce for whatever was going on in that garage. That was a promise, one she felt sure Katie would support.

27

KATIE

Thursday, August 4th

Vivian's arrest was on every television newscast, front page, above the fold in every small-town newspaper. It was spreading like wildfire over social media—the video of the once-proud mother as she was marched out of the hospital in handcuffs—shared hundreds of thousands of times and counting. Vivian had already earned a name, and it wasn't a good one. Murder Mom. That was what the conservative media outlets were calling her, and it was news gold, selling like mad.

Katie was trying to keep track of the comments and shares, to follow the threads of the flame as they continued jumping from one account to the next, but it was an impossible task.

"Do you really think all that's worth it?" Ashley's voice cut through the silence, causing Katie to jump.

Katie's tired eyes shifted away from the computer, settling on Ashley's thin, waifish frame standing in the doorway. "I'm only focusing on Iowa locals, Brine County first, then the closest counties after that." She had a running list of names of those who shared or commented on the news stories. Each comment had a snapshot, each name with a folder.

"Change of venue motion?"

"Yup."

Katie had worked with Ashley long enough to know that a Change of Venue Motion was coming. It meant that Ashley would try to move to a larger county with a more liberal jury. This kind of research was the start of it. To get a change of venue, Ashley would have to prove that a Brine County jury had been too tainted by news stories for Vivian to get a fair trial. At this point, it seemed like they were off to a great start. She had fifty separate folders already, and she was adding new ones every few minutes.

"Good thought," Ashley said. She came into Katie's office and dropped into one of the chairs across from her desk, sighing heavily as she flopped down. "What do you have going on today?"

It was early morning, shortly after seven o'clock. Since Vivian's arrest, Katie had been coming in earlier and earlier each day. Ashley had done the same. Katie rubbed her eyes and flipped open her paper calendar. She didn't like electronic calendars. There was something about writing her day out by hand that helped her process the upcoming events before they arrived.

"I've got a meeting with Sheriff St. James. He's supposed to give me the records of the BMW Oliver was driving."

Vivian had taken so much of Ashley and Katie's focus over the past few days, but she wasn't their only client. Oliver's case was still pending, and Katie needed to continue working on her investigation. At this point, they believed the car belonged to Bruce Ross, but they didn't *know*, and they had no proof. To be admissible in court, they needed tangible evidence. Documents stating *Registered Owner: Bruce Ross*. That was why Katie had scheduled a meeting with the Sheriff.

"Oh, good," Ashley said, raising a hand to her mouth and yawning. "I emailed the prosecutor about that a while ago, and he never responded. I told him it was exculpatory. I assumed he was ignoring me, so I was going to follow up with him, but I've been swamped with other things."

Exculpatory evidence was evidence that could prove the Defendant's innocence. If some existed and it was within the prosecutor's possession or easily attainable by the prosecution, then the State had a duty to disclose it.

This rule primarily existed because prosecutors had County Attorney subpoena power and other tools for investigation that Defense attorneys did not have at their disposal. County Attorneys could subpoena evidence without a hearing, defense attorneys could not. Since motor vehicle purchase records were not public record, they needed to get information about Oliver's car from the State.

"Did you want to meet with Oliver as well? I have an appointment with him at one o'clock today," Katie said. She'd scheduled it after the hearing to revoke his probation. They needed to start going through discovery.

"That'll depend on the stuff you get from Sheriff St. James."

"Okay." Katie penciled *Ashley?* next to Oliver's name.

"Do you have time to check on Penny?"

Katie didn't. Her schedule was jam packed with other private cases and meetings—her father had been scheduling more and more so their business could stay afloat—but Vivian was technically still a client, which meant Katie was technically still investigating Bruce. She could justify stopping by the house. She'd been doing it several times each day, mostly to make sure nobody was abusing or neglecting Penny.

"I'll go over there now," Katie said, rising to her feet and stretching with her arms out wide. "Wanna come?"

Ashley's gaze shifted to the door, then to her watch. "I probably shouldn't. I've got a million motions pending. Which means I've got a bunch of hearings to prepare for, but I also won't be able to focus until I've heard news of Penny."

"Well, come with me then," Katie said, motioning for Ashley to follow as she grabbed her keys and headed for the back door. She didn't wait to see if Ashley was coming. She could hear Ashley's heavy footsteps against the carpet as she followed.

They got in Katie's old, but trusty Impala. Katie had the engine on and was backing out before either of them even had their seatbelts buckled.

"She'll be in kindergarten soon," Katie said, as she drove the now familiar path toward Penny's house.

Katie would feel much better once little Penny was in school. Teachers were mandatory reporters. Meaning, they had to contact social services if they received any evidence of child abuse. If Bruce lost his temper even once, Penny would have a whole staff of adults ready and willing to report it.

"Yeah, if Bruce bothers to sign her up."

"Vivian already did it."

"She did?" Ashley asked. "How?"

Katie shrugged. "Beats me. Maybe she did it before her arrest. I just know she did. I have a friend who works at the school. She checked the records."

"And she told you?"

"Yup."

"That's illegal."

"Are you going to report it?" Katie said, glancing over at Ashley and raising an eyebrow.

"No." They were silent for a long moment, then Ashley said, "You've come a long way."

"From what?"

"From the days when you followed every rule, no matter how dumb."

"I've spent a lot of time around some bad influences," Katie said, a smile tugging at the corners of her mouth. Because Ashley was right. She used to be such a rule follower. A rule bent was a rule broken. But now, well, she was becoming more and more like Ashley every day.

"I'd say you've spent a lot of time around *good* influences."

Katie shrugged. "Semantics." She pulled off to the side of the road, directly across the street from the large modern-style home owned by the Ross family. "We're here."

"I can never quite understand why some people want so many windows. It's like living in a glass house."

The Ross home was exactly that, a home of windows, but the garage was the opposite. There were few windows and those were covered. Katie hadn't been close enough to determine what Bruce had used to black out the windows of the garage, but she suspected it was tin foil.

"I can see into virtually every room," Ashley said.

Penny was in the kitchen, pouring herself a bowl of cereal. Nobody else seemed to be home. That, or they weren't awake yet.

"Come on," Katie said, getting out of the car, and heading toward the front door.

"What are you doing?" Ashley said. "What if Miranda is here?"

"She isn't. She leaves at night. Sometimes she goes to the garage, sometimes she goes somewhere else, but she never stays the night with Penny."

"Yeah, well, it isn't night anymore."

"Miranda never comes before 9:00."

"You're sure about that?" Ashley said, following closely behind Katie.

Katie knocked on the door, her knuckles rapping against the glass. "Pretty sure."

"This is going to be a disaster," Ashley said, placing a hand against her forehead and shaking her head.

"Oh, come on, Ashley. Where is your gumption? You never used to care what people thought of you."

"I don't care now. I'm worried about Penny's safety, not the opinion of her father or Miranda. Those two can go suck an egg."

Katie barked a laugh just as Penny made her way into the main hallway. She paused for a moment as her gaze settled on them. Then a wide smile split her face and she came running to the door, unlocking it, and pulling it open.

"Are you here to pick me up?"

"Umm, no," Katie said.

Penny's face fell. Katie didn't like upsetting her, but honesty was important. They couldn't take Penny without her father's permission, and he'd never grant it.

"Sorry, Pen," Ashley said, dropping to her knees so she was eye level with the little girl. "We would if we could. We just wanted to stop by and tell you that we are watching out for you."

Penny's smile returned. "Like guardian angels?"

"Umm," Ashley pursed her lips. She wasn't a religious person.

"More like the angel and the devil on your shoulders," Katie said. "You know, like they show in the cartoons."

Penny looked from Ashley to Katie, "Which of you is the angel?"

"Okay, fine. Maybe the devil and the devil on your shoulders," Katie said. "Either way, we're making sure you have everything you need, and Miranda and your father are treating you right."

"They're okay, I guess. Nothing's changed with Bruce, and Miranda ignores me most of the time. It's like living alone. How is Mommy? Will she get out of jail soon?"

"Not soon enough," Ashley said. "But we're working on it, okay?"

Penny nodded. "I know. I trust you."

"Thanks," Katie said, but she couldn't help feeling the trust was misplaced. If not for Katie and Ashley's in-court shenanigans, Vivian would probably still be home.

"I found something. It could help," Penny said. She was wearing a pajama t-shirt and shorts with unicorns on them, with a matching robe over her shoulders. She reached into the pocket of her robe and produced a letter, roughly the size of Ashley's hand.

"What is it?" Ashley asked.

"I saw it in the mail. I grabbed it before Miranda noticed. I saw Mommy's name on it. She has two Vs in her name."

Ashley accepted the letter and placed it in her pocket. "Thank you. I'll take a look at it when we get back to the office." She looked over her shoulder. "We should probably go before Miranda catches us."

"Okay," Penny's gaze shifted to her bare feet.

"We'll keep watching," Katie said. "The devils on your shoulders. Okay?"

Penny nodded. "It's hard to tell who is devil and who is angel these days. Everything seems all mixed up."

"Most everyone is a little of both," Ashley said, a little off balance by the small child's maturity. Penny sounded like an adult, yet she was still so young. "Some more than others. We'll see you soon, okay? Don't worry."

Penny nodded slowly. Ashley and Katie turned around and headed toward Katie's car. They got inside and Katie started the engine.

"Let's get out of here before someone sees us."

"What's in the letter?" Katie said, heading down the street.

Ashley pulled it from her pocket and opened it, her mouth dropping open.

"What is it?" Katie said, glancing over at Ashley while also trying to keep her eyes on the road.

Ashley said nothing.

"Come on. Seriously? Say something."

"It's..."

"It's what?"

"The smoking gun."

28

ASHLEY

Those words *the smoking gun* sounded overly dramatic, even to Ashley's ears, but she couldn't think of a better way to explain it. This letter was a potential tie between two seemingly unrelated incidents.

"What do you mean, Ashley?" Katie asked. She was having a hard time keeping her eyes on the road. She leaned toward Ashley, trying to see the document in her hands, causing the vehicle to swerve, narrowly missing a mailbox.

"Don't crash," Ashley said, reaching up and grabbing the *oh shit* handle above her door.

"You can't say something like that then go silent."

"Fine, fine, just keep your eyes on the road."

"Then spill."

"It's not a letter, it's a bill."

"A bill. How is that a smoking gun?"

"Smoking gun was a little over-the-top," Ashley admitted. "It's not *that* big."

"I don't know what to do with that." Katie's hands tightened on the wheel. Ashley could see her knuckles turning white. "You aren't telling me anything."

"It's a bill from Planned Parenthood in Illinois."

"For..."

"The abortion pill."

"I don't see why you are smiling," Katie said, her eyes cutting toward Ashley and then back to the road. "That's bad for us. As in, this is the smoking gun for the State. It provides motive—that Vivian never wanted the baby and was desperate to get rid of him. It will be the last nail in Vivian's coffin."

"I mean, maybe. It's definitely not good for Vivian, but that's not what I mean."

Ashley hadn't even considered the ramifications to Vivian. Her mind hadn't quite made it that far yet. She was focused on the name listed on the bill and the date of service.

Katie huffed an exasperated sigh. "Then what do you mean?"

"This bill wasn't sent to Vivian."

"Then why was it in her mail?"

"It was sent to her. But not originally. It was forwarded."

"From who?"

Ashley's gaze shifted to the top corner of the page. "Bambi Clark." Ashley paused, studying Katie's face, waiting for her to make the connection. "That's the name on the bill."

"Bambi Clark. She's a druggie, right?"

Bambi was a Brine County local. Her biological mother, Gretta, still lived in town, although she had no permanent address. Gretta was an alcoholic who couch-surfed part of the year and spent the remainder sleeping on the streets. Her father was a local businessman who rarely acknowledged his daughter even before the drugs, but now, she was practically dead to him. He was remarried with a new wife who spent her time rubbing elbows with people like Bruce Ross. Bambi had no chance.

"She's used meth in the past. I've only represented her once for possession, but she's only nineteen." Ashley would not know of Bambi's brushes with the law before she was an adult. Those incidents would have been handled by juvenile court and she did not do juvenile work.

"Why is that significant?"

"The date of service is May seventh."

"Okay..."

"Still not ringing any bells?"

"Just tell me. Your little guessing game is exhausting."

"Okay," Ashley said. "Bambi is the victim in Oliver Banks' case. He hit her while she was walking on the road." Ashley paused, waiting for Katie to connect the dots. "On May thirteenth. That's a week after she was prescribed the abortion pill."

Katie's expression remained puzzled.

"The appointment was telehealth. It would take some time for the mail to get to Bambi."

"I don't see the significance. You're saying this is a tie between Vivian and Bambi's attempted murder."

"Potentially."

"But who sent the bill to Vivian and why?"

"That's something you'll have to find out. I have a hunch, and it's going to result in us withdrawing from Oliver's case as his attorney."

"And that's why you're smiling."

"Yeah."

Ashley hadn't admitted it to herself or to anyone else, but she did not like Oliver. It wasn't anything he'd done; it was more in the way he presented himself. There was a creepiness to him that caused the hairs on the back of her neck to stand on edge. She'd criticized Vivian for testifying against him in the Bond Review hearing, but Vivian hadn't been completely off base. It would be disturbing to find him skulking around a schoolyard.

"You think there is a connection between Vivian and Bambi," Katie said.

Ashley held up the letter. "There seems to be."

"But who sent the bill? If it was in Vivian's recent mail, then it couldn't have been Bambi. She's been in the hospital for a long time."

"That's something you'll have to find out."

The information was important for Ashley to complete a conflict-of-interest analysis, but also because it meant that someone else out there knew Vivian did not want to carry her pregnancy to term. She had to find that person before the state did. She couldn't ensure their silence, but the sooner she found the person, the sooner she could start looking for a way to discredit their testimony.

Katie parked in the lot behind the Public Defender's Office. "I have a meeting with Oliver today. I told you about it this morning. Do you want me to cancel it?"

"Yeah." Ashley got out of the car, the sticky summer air clinging to her skin. "We need to connect some dots before getting too far into his case."

Ashley didn't get to choose her clients, but when two clients' interests clashed, she got to choose the case for which to file her withdrawal. She didn't like either Vivian or Oliver on a personal level, but she cared about Penny, and Penny's happiness was tied to Vivian. Choosing between the two clients was not a difficult task for Ashley.

"Should I cancel the meeting with the Sheriff, too?"

"No. Keep that one. That information may still come in handy."

"For Vivian's case?"

"I don't know," Ashley answered.

It was an honest answer, but she felt sure there was more to the tie between these two cases. Bambi and Vivian had no obvious connection, which meant Ashley was missing something. Someone sent this bill to Vivian, because they thought Vivian was the one who needed to pay it. That wasn't an accident. Or maybe it was. Either way, Ashley had to find out.

29

VIVIAN

The days were long and empty. The jailers were cold and impersonal. There was nothing to do but sit around. It had been that way in the hospital, but days were even worse now that Vivian had been transferred to the Brine County jail.

She had a cell of her own, which was equal parts blessing and curse. There was nobody there to bother or harass her. No Bruce to burst in making wild accusations or strange demands. She finally felt safe for once. But after only one day, the solitude was already weighing on her. The emptiness felt like a physical weight on her shoulders. Nobody needed her, at least not in any way she could accommodate. This nothingness was foreign to her. She'd spent the last five years of her life dedicated to Penny. Now, at such a young age, Penny was on her own.

Vivian could feel every ache and pain in her body. Her incision was healing, but she couldn't take much medication for it. She had prescription strength Ibuprofen tablets to take "as needed," but those were only doled out when the jailers saw fit. Her breasts were swollen and heavy, full of milk that would never feed a child. They were a constant reminder of the little boy that she should be holding in her arms. She mourned the baby and hated the baby at the same time.

Ugh, Vivian thought. *I've created such a mess for myself.*

A jailer came by. A woman who had previously introduced herself as Theresa. She hadn't said a lot to Vivian, but the few things she'd said were not cruel, which was far better than any other jailer had done.

Theresa walked down the hallway, headed toward her. Vivian watched her, not daring to hope that she was coming for her. The jailers often walked right past her, refusing to make eye contact or say a single word, like a visitor to a pound ignoring a mangy dog that they'd never adopt. But Theresa started to slow as she approached Vivian's cell. Ashley could not get her released this soon, could she? *No, no, stop it,* Vivian chastised herself. She could not get her hopes up.

Theresa stopped in front of Vivian's cell. "You have a visitor." She placed a key in Vivian's door and unlocked it, allowing it to swing open. She held what looked like a long chain in her hands. It reminded Vivian of the chains in *A Christmas Carol*, the ones that Jacob Marley had to drag for all eternity. "I'm sorry, but I've got to put these on you," Theresa said, her gaze soft and apologetic.

Vivian nodded.

"Have a seat over there." Theresa nodded to the small cot, chained to the wall. It was nothing more than a large piece of metal with a small, thin, mattress on top. "These things can be a little awkward the first time. You'll have to figure out how to balance."

Vivian sat down, the cold steel biting through the mattress and through her thin, jail-issued jumpsuit, causing a chill to run up her spine. From the moment Vivian stepped into this building, she hadn't been able to keep warm. Not for a second. Part of her wondered if it was all mental, or if this was a special form of torture created by the jail staff—keep them cold, but not cold enough to freeze.

Theresa looped two manacles around Vivian's hands and two around her feet. A chain linked the wrist manacles together, and a separate chain attached the ankles together. A third chain tied the center of the wrist manacles and the center of the foot manacles together. She hadn't even stood yet, and Vivian already knew they'd be heavy. She wondered if the chains were going to cause problems with her incision. She was not supposed to lift anything until her incision completely healed and she'd been cleared by a doctor. Neither of those things had happened yet.

"Can you stand?"

"I think so," Vivian said.

She pressed her heels into the ground and used her thighs to push off the cold bench. Pain ripped through her, but she didn't complain. She didn't care much for her own health anymore. Besides, the discomfort felt like punishment, something she deserved but couldn't fully accept because she needed to get out—for Penny.

"Follow me," Theresa said, leading the way down a long, gray hallway.

At first, Vivian struggled to get her footing. The chains were short, preventing long strides, but they were also heavy. This made movement stilted and awkward, especially with her incision. At first, she tried walking as she normally would, except using smaller steps, but that was too painful, so she shifted to shuffling her feet, sliding the soles of her flimsy shower shoes across the cement floor.

"Are you doing okay?" Theresa slowed to match Vivian's pace.

"I'm not sure what that is anymore."

"I mean physically. I know you must be struggling with all the other stuff."

Vivian gave her a probing look, and Theresa lifted her hands in a gesture of surrender.

"I'm not asking you to say anything or even agree with me. Ashley would have my head for saying something like that to you. I'm just trying to tell you that I understand." She paused. "Well, I don't *really* understand, but I can imagine, and it has to be challenging."

"Thank you. Physically," Vivian said, "I could be better."

"The chains are too heavy, aren't they?"

Vivian was a slight woman. Tall, but slim. Thanks to the morning sickness, she hadn't gained much weight during pregnancy. She would have struggled with the weight of the chains even without the recent surgery.

Theresa put a hand at the center of her chains, lifting them. "How's that?"

"Better." Walking was still awkward, but it wasn't quite so painful.

They continued down the hallway until they stopped in front of a door. Theresa said something into a radio on her shoulder. There was a loud click, and Theresa pulled the door open, gesturing for Vivian to enter.

Inside the room, Ashley was seated at a beat-up desk. An empty, blue plastic chair sat on the other end of the desk, closest to Vivian.

"Go on in," Theresa said, slowly lowering the chains and handing the weight back to Vivian.

Vivian shuffled into the room, wincing with every step. When she reached the chair, she pulled it out and sank into it, her knees facing to the side. She took several breaths, then willed her body to turn her knees toward the middle.

"Sorry about that," Ashley said. She was writing in a file folder and hadn't bothered to look up.

"About what?"

Ashley paused, lifting her gaze. "That," she said, gesturing toward the manacles with the end of her pen. "It's jail policy that inmates wear chains when they meet their attorney in person for the first time. I've told them a million times that I am not afraid, but they don't care."

Vivian blinked, unsure if she was supposed to respond.

"It has nothing to do with actual safety, it's about liability."

"Listen," Vivian said after a brief, awkward silence, "I'm sorry for the way I treated you. I was..." she swallowed hard. Vivian had never been gifted when it came to apologies. She was more of a master of the non-apology. The *I'm sorry you felt hurt*, and *I'm sorry but you're too sensitive*, those kinds of things. "I was unkind, and you didn't deserve it."

Ashley snapped the file she'd been writing in shut and stuffed it in her laptop bag. "No need to apologize. I'm partially responsible for your circumstances, so I suppose we're even."

"I'm not sure that makes us even..."

Ashley had been part of the storm that led to Vivian's incarceration. The past six months had been a bit like global warming with no clear culprit, but rather everyone contributing a bit to the demise of Vivian's freedom. Ashley certainly wasn't innocent, thanks to her evidence presentation at Oliver's bond review hearing, and that was the only reason the prosecutor could have known about Vivian's treadmill escapade. Bruce was most certainly in the prosecutor's office now, demanding that something be done about Vivian. Even now, he could still punish her. He still held all the power.

"What were you masking anyway?" Ashley asked. "With the haughtiness. You've completely changed over the past few days, and that is not common. It leads me to believe your old self was an act. Something you used as a mask. What were you hiding?"

"Masking?" Vivian was caught off guard. "What do you mean?"

Ashley spun her pen around her finger. "For some it's drugs, booze or gambling, but that's not you."

"No."

"For others it is childhood abuse, sexual, physical, mental, that's also not you."

"I was mostly ignored as a child."

"So," Ashley leaned forward in her chair, "What is it then? You aren't inherently an asshole—or are you?"

Vivian flinched. She couldn't remember the last time someone cursed in her presence—aside from Bruce, of course—but Ashley didn't seem to notice. She kept right on talking.

"I say that because your daughter is such a good person. Penny really, truly has a pure heart and soul. Part of that is because she's a child, but she's old enough to have learned some of that as well. I know Bruce isn't the reason for that. She doesn't have any grandparents and knows few people in town. So...that leaves you." Ashley's eyes flicked up to meet Vivian's gaze, then back down to the pen, spinning it around her fingers.

Tears pooled in the corners of Vivian's eyes. Should she wipe them away? Should she blink really hard to force them back? What would be least noticeable?

"How is Penny?" Vivian finally choked out.

"I saw her before coming here. She's fine. Bruce is still holed up in the garage."

"Oh, thank God," Vivian said, her chains jingling as she brought a hand to her chest. It didn't mean Penny was safe, but it did mean that things hadn't changed much. Bruce was still ignoring the little girl. If he didn't see her often, there would be less of a chance that he'd get angry with something she did or said and hurt her.

Ashley's eyebrows shot up and she dropped her pen. "That's a strange response."

Vivian shrugged.

"Care to expound on that?"

She didn't. Vivian was thankful for all of Ashley's help, but she wasn't ready to divulge all her family secrets. She'd taken enough hits to her ego over the past few days. She couldn't quite bring herself to accept the brand of *victim*.

"No? Then how about this," Ashley slid a document across the desk, allowing it to stop in front of her.

Vivian's heart fluttered, and her gaze shifted down. It was a bill. She scanned the top, her eyes shifting from the top left to the right. There was a name, and it read "Bambi Clark." *She knows. How does she know?* Vivian thought.

"What is it?" Ashley asked.

"A bill."

"Why was it sent to you?"

A whoosh of relief flooded through Vivian. Ashley didn't know. She wouldn't be asking if she knew. Vivian shrugged. "Post office error?"

"That's not it. You know how I know that?"

Vivian waited, too afraid to respond.

"There were two envelopes. The inside envelope was sent to Bambi. That one was stuffed inside another envelope addressed to you."

"Okay."

"Bambi Clark is the alleged victim in Oliver Banks' hit and run case. Did you know that?" She was looking down at her nails, feigning nonchalance.

It irritated Vivian. If Ashley wanted to make a point, she should come right out and say it. This toying with Vivian was cruel. "What is your point?" She tried to force some of the old haughtiness back into her voice, but it cracked. "I can't take this guessing game."

Ashley's gaze flicked up, but she didn't apologize. "What is the connection, Vivian? You and Bambi have nothing in common. Nothing. There is a decade age difference, you're high class—she's not. She's a drug addict, you aren't. I could go on, but I'll stop there. So why would someone—we can discuss who in a minute—be sending you a bill in Bambi's name?"

Vivian opened her mouth, then closed it again.

"And don't say it's charity. It isn't charity." Ashley grabbed the bill and waved it in the air. "This isn't how charities work."

"I..." Vivian's voice trailed off. She didn't know how to answer the question. If she even wanted to answer it.

"You have got to trust me, Vivian. Otherwise, this relationship," she gestured from Vivian to herself, "is not going to work."

"Is Bambi okay?" Vivian asked. Now that Vivian was in jail, she couldn't follow the news as closely. Last she'd heard, Bambi was hanging on by a thread, still hospitalized.

"No. She's not okay. She died last night. Oliver's attempted murder case has now morphed into a murder or manslaughter charge. I'm still waiting on the prosecutor to amend the Trial Information."

Vivian closed her eyes and shook her head. This was all her fault.

"What is the connection between you and Bambi?" Ashley asked again, this time more insistent.

"Fine," Vivian issued a heavy breath. "I hired Bambi."

"Hired her? For what?"

"To get me the abortion pill."

"Where at?"

"I don't know. I think she went to Illinois to get it, but I didn't know. She could have done telehealth."

"Why her?"

"She was pregnant, too."

"Bambi was pregnant?" Ashley's eyebrows shot up and she jotted a note on her notepad. "I guess that's something that will eventually come out with the autopsy," she muttered to herself. "How did you find out?" She asked, looking up again.

"Bambi's stepmother is a friend of mine."

"A friend," Ashley said, incredulous.

"Okay, she's an acquaintance. I was at an event for May Day and she was telling everyone who would listen that her 'promiscuous drug addict stepdaughter' was 'knocked up *again*.' Her words, not mine."

Ashley's brow furrowed in disgust.

"Yeah, I know. Bambi's stepmother is a real lovely lady," Vivian said sarcastically.

"But Bambi was keeping the baby?"

"She intended to, but if her stepmother was to be believed, that wouldn't last long. Social services would come to get the child after birth. Something about drugs and testing the umbilical cord."

Ashley waved a hand as if to shoo away Vivian's last comment. "Bambi got the pill to bring it to you."

"That's what I paid her to do."

"Why didn't you go get it yourself?"

"I couldn't let Bruce know."

"Why not?"

Vivian pursed her lips. She didn't have the energy to discuss Bruce. Not yet.

Ashley waited several long moments, watching Vivian closely, but she didn't press the issue. "And Bambi never made it."

"No. She was walking to my house. That's when Oliver hit her."

"Allegedly."

Vivian looked up, narrowing her gaze. "Whatever."

"That's why you testified against him. You wouldn't go on record saying these things, but you wanted him punished, so you tried to revoke his bond."

"No. I mean, a little, but not entirely. He was following us. Me and Penny. I saw him hiding in the forest while we were at the park. I wasn't lying about that. I see him at the grocery store, watching us closely. I don't know what the deal is with him, but he's obsessed with us. I wanted to get rid of him. For Penny's safety."

Ashley sat back. "Wow. Okay. Well, it's a good thing Penny pulled this out of the mail before Miranda found it."

"Miranda? Why would she..." Vivian voice trailed off as her mind whirred. Bruce used to always talk about Miranda when they were young, but he hadn't brought her up in over five years now, not since before Penny was born. "They are seeing each other, aren't they?"

Ashley shrugged. "It doesn't actually seem that way. I thought so at first, but it seems more like Miranda is acting as a babysitter."

Miranda watching Penny was better than Bruce doing it, but not by much. Vivian didn't know anything about Miranda anymore, but what she had known of her involved heavy drugs and risky decisions. Definitely not a person she wanted around her daughter. Still, Vivian had never seen or heard that Miranda had been cruel. Drugs or no drugs, that made her a better option than Bruce.

"You don't seem all that upset," Ashley said. "About the potential of an affair, I mean. But isn't that why you originally hired Katie?"

"I hired Katie because Bruce was acting strange."

"Do you want to expound on that?"

Vivian leaned forward, pressing her hands to her incision. "Can we take a break? I just, I need a bit of a rest." She was buying time, and she suspected Ashley knew it.

"Fine," Ashley said, rising to her feet. "We can stop there, but I'll be back soon. When I come back, I want your family background. You are leaving something out, and I think it has a lot to do with Bruce."

Vivian nodded, swallowing the large lump that had formed in her throat. She couldn't promise anything, but she'd try.

30

KATIE

Entering the law enforcement center always brought a mixture of emotions. Anger. Nostalgia. Déjà vu. Jealousy. Katie had thought the feelings would fade with time, but that hadn't been the case. They continued to war within her, causing her stomach to twist and her heart to flutter as she approached the front door. She paused, taking a deep breath before gripping the handle and pulling it open with a soft *whoosh*. Cold air greeted her. Physically, the air conditioning was a welcome respite from the sticky late summer heat, but emotionally, it grated on her nerves.

Katie had once worked in this building as a police officer. There had been no extra money to run the air on high. Back then, she thought her whole career would be dedicated to serving the city of Brine. She'd been young, impressionable, idealistic. She could never have imagined how much her life, and she, herself, would change over the years. She knew for certain that her former self would not approve of the person she was now, just as she no longer approved of the person she'd been.

She shivered and stepped over the threshold, making her way toward the glass window with a large "Sheriff" sign hanging above it. When she'd worked there, the sign had read "Law Enforcement," because there had also been a police department. A slow, methodical defunding of the police department resulted in its eventual closing. Now, the Sheriff handled everything in Brine County and Brine City.

As she approached, the glass window slid open, and a middle-aged woman with tired eyes greeted her. "Hello, there, Katie."

"Hi, Theresa. I didn't realize they'd moved you to front desk duty."

Theresa was a jailer. Katie had never seen her working outside the jail, but the jail was run by the Sheriff's Department, so they were all employed by the same entity.

"For now. We're short staffed. It's overtime. Today is supposed to be my day off, but I need the money." She shrugged in a *what can you do* sort of way.

"Don't we all," Katie said. "Mortgages don't pay themselves, and it seems like everyone is looking for employees these days."

"I think there's a 'help wanted' sign in every business window. But you didn't come here to chat about my financial situation. What can I do for you?"

"I have a nine o'clock meeting with Sheriff St. James."

Theresa turned to her computer and pressed a few buttons.

"I'm a little early..." Katie said after a long pause.

"I don't see it on his calendar."

A flush of irritation curled its way up the back of Katie's neck. They'd scheduled this appointment on Monday. She hadn't wanted to meet with the sheriff himself. All she wanted was information. Any deputy could have given that to her, including George, who she saw regularly after hours. It was the Sheriff who had insisted upon personally meeting with her.

Theresa picked up the phone receiver next to her. "Let me give him a call."

She was dialing before Katie could respond. Not that Katie would have had much to say. He'd forgotten. It was as simple as that. Katie would love to rage at someone, really give them a piece of her mind, wasting her time like that. Time was money, and Theresa wasn't the only one with a mortgage to pay. Katie also had a business to run, one that wasn't exactly flush with cash. Yet, none of this was Theresa's fault. Shouting at her would only result in Katie apologizing.

"Yes, Sheriff," Theresa said, turning to the side for partial privacy. "Katie

Mickey is—" She abruptly stopped talking, pausing for a long moment. "Yes, I know but—" Another pause. "Okay. I'll tell her."

That didn't sound good.

Theresa cradled the phone and looked up.

"He's too busy, isn't he? He forgot, and now he's too busy." It was typical. The sheriff considered his time precious, but hers, it could be wasted as though it was worth nothing.

"No, well, I don't know."

Katie rolled her eyes. "How long until he's available?"

"Actually, he has a meeting with someone else."

"Of course, he does."

"But he's going to move it. He said he'd be out in just a minute."

Katie was already turning to go. She stopped, then abruptly turned back. "He's what?"

"He's going to clear his calendar. He apologizes for the wait, but he said five minutes max."

"Okay..." Katie wasn't sure what to say. She's been fully prepared to march out of the building in a huff, but now, she didn't know what to think. Sheriff St. James was not a kind man. He was not doing this out of the goodness of his heart. So, what did he want?

"Katie," Sheriff St. James said as he came around the corner and up to the front desk. "Good to see you." His voice was deep and gravelly, reminding Katie of a cowboy in an old western movie.

"Umm, likewise," Katie said.

The sheriff opened the "employee only" door next to the window, stepping aside and motioning for Katie to enter. She walked through.

"We can talk in my office," he said.

Katie nodded and followed him down the long, winding corridor, still dumbfounded by his apparent kindness.

"Coffee?" He called over his shoulder as they passed the kitchenette area.

"No, thanks," Katie said.

She could always use coffee—especially since Vivian's case was taking on a life of its own—but she didn't want to accept anything from him. Sheriff St. James had always been the type of man who kept score. Even though coffee was a small thing, she preferred to keep things even. She'd accept nothing from him, and she'd offer nothing to him.

"Suit yourself," he said.

They continued down a few more corridors. He stopped outside a large, corner office. A placard on the open door read, "Patrick St. James, Brine County Sheriff." The light was on, and there was nobody inside.

"Go on in, have a seat."

Katie stepped inside and chose the chair across from his executive-style desk, the one closest to the door. He followed close behind, walking around his desk and sitting in his high-backed office chair. He was a small man, short and stout, but he moved lithely, like a cat stalking its prey. Despite the plush comfort of his chair, he remained sitting upright, his back straight. A remnant of his military background, no doubt.

"You wanted to meet with me about Oliver Banks, is that right?" He asked.

"Yes. I need the ownership records for the BMW."

"Here it is," Sheriff St. James slid a document across the desk.

Katie picked it up, studying it, looking for the name on the title. She found it near the top of the page. It read, *Ross, Winters, and Associates, PLLC.* "That's Bruce Ross's law firm," Katie said aloud. She'd suspected a connection between Oliver and Bruce, but she hadn't thought it would be this easy to prove. She thought for sure it would be far more complicated. A shell company that led to a shell company that was owned by some distant, barely known relative of Bruce Ross. But his own firm? It was almost too easy.

"Yes. It seems that Mr. Banks was driving a vehicle owned by Bruce Ross's firm. I will also point out that the vehicle was reported stolen."

Katie looked up. "When?"

"A couple days after Oliver hit Bambi Clark."

"Allegedly."

"Whatever," the Sheriff said, waving a dismissive hand. "You don't have to do that defense nonsense around me. I know you are an officer of the law. Even if you don't work on our side anymore. You don't believe that bullshit."

He was right, but only to a degree. They both knew Oliver was guilty, so there was little point in standing on pretense, but Ashley had taught her the importance of the concept of innocence until proven guilty in a court of law. Nobody truly followed it anymore, but it was important.

"That's the reason I've asked you here today," the sheriff said.

"I don't follow."

"You know I could have sent this little document over with one of my newly hired peons. I didn't need to meet with you."

"Yeah."

"But I wanted to discuss something with you. I understand time is limited for you, but this is important. I want you to come back."

"Come back?" Katie repeated. "Come back to what?"

"To law enforcement."

Katie blinked several times.

"Come back to our side. Be one of my deputies."

Katie sighed, exasperated. "I have a business of my own."

"I'll make you sergeant."

"My father works with me."

"A criminal who left you on your own and destitute as a teenager."

That was true, but they'd been working on rebuilding their relationship. If she bailed on her father now, she wouldn't be much better than he had been when he committed the financial crimes that placed him in prison.

"Ashley depends on me."

"Ashley's applying to be a judge. What then? Who will you work for if she leaves you? Your business is going to struggle."

She hated to admit it, but he had a point. There was a fifty percent chance that Ashley would become the next District Court Judge. There was no telling if the new public defender would want to work with Katie. If they didn't, she'd be left to a career of investigating cheating spouses and custody matters. That was a fate she did not want to face. She'd lose her mind.

"You don't have to answer today. But Sergeant comes with a nice salary and benefits. You'd work for the government, so you'd be part of the pension plan as well. You could do worse."

Financially, she was doing worse. She was barely scraping by. She had no savings. No retirement. Nothing to ensure a comfortable future.

"I'll think about it."

"Yes, do think about it," the Sheriff said, a wide grin splitting his face. It transformed him from the stern man she'd known, to something a little softer. Then his features hardened. "I'll expect an answer by the end of next week."

Katie stood, grabbing the BMW vehicle registration information from his desk. "I'll let you know before then."

It would be nice to dismiss him off hand. To immediately say *I don't need your handout*, but she couldn't do that. Small businesses were hard to run. She hadn't expected it to be quite so challenging. Now, the Sheriff was offering her a high-ranking position within the Sheriff's Department. It was enticing, but she didn't know if she could let Ashley and her father down like that. Yet, if finances continued in the same manner, she wouldn't have a choice.

31

ASHLEY

Monday, August 8

It was a district court day. Mondays always were. District Court was the highest lower court, meaning it was the most powerful court aside from the Court of Appeals that critiqued their work, and the Supreme Court that critiqued the Court of Appeals' work. It was the court that would hear Vivian's case if it went to trial, Oliver's case, also if it went to trial, and Ashley's many, many pending motions to suppress.

Ashley arrived at work unusually early. It was barely five o'clock in the morning when she parked and entered through the back door of the office. She had a full day of motion hearings, all set in front of a new Judge. Judge Ahrenson was officially retired. His seventy second birthday had passed, which meant he was no longer able to serve on the bench.

She sat at her desk and turned on the local talk radio station. The radio host was Bill Roberts, a local City Councilman who spent a good deal of time spewing nonsense about politics. Ashley did not care for politics. She should care, but she didn't have the stomach for it. She had enough stress in her job, and she didn't need or want to add to that. The primary reason she'd started listening to Bill Roberts was because he'd started discussing the court system, including some of her cases on his show.

"Good morning, early birds," Bill's voice was weathered and gruff, not ideal for radio, but he wasn't hard to follow. "It's five thirty on the dot, so let's get started on the show. For the late bloomers out there, don't worry, you can catch a rerun at ten o'clock and noon, right here on Brine's own talk radio."

Ashley turned to her case files, grabbing off the top of the stack and flipping it open. *Amanda Birch*, she'd been charged with possession of methamphetamine with intent to deliver. This wasn't Ashley's first time representing Amanda, but it was the first time she'd wondered if Amanda and Miranda were related. She hadn't realized Miranda had any siblings, but this girl also could be a cousin or some other distant relation. Or no relation at all, and Ashley was trying to find connections where they didn't exist.

"We have Bruce Ross here in the studio today," Bill Roberts said.

Ashley froze.

"He's here to discuss his wife's criminal case. How are you holding up, Bruce?"

Ashley looked up, slowly lowering her pen, setting it down on her desk. She turned her full attention to the local radio station blaring out of her computer audio.

"I'm doing the best I can, considering," Bruce said. His voice was reedy, not at all like himself.

It sounded to Ashley like a failed attempt at sadness. She wasn't buying it, but others probably would. He was manipulative. Ashley had worked with her fair share of manipulative men, and she knew where to look, what to believe. She knew how to read between the lines and catch the unsaid lie hidden between his words.

"Your wife, she has an arraignment today, is that right?"

"Yes. That's what the most recent court order says. She's to be arraigned today."

"How do you feel about that?"

"I don't know. An arraignment is just a formal hearing. It is where the judge will read the charges and she'll enter a plea of not guilty. It's hard to feel anything about it."

"That sounds like something a lawyer would say."

"I am a lawyer."

Bill chuckled. "I forgot you were a lawyer, Bruce."

Ashley smiled, that comment would stick in Bruce's craw. He was the type of man who thought everyone should know everything about him, while he neither had the time nor interest to return the sentiment. He was that important, or so he thought.

"How do you feel about your wife?"

"I feel like I wish she'd never done it."

Done what, Bruce? Ashley thought bitterly. *Got knocked up by your dumb ass? I bet she is sorry for that.* She could have been with someone so much better, but instead she'd chosen Bruce.

Over the past week, Ashley's opinion of Vivian had completely changed. She now saw Vivian's haughtiness as a form of armor, much like Ashley's sarcasm. She wore it as a shield from something. Ashley hadn't quite determined what that something was, but she knew it had to do with Bruce. It was only a matter of time before she found out. And once she did, she doubted Bill Roberts would invite her onto his radio show to discuss it.

"Your wife, she's been charged with child endangerment causing death," Bill said. "And before we go any further here, I am *obligated*," he put emphasis on the word obligated, "to tell you that an arrest is not a conviction. Vivian is presumed innocent until she is proven guilty beyond a reasonable doubt."

"Oh, there's little doubt," Bruce said. "She was pregnant. When she went into labor, my son was born alive, and then he died. And it was her fault. It's her fault I am not holding my little boy in my arms," Bruce's voice broke at the end.

This emotion felt genuine to Ashley. She did believe that he was hurting because he lost his son. That was a common emotion. The uncommon response was for him to blame it on his wife. He should be defending her. Telling the world that these things happen. That's why giving birth is done in hospitals, things can go wrong. One tragedy should not lead to another. Vivian was a mother already. She had a daughter at home who needed her, who missed her. Her conviction would take her away from Penny for the remainder of her childhood. That, too, was a loss. But Bruce said none of that.

"Did you have a name picked out for your son?" Bill's voice had softened at the edges.

"His name is Ronald Reagan Ross."

"That's a wonderful name."

It was not a wonderful name. It was disgusting. Bruce's daughter was named Nancy Reagan Ross. To name siblings after a married couple was disgusting. *That's encouraging incest you gross motherfucker*, Ashley thought. But, of course, Bill didn't think anything of it. Especially since there had been no mention of Bruce's living, breathing, daughter. It was as though she didn't exist to him. Perhaps she didn't. At least not unless he could use her to benefit himself in some way.

"I have arranged a funeral for him. It will take place this Saturday, August thirteenth."

"Will Ronald's mother be present at the funeral?"

"No. My wife will not be there." Bruce's tone was firm, confident. Like there was nothing anyone could do to change it.

"Fuck that guy," Ashley said, shaking the mouse of her computer and opening Vivian's electronic file, creating a document entitled, "motion for temporary release to attend son's funeral." Ashley began typing out her request, banging the tips of her fingers against the keyboard with hard, violent strokes. This was so unfair. Vivian had carried that baby. She hadn't had a choice in that matter, yet she'd done it.

Sure, she wasn't perfect in the way she'd done it, but she could have been worse. She could have drunk alcohol, smoked cigarettes and used drugs. She didn't do any of that. She'd ignored a bed-rest order. She got up, walked around, ran once, and that led to her arrest and now seemingly her inability to grieve for her lost child. Like her loss was somehow less than Bruce's.

Ashley finished the motion and opened the electronic filing website. She uploaded the document and submitted it to Vivian's case.

"There," Ashely said to the voices coming from her computer. "Try to keep her out now."

Neither Bruce nor Bill had heard her, of course, but they would understand what she'd done. Vivian would be at her son's funeral. She would get to mourn and be seen mourning in the same way as Bruce. He knew full well what he was doing. He was trying to manipulate the process. He was trying to make himself the face of Vivian's criminal matter. To punish her. And Ashley was not about to allow that to happen. Vivian lost a son, too, and the public would know it. They would see her grieving. They would see her with Penny. Mostly, they would see her as human, not a set of facts that led to a criminal charge.

32

VIVIAN

"It's time," Theresa said, guiding Vivian down the hallway toward the doors that would take her to the courthouse.

"This hearing is just a formality, right?" Vivian asked. She had a panicky, fluttery feeling in her chest. She didn't want to go, but she knew she had to. "That's what Ashley told me. She said the arraignment is when the judge reads the formal charges filed against me and I enter a plea of not guilty."

"That's true, but there's a new motion that the judge has also set for hearing."

Vivian's heart seized, and she had to stop. It was difficult enough walking with the heavy, awkwardly placed chains, but now she couldn't breathe. She had never realized the criminal justice system was so unpredictable. She'd planned for one thing, worked it all out in her head, and now she was being confronted with something entirely different.

"Don't worry," Theresa said, patting Vivian on the shoulder. "It's Ashley's motion."

That eased some of the tension, but not all of it. "What is the basis for the motion?"

Theresa sighed heavily. "Bruce is having a funeral for your baby. Ashley wants you to be able to go."

"She does?" Tears sprang to Vivian's eyes.

Vivian had known about the funeral. She'd been watching the local news on the TV in her cell when they covered it. Bruce's face had filled the screen, standing next to a reporter, face solemn and eyes puffy. Vivian scrambled to find the remote. She couldn't handle seeing Bruce. Even in jail where he could not get to her, his presence caused heart palpitations. The reporter outlined the reason for Bruce's interview before Vivian could get to the remote. Ronald's funeral.

Ronald. What a terrible name for an infant. Vivian would have never chosen that name, but even if circumstances were different and the baby had lived, his name would still have been *Ronald.* Bruce got his way, and if he didn't, he'd hurt her. He'd do something cruel, but untraceable, like keep the baby away from her while also hiding her breast pump so her breasts would fill with milk and grow hard and painful. He'd pull her hair until it felt like it would come out at the roots. He'd separate her from her son. As her son grew, Bruce would turn him against his mother unless she did everything that Bruce asked in the exact way he wanted it done, which was impossible.

The reporter had asked Bruce about the date and location of the funeral as Vivian's hands closed around the remote. She shut the television off before he could respond. She'd heard enough.

"Come along," Theresa's soothing voice cut through Vivian's thoughts, pulling her out of the past. "The judge is waiting."

Vivian nodded and they started moving again. "I didn't realize Ashley cared about things like that—allowing me to attend my son's funeral."

"She's a hard woman to get to know, but Ashley Montgomery has a lot more layers than anyone thinks. Here, I'd say she cares about fairness. It seems unfair that Bruce gets to mourn his son, but you don't get to do the same."

Vivian bit her lip to keep a sob from escaping. She had misjudged Ashley Montgomery wholly and completely. These days, it was becoming more and more clear that she'd misjudged everyone. Those she'd chosen to bring close to her were egotistic self-important psychopaths. The people she believed were beneath her were people like Ashley. Good, kind, hard-working people.

"We better pick up the pace," Theresa said, glancing at her watch. "We're going to be late."

Vivian nodded and began walking as quickly as she could. They had to go outside to make their way toward the courthouse, and she was surprised to see the flash of cameras greeting her the moment she stepped into the morning sun. She froze once again.

"News station," Theresa said. "Just look straight ahead or down at the ground. You'll be fine. Don't let them intimidate you."

At Theresa's kind words, Vivian found the strength to keep moving forward.

"That's right. One foot at a time," Theresa coaxed.

The distance across the street felt like a marathon. Voices shouted her name. Lights flashed. People jostled to get a better look at her. But then, they were in the safety of the Courthouse, and Ashley was waiting for them just inside the doorway.

"Good morning, Vivian, Theresa," Ashley said, nodding at them in turn.

"Morning," Theresa said.

Vivian pursed her lips. She was afraid that if she said anything, she'd burst into tears.

"Are you ready to head up to court?" Ashley asked.

Vivian nodded.

They made their way to a rickety elevator, and they all stepped inside. Vivian held her breath as they ascended. She was never one for elevators, especially those that looked like they'd been built in the seventies and last serviced around the same time. They got off at the second floor, and Ashley led her into the courtroom.

To Vivian's surprise, the gallery was full. Bodies filled every space in the bench seating, pressed in, shoulder to shoulder.

"Why are so many people here?" Vivian whispered to Ashley.

"Social media. Some of the right people—or potentially wrong people, depending on how you look at it—got ahold of the story. It's blowing up into a big political thing."

"Politics. That can't be good for me."

Ashley shrugged. "If there is one thing people don't budge on, it's their politics. As long as you have one person on that jury that is a hard democrat, the state will never be able to convict you. The jury will keep hanging until the end of time."

"That's...good."

"It isn't bad."

Ashley led Vivian down the aisle to the partition that separated the parties from the onlookers. Vivian kept her gaze lowered. While Ashley had said that at least some of these people were there to support her, she couldn't bear the judgment that would inevitably come from someone who was not.

There were two tables, one set up for prosecution, one for defense. Two people sat at the prosecution table, but Vivian didn't look at them either. She followed Ashley, who led her to a seat at their table that was farthest away from the prosecutor. Once they were seated and situated, she made the mistake of looking over at the prosecution bench. There, sitting next to the prosecutor, was Vivian's husband and tormentor, Bruce Ross.

The prosecutor was an enormously overweight man. Court documents identified him as Charles Hanson. Vivian had never met the man before, but she had heard his name mentioned over the years. She had heard that he wanted to be a judge, but he hadn't made it the final two. Bruce had told Vivian that Charles would have made it through committee if, "he wasn't such a fat ass."

Bruce had always thought Charles was beneath him. After all, Charles worked for the government and had a capped salary. It was almost ironic to see the two of them together now. Probably as ironic as it was to see Vivian and Ashley seated side-by-side.

Ashley took a few moments to remove her laptop, two notepads, and multiple pens from her laptop bag. She placed one notepad in front of Vivian, and another in front of herself. Then she turned to the prosecutor and hissed, "What is he doing here?"

"It's a public hearing," Charles retorted, tucking his face back so his chin disappeared into the folds of his neck.

"Yeah, it's a public hearing, that's why they are here," Ashley gestured to the gallery. "He isn't allowed up here. He isn't a party," Ashley nodded at Bruce.

"I'm an attorney," Bruce said.

"No shit, sherlock," Ashley said, "but that doesn't mean you get to be up here. You aren't a party to this action."

"I'm the victim."

"Nobody's the victim, except Vivian here." Ashley's gaze shifted to the prosecutor. "Get him out of here or I'm going to ask the Judge to do it. I'm not playing games. He's a witness at the very best. Witnesses don't sit at counsel table."

"This is ridiculous," Bruce said, his face reddening.

Ashley blinked several times. "No, sir. What's ridiculous is that you think you have the right to do whatever you want. Well, this is a court of law. Something I understand you have absolutely no understanding of even though you are, in fact, an attorney. Non-parties do not sit at counsel table. That's how this works. You don't get to do whatever you want just because you want to do it."

"Can't you make an exception?" Charles said, his eyes pleading.

"Oh, like you always make for my clients. That kind of exception? He's free to sit up here during every hearing if he wants to sit in the Defendant's chair."

Charles didn't answer. It was obvious the question was rhetorical, but Bruce, of course, thought he had every right to interject, so he added a quick, "No."

Ashley ignored him. "In that case, I should come down harder on him. Is there anything you've done that would place you in the hot seat, here? Did you slap Vivian around a little bit while she was pregnant?"

Vivian froze, her gaze moving up to meet Bruce's for the first time. A flash of fear passed across his features, but it was quickly replaced by anger. Vivian gave a small shake of her head. She hadn't told. Ashley had guessed. She hadn't told. He had to believe her. For Penny's sake, for Penny's safety, he had to know that she had heeded his warnings to stay quiet.

"Anything at all?" Ashley continued, "Because if you have done something, my investigator is going to find out."

Ashley's gaze flicked toward the audience, and Vivian followed it. Katie was seated near the middle, watching them all with interest. She lifted a hand and waved, moving only the tips of her fingers.

Bruce's expression went dark. Vivian hadn't seen him this angry in a very long time.

"That's enough," Charles said, cutting through the tense silence. "He can sit behind me." Charles turned and motioned for several people in the gallery to scoot closer, making space for Bruce.

Bruce's expression had gone from dark to wild, but he did stand and move around so he was seated in the gallery. He withdrew his phone and began texting the moment he lowered into his seat.

Penny, Vivian's thoughts flew to her daughter. The exchange between Ashley and Charles had felt empowering, but Vivian already regretted every second of it. Bruce would be looking for a way to punish Vivian, and what better way to do that than to harm the one person she cared about most.

"Someone needs to check on Penny," Vivian whispered to Ashley.

"Now? Why?"

Vivian's gaze cut toward Bruce. "I just need to know she's safe."

"I knew there was something off about that man." She removed her phone from her computer bag and began texting. "I'll tell Katie to head over there."

"Thank you. Thank you. You have no idea."

Ashley did have no idea, but after this hearing was over, Vivian was going to tell her. It was time to reveal everything. She hadn't wanted to discuss Bruce because she thought that it might keep Penny safe, but she now knew that it wouldn't. It was time to tell the whole truth.

33

KATIE

Katie was in the gallery, watching what she assumed was an entertaining exchange between Ashley, Bruce, and Charles, but she wasn't close enough to hear the words. The facial expressions were clear enough to tell the story, though. If looks could kill, Bruce would have murdered Ashley right there in the courtroom. After what felt like a long standoff, Bruce stood up and moved to a seat in the gallery. The moment he sat down, he had his phone out, and he was pounding at the screen with short jabs of his index finger.

At that moment, Katie's phone buzzed in her pocket. She ignored it and continued watching Bruce. If she took a photo of this moment and framed it as art, she'd call the project *angry man texting*. But after a few moments, her phone buzzed again. When she still hadn't reached for it, Ashley turned around in her seat and mouthed the words, "read your texts." Katie removed her phone from her pocket, unlocked it and clicked on the messaging app.

"Can you go check on Penny?" Was the first text.

"Vivian is worried." Was the second.

Katie looked up to see Ashley and Vivian looking back at her, both wearing tense expressions. *Now?* She mouthed.

Ashley nodded.

Katie sighed and tapped a response back. "On it." Then she stood and exited the courtroom.

This concern over Penny's wellbeing was overkill, at least in Katie's opinion. She would have preferred to stay and see how the hearing ended, but she was working for Ashley, so she got up and left. She made her way down the aisle toward the back of the courtroom. Ashley had such a soft spot for the little girl, and it clouded her judgment. Checking on Penny's safety was the job of a social worker, not an investigator. Ashley was using Katie in all the wrong ways, which was not common. She never allowed personal emotions to impact a case.

This couldn't continue. Katie was going to have to discuss this with Ashley, and she wasn't eager to do it. But they simply did not have the resources to keep doing this. She pushed the back door open and stepped out into the hallway, thankful to be away from all the curious eyes of those in the gallery watching her leave before the hearing had even begun. George Thomanson was out in the hall. He came up to her when he saw her step out into the hall.

"Where are you going?" George asked.

"If I said, 'the bathroom' you'd be pretty embarrassed."

"But that's not where you are going."

"Very astute of you, sir. I am going to check on little Penny Ross."

"Why?"

Katie huffed. "Honestly, it beats me."

"Want some company?"

"You don't need to stay here?" Katie nodded toward the courtroom.

"No. They haven't asked for security or anything. I'm just here because I knew you would be." He winked.

Katie rolled her eyes. "You know me too well."

"Come on," he made a *follow me* gesture, "we can take my patrol car. It'll look more official."

"Are you sure?" Katie didn't know if Sheriff St. James would appreciate George using county resources for a side jaunt for a non-employee.

George shrugged. "It's essentially a welfare check."

A welfare check was something law enforcement officers did often, but it wasn't something many people in the public understood as part of their job. Most people saw deputies as law enforcers, not peace officers. A welfare check was part of the "peace officer" portion of the job. It was when a concerned family member or friend called law enforcement requesting that they check on an elderly relative or someone who had made concerning suicidal statements over social media. The purpose was to check on the person, ensure they were safe, and offer services if they were not.

"Lead the way," Katie said.

George led her through the hallway, down a side set of stairs, and out a side door. His patrol vehicle was parked right there, and they got inside.

"It's been a while since the two of us were in one of these together," George said, cracking a smile.

Katie nodded.

"Have you come to a decision about the Sheriff's offer?"

Katie had told George about the employment offer. He hadn't been pushy, but he had made it clear that he wanted her to take the position so they could spend more time together.

"I haven't. It will depend heavily on whether Ashley gets the judgeship or not."

"Sheriff St. James is not one to wait. Are you sure he will give you that long before he wants an answer?"

Katie exhaled heavily. "I hope so. Otherwise, I don't know what I'll do. Financially and personally, it is probably the right decision."

"Then, what makes it the wrong decision? It seems like financial and personal are the only two things to consider in this particular decision-making process."

"Yeah, it would seem that way, but you know me. I don't want to let anyone down. And before you go pointing out all of my father's flaws, none of that matters. What matters is that I gave my word that I'd work with him, and taking this position would be bailing before we gave the investigative firm a real chance to get up and running."

"I understand," George said, pulling up outside the Ross's home.

He put the vehicle in park and they both got out and approached the door. George knocked and Katie stood slightly behind him. They waited several moments, but nobody answered the door. George knocked again, this time harder. Still no answer. Yet all the lights were on inside the house, and they could see movement somewhere upstairs.

"What the hell is going on?" George asked.

Katie motioned with her head. "Let's walk around back."

They walked around the house, making their way toward the second, unattached garage. Bruce's garage. They found the BMW with a heavy dent in the front parked behind the house where it couldn't be seen from the road. There was another vehicle parked next to it—a Jeep Wrangler.

"Is this the car that hit Bambi Clark?" George asked, stunned.

"I believe it is."

"What's it doing here?"

"Good question."

Katie had seen it at this residence once before, but she hadn't told George. She'd learned about the car through her work with Ashley, and releasing it to George would be a betrayal to the defense. It made her relationship with George like walking a tightrope. Some things she could tell him, others she had to keep secret. He was likely doing the same. It was fine for now, but it would get harder as time went on. If she remained in this relationship, she was going to have to switch jobs.

They walked back around the house and began banging on the door again. This time George shouted, "Sheriff's Department. We're here for a welfare check."

There was more movement upstairs, and an uneasy feeling began settling into Katie's chest. What was going on? Katie started taking steps back, moving away from the house so she could get a better look at what was going on upstairs. The house wasn't all windows, but there were quite a few of them. She could see two large figures moving around upstairs. Adults, both dressed in dark colors.

George banged on the door again, this time putting all his strength behind it. "Sheriff's Department. Someone better get to this door before I break it down."

The adult figures froze, and then they both scuttled toward the stairs. They reminded Katie of a couple of cockroaches, fleeing from the light.

"I think they are coming," Katie said as she returned to George's side.

"They'd better be. The next time I knock, I'm going to draw the attention of the whole neighborhood."

The door was solid, but there was glass on either side. Katie leaned over to see the woman who had come to her office the other day looking for Penny, Miranda, and another person following behind her.

"They'll be here in a second."

"Is the little girl with them?"

"Nope," Katie said. The word carried a heavy sense of dread.

Katie hadn't seen anyone else in the house when she'd been looking through the windows. Not every portion of the home was windows, so Penny could be somewhere that wasn't visible from outside, but Katie didn't have a good feeling about it. And she couldn't be anywhere else other than the house. She wasn't in daycare, school hadn't started yet, and both her parents were in a district court hearing.

"We'll find her," George said. He must have sensed her anxiety.

"I hope so."

And just then, the door swung open.

34

ASHLEY

A court reporter poked her head from the door leading to chambers. She was a tall, slender woman, built a lot like Ashley, but the grooves on her face indicated she was older by a good ten years. Her gaze shifted from defense table to prosecution table, then she nodded and disappeared back into chambers.

"Who is the judge?" Vivian asked. She seemed nervous.

"I don't know," Ashley answered honestly.

Judge Ahrenson had retired, so it couldn't be him. Ashley hadn't recognized the court reporter, which likely meant she wouldn't know the judge. In district court, court reporters were assigned to a specific judge. They went to every hearing together, judge and reporter. Which meant that whoever the woman was who had looked into the room a moment earlier, she was always with the same person on the bench.

"All rise," the tall court reporter said as she strode into the courtroom. "The honorable Judge Steinkamp presiding."

"Fuuuuck," Ashley groaned.

Vivian's eyebrows shot up. "What is it?"

"Stand up, he's coming," Ashley said, motioning with her hand.

"Do you know him?" Vivian whispered as she rose to her feet.

"Not anymore."

"What does that—" Vivian was cut off by the entrance of the judge.

Judge Steinkamp was a tall man with white hair that was once brown. It contrasted with his dark eyes, making him even more handsome than he had once been. His black robe cloaked his figure as he strode into the courtroom, but Ashley could see his shoulders were still broad. She hadn't seen him for years, but he looked mostly the same, aside from a few new crinkles at the edges of his eyes. He flashed her a mischievous smile that she had known so well, but it disappeared as quickly as it had come. A grin just for her. He hadn't changed a bit.

The courtroom was silent as the judge and his court reporter took their places at the bench.

"Is everyone ready to proceed?" Judge Steinkamp said, looking from Ashley to Charles Hanson.

"Yes, your honor." The words *your honor* sounded odd when directed toward him.

"Yes, your honor," Charles parroted.

Vivian shifted her weight, leaning closer to Ashley, as though drawing from Ashley's strength. Which was something that Ashley, unfortunately, didn't have in reserve. The sudden appearance of her law school boyfriend had unnerved her. She'd heard he'd ascended to the bench, but she never thought he would run *her* courtroom.

"We're here today to address two issues. The first is the Defendant's arraignment, the second is the defense's motion for release," Judge Steinkamp squinted at his computer screen, scrolling through what Ashley assumed was her motion. "You're asking for temporary release only?" He looked up and met Ashley's gaze.

Ashley rose to her feet and cleared her throat. "That's what I've included in my motion, but if your honor would be willing to consider the release of Ms. Ross, the Defense would make oral motion for that now."

She hadn't included full release in her motion because Judge Ahrenson would not have even considered it. Vivian's charges were too political, and he had shied away from anything that would make him a target.

"Your honor," Charles said, shooting to his feet far faster than Ashley had ever seen him move. "The State is not prepared to proceed on such a motion."

Judge Steinkamp cocked an eyebrow. "Surely the evidence would be the same whether you are resisting temporary release as opposed to full release. Release is release, right?"

Ashely had heard that, before taking the bench, Judge Steinkamp—back then Darren Steinkamp—had been a career prosecutor. On the surface that didn't sound good for the defense, but it would depend on the type of prosecutor he had been. Had he been an empathetic prosecutor or an overly zealous one? The jury was still out on that question. His ruling here would be a clue.

"I suppose so, your honor. The State was not going to present any evidence. I was merely going to make a professional statement."

"So, make your statement," Judge Steinkamp said.

"Right, okay," Charles said, clearing his throat.

Ashley slowly lowered back down into her seat to wait for her turn to speak.

"The State resists the Defendant's release in any capacity, whether temporary or otherwise. The Defendant is accused of committing a heinous, awful crime against a poor, defenseless baby. That baby's death was violent and completely avoidable. And for those reasons, the State believes that the Defendant is a danger to the community and asks that her bond remain at five hundred thousand cash only."

A cash only bond meant that a bondsman could not bail Vivian out. She would have to come up with the full amount in cash for release. It was impossible, even if Bruce wanted her out. Few people had that kind of money in cash. Even rich people had most of their funds tied up in investments.

"I'll post the bond," a familiar voice said from somewhere in the gallery.

Ashley turned around to see Stephanie Arkman standing near the back of the courtroom. Stephanie's family was extremely wealthy with ethanol plants and an immense amount of farmland throughout all of Iowa. They owned multiple businesses, and Stephanie was the one with the most busi-ness sense of the bunch. She was even more savvy than her father and grandfather, which was saying something. She was probably the only person in a five-county radius who could easily post that bond. Ashley would wonder why she was even offering, but she already knew the answer.

Stephanie was Rachel Arkman's aunt. Rachel was another one of Ashley's former clients. Rachel had been accused of killing her stillborn baby and was later acquitted, but not until after she'd spent a significant time in jail. Stephanie hadn't been there for Rachel, and she'd always regretted it—or so Rachel had told Ashley. This must be an attempt to try to make up for her previous shortcomings.

"You can't do that," Bruce Ross said, turning to face Stephanie.

"Why not? It's my money," Stephanie retorted.

Ashley watched them for a moment, then turned back toward the judge, wondering how long he was going to let the fighting continue. The answer was, not long.

"That's enough," Judge Steinkamp said. His voice was stern, but there was laughter in his eyes. "Those in the gallery should stay quiet through the remainder of the hearing, or I'll have you escorted out." He focused his gaze on the gallery for another moment, then shifted his attention to Ashley. "Ms. Montgomery. I'll hear from the defense."

Once again, Ashley rose to her feet. "As the Court knows, bond is only required when a person is either a flight risk or a danger to the community. Ms. Ross has lived in Brine nearly all her life. She grew up here, her daughter is growing up here. Her daughter starts kindergarten in a few short weeks. Ms. Ross has already enrolled her in school. Ms. Ross owns a home in town. The only time Ms. Ross has left this area was when she attended college, and she returned almost immediately after graduation."

Judge Steinkamp was nodding along with Ashley's statements, which was encouraging.

"Ms. Ross has no prior criminal history. The allegations here are that she acted in a way that was contrary to a child's health before the child was even born. If she is a danger to anyone as the State alleges, it is only to fetuses, and she is obviously no longer pregnant."

"Ms. Montgomery has a point," Judge Steinkamp said, turning his attention to Charles. "Do you have any counter to her very compelling arguments?"

"Just that she's dangerous," Charles said, standing again and pulling at the collar of his shirt. A bead of sweat ran down his cheek. "And the State urges the Court not to release her."

"Alright," Judge Steinkamp said, leaning forward, "I'm prepared to rule. The Defendant is released. No bond. On her own recognizance."

"Your honor," Charles said with a gasp, "at least add the supervision of the Department of Correctional Services."

Charles was asking that Vivian essentially be placed on a pretrial probation. Release with supervision meant that she'd meet with a pretrial release officer monthly, just as a probationer would. She'd have travel restrictions and any other restriction the Department of Correctional Services saw fit.

The judge's playful gaze turned steely. "Last I checked, I'm the one wearing the robe here, Mr. Hanson. And I don't see a point in requiring supervision. You've given no reason to believe that Ms. Ross will run. You've given me no reason to believe that Ms. Ross is a danger to this community. I'm starting to think that you've given me no reason to believe that Ms. Ross has even committed a crime."

Several members of the audience audibly gasped.

"I am not prejudging this case, Mr. Hanson, but if your allegation for child endangerment is based on actions made by Ms. Ross in utero, I have serious doubts that there is probable cause to even bring a charge against Ms. Ross."

"Your honor," Charles said, swiping sweat from his forehead. "A district court judge signed the trial information based on those facts."

"Well that district court judge wasn't me," Judge Steinkamp said. "I've made my decision. This hearing is over." His gaze shifted to Ashley. "Are you going to file a written arraignment, or do you want me to make a record on that as well?"

Arraignments could be done in writing or in person. Ashley was going to have the judge do it in court, but he had thrown her and her client such a bone that she would have done anything he asked at that point. He clearly wanted her to do the arraignment in writing, so she would.

"We'll complete a written arraignment and have it filed within the hour," Ashley said.

"I assume the defense is planning to file an additional motion regarding this matter. The court's calendar is a bit jammed with some of defense's other motions. Defense may want to reconsider some of those pending motions if she wants the Court to schedule it in a timely manner."

"I understand, your honor."

It was the best thing he could possibly have said, but the request was double edged. He was hinting she should file a motion to dismiss in Vivian's case, and he would entertain granting it. That would be a win before they even got to trial. But the flip side of it was that Judge Steinkamp also wanted Ashley to withdraw her prior suppression motions in all her other cases.

She'd filed those in a fit of rage after the *Dobbs* decision had come out. It had felt like she was doing something at the time, but she was starting to realize that she wasn't actually doing anything except clogging the justice system. That could be positive for some clients, but it could be negative for others.

Judge Steinkamp stood and left the courtroom, his reporter following behind him. Voices in the courtroom gallery picked up the moment he was gone. At first it was only a few murmurs, then those murmurs rose in volume and inflection. Ashley turned around to find the gallery split into two separate groups. Bruce Ross at the head of one group, Stephanie Arkman at the head of the other. Vivian was the topic of the argument, but it wasn't actually about her. The arguments were not physical, but it seemed as though the situation could rapidly deteriorate.

"I think we ought to get going before things get worse," Theresa said.

Vivian was still in the care and custody of the Brine County jail. If this argument turned into a mob and Vivian was hurt, they'd be liable.

"Good point. I'll have you sign a written arraignment at the jail. It'll take Theresa a while to process you out anyway."

When someone was released from jail, it wasn't as simple as unlocking the chains and letting them walk out. The Court had to issue a written order, and that order was processed by the clerk's office and then sent to the jail. Once the jail received the order, they could start the paperwork for Vivian's release. It would take the better part of an hour even if Judge Steinkamp filed the written order immediately—and judges were easily distracted. Everyone wanted their attention. Another attorney could swoop in, calling the judge or appearing in chambers thinking their issue was most pressing.

Vivian nodded and Theresa led them through the crowd with Vivian in the middle and Ashley at back.

Bruce's face was bright red as they passed. He shouted, *"You can't do this! You'll be sorry!"*

Ashley didn't know if he was aiming his words at Vivian or Ashley—maybe it was both—but Vivian's face turned ashen. She didn't look at her husband, but Ashley could tell it was taking a good deal of effort.

Theresa picked up the pace, and Vivian was struggling to keep up, her gait awkward from the chains. They made it outside, Vivian stumbling and Ashley doing everything she could to steady her client. Once they were outside, they were greeted by news stations and flashing lights. Vivian froze.

"Keep moving. It'll be okay." Ashley had been in this situation before and moving forward was the only way to safety. They needed to get to the jail and call a law enforcement escort once Vivian was processed out and ready to leave.

Vivian nodded and they shuffled ahead, making their way back to the jail. When the heavy doors of the law enforcement center closed behind them, she issued a great, heavy sigh. Vivian did the same. She appeared calm for a beat, then her eyes grew wide.

"Penny. Where is Penny?" Vivian said, turning so she was facing Ashley.

"I'm sure she's fine," Ashley said with more confidence than she actually felt. "Katie went to check on her. I'll call her once we get into the jail." Ashley removed her phone from her back pocket and displayed it to Vivian.

They made their way through the law enforcement center and into the jail, Vivian still wearing the same expression of anxiety. Now that Ashley thought about it, it was odd that Katie hadn't yet sent any updates. She hadn't called or texted. Usually, she'd say something. Even if it was as simple as a text saying, "she's good." That meant something was going on with Penny. But what?

35

KATIE

The door swung open, and two individuals stood before Katie and George, neither of which were part of the Ross family.

"Can I help you?" Miranda said.

Next to her stood Oliver Banks, arms crossed and eyes narrowed. The two held themselves in the very same way, backs straight but a slight stoop to their shoulders, like they were fighting it, but the weight of life was making its mark. Both had dark hair and light skin. Both had piercing blue eyes. Both were long and lean.

"You're related," Katie blurted.

"Excuse me?" Miranda lifted an eyebrow. "That's none of your business." She turned her attention to George. "I didn't realize deputies made genealogy house calls."

"We don't," George said.

"Then what's the deal?"

How had Katie failed to see it before? Standing like that, side by side, Oliver and Miranda looked like near mirror images except one version was male and the other was much older. "Ashley never said you had a brother."

Miranda's gaze shifted back to Katie. "Ashley doesn't know everything about me or my father. We grew up together, but she wasn't exactly a friend. She definitely wasn't someone I would tell about my father sticking his dick into everything that moved. But, yeah, Oliver here," she gestured to her half-brother, "is an obvious testament to that." She paused, her gaze flicking back to George. "But again, you're not here for a genealogy house call, so what is it?"

"We're here on a welfare check."

"As you can see, everything is fine," Miranda began to close the door, but George stuck his foot out to block it.

"A welfare check for Nancy Reagan Ross. Is she here?"

"Obviously not."

"Then where is she?" Katie asked, her heart thudding in her chest. What had these two done to that little girl while they were all focused on Vivian's hearing? Oliver was not a trustworthy man. He'd hit someone with his vehicle. On purpose. What would he do to a small girl that got in his way?

"I'm not her keeper."

"Then who is?" Katie said.

"Her parents, obviously."

"Mind if I have a look around," George said, shoving past Miranda before she could respond. Katie followed close behind.

"Hey, you can't come in here."

"Looks like I already did," George said.

"I will have your badge for this."

"Here," he removed his badge from his pocket and mimed tossing it to Miranda. "Have it. I'd rather give it up and ensure the safety of a small child than the opposite. Where is she?" George said, opening a hall closet. "She's here. I know it."

"Bruce is going to be upset when he gets home," Miranda said, her voice rising, almost as though she was afraid of Bruce. But that didn't seem possible. Katie had dealt with lots of Mirandas in the past, both as a police officer and as a personal investigator. Miranda wasn't the type of woman who scared easily.

A loud banging noise came from upstairs. *Thump, thump, thump*, like an object striking a wall or a door.

"What was that?" George said looking up.

Nobody answered.

"Was that her?"

Still no answer.

George strode toward the stairwell and up the stairs, taking three at a time. Miranda followed him and Katie followed her. Oliver remained in the doorway. He lingered there for as long as it took for Katie to get to the top of the stairs, then she heard the door open and close. He'd left. That was not a good sign.

"Penny!" Katie shouted so loudly that her voice broke. "Penny! Where are you?"

Thump, thump, thump.

"It's coming from this way," George said, pointing down a hallway. He followed the sound into a bedroom decorated for a child much smaller than Penny. The walls were a sky blue with cloud decals pasted so they looked as though they were floating across the room. An ash grey crib sat at the center of the room and a matching wardrobe blocked the closet door.

Thump, thump, thump.

"It's coming from the closet," Katie said.

George gave Miranda a hard look.

"I can explain," Miranda said.

George ignored her and went to the side of the dresser, pushing it so it no longer obstructed the door. Katie rushed toward the door and wrenched it open. Penny was lying on the floor, her hands and feet duct taped together, and there was a piece of tape over her mouth.

"Jesus Christ," Katie hissed. She ran to Penny. "Hi, sweetie. We've got you now," Katie said. "I'm going to pull the tape off your mouth now, okay?"

Penny nodded.

"It might hurt."

Penny nodded again.

Katie gripped the corner of the tape, peeling it back slowly. In her experience the whole "ripping off a Band-Aid" thing only worked with Band-Aids. If she did that with duct tape, she'd likely rip off the top layer of Penny's skin along with it.

"She did this," Penny said, glaring at Miranda. "A little while before you came."

"Do you have some scissors?" Katie asked George. She was trying to grip the corner of the hand restraints to peel them off, but her hands were sweaty, and her fingers kept slipping. The process would go a lot faster if she had some scissors.

"You said you could explain," George said to Miranda. "Now's your chance. Get to explaining."

"There are scissors in the kitchen," Penny said to Katie.

"Where in the kitchen?"

"Top drawer beside the stove."

Katie was torn. She wanted to hear what Miranda was about to say, but she also couldn't leave Penny in her restraints. Not even for a moment longer. She hesitated for a fraction of a second, then nodded and stood, dashing downstairs, down the hall, and into the kitchen as fast as she could. She found the scissors and was back up the stairs in record time. If stair running was an Olympic sport, she felt certain this display would qualify her for the team.

"It wasn't my decision," Miranda was saying as Katie reentered the room.

Katie dropped to her knees, running the scissors along Penny's feet and then hand restraints, freeing her. The little girl's wrists and ankles were angry red. She'd been fighting against her restraints, trying to get free.

"It wasn't your decision to tie up a four-year-old child and lock her in a closet. Is that what you are saying?"

"Five," Penny said. "My birthday is tomorrow."

This was where people usually said *Happy Birthday*, but this was not an ordinary situation, and Penny hadn't said it in a "you should congratulate me" sort of way, it was more in a "trying to get the record straight" sort of way.

"Right, five-year-old child," George amended. "Whose decision was it?"

Miranda didn't respond.

"Was it Oliver's?" George paused, looking around. "Where is he, by the way?"

"He bailed," Katie said. "Straight out the front door. Left you to fend for yourself, Miranda. My guess is the person who gave you your instructions to lock Penny up will do the same."

Miranda pursed her lips.

"It was Bruce," Penny said. "I didn't hear him say it, but she was on the phone with him, and she did this right after they hung up. He was punishing me. Like he does with Mommy."

Katie narrowed her eyes. "Punishing you. Does he do that often?"

"Not to me. This is the first time he's ever done something like this to me. But he does it to Mommy all the time. They think I don't know. She's scared of him."

"You know what, this is probably a conversation better had down at the station, don't you think, Miranda?" George asked.

Miranda didn't respond, but she followed George as he began walking toward the door.

"Can you call social services?" George said to Katie.

"Yeah," Katie said, removing her phone from her pocket.

"I don't want to go to foster care," Penny said.

Katie understood wholeheartedly. When her father was incarcerated, she'd been old enough to fend for herself. But even then, she had felt the same way about foster care. She didn't want to be at the mercy of a family she didn't know, living in their home, following their rules, eating their food, and Penny didn't want that, either.

"I'll call Ashley. Maybe she has a suggestion."

She couldn't avoid calling social services. As a deputy, George was a mandatory reporter. He had to report this to social services. If he didn't, he could get in trouble with his job. Which meant that if she didn't, he'd be in trouble. She'd promised to do it for him, and it didn't seem fair to back out now.

Katie unlocked her phone and opened contacts, pressing Ashley's name.

"Hey, Katie," Ashley said after only one ring. "Have you seen Penny? Vivian's worried sick."

"I found her, but you aren't going to like it."

Ashley grunted. It was her way of saying *go on*. Katie explained the circumstances surrounding her and George's discovery of Penny.

"Good thing George was with you. They wouldn't have let you in other-wise. Honestly, George probably shouldn't have gone in at all, but I'm glad he did," Ashley said.

"Me too. My question now, though, is what to do with Penny? George has to report it, and I told him I'd do it for him, but Penny doesn't want to go to foster care."

"She won't have to," Ashley said with more confidence than Katie thought she should considering Penny's father had ordered her maltreatment and her mother was incarcerated.

"How are you so certain?"

"Because the judge released Vivian today."

"He released her?" Katie said, dumbfounded. "Like for the funeral, right?"

"Nope. Pretrial release. She's coming home."

"Wow. When?"

"As soon as they can get her processed out."

Katie lowered the phone, holding it out between herself and Penny, and clicked the speakerphone button. "Say that again. Penny is right here."

"Penny, honey," Ashley said.

Penny nodded, not realizing that Ashley couldn't see her.

"Your mother is coming home."

In that moment, Penny burst into tears, sobbing like a child of her age should considering the horrible circumstances that had befallen her over the past few weeks. An hour earlier, she'd been locked in a closet, held against her will by a woman she hardly knew. Now, she'd be back in the care of the one person who loved her more than anyone else in the world.

Life was strange that way. It could turn on a dime. Katie hoped Penny's closet incarceration was the last negative turn Penny and Vivian would have to endure. That was the problem with hopes, though. They were just as tangible as wishes and dreams. Few came true.

36

ASHLEY

Friday, August 12

It was early morning and Ashley had already been in the office for hours. Katie had been there almost as long, but they'd been busy in their respective offices, catching up on paperwork. At seven thirty, Katie came into Ashley's office and plopped into a chair, draping herself over it so she was sitting sideways with her legs hanging over the side.

"Have you seen the local paper?" Ashley asked.

"No. What does it say?" Katie said, stifling a yawn.

"The headline article is about Bruce and Vivian."

Katie sat up straighter. "Good or bad? For Vivian, I mean."

Ashley had filed Vivian's motion to dismiss, but that wasn't set for hearing until the next district court service day, which wouldn't be until August twenty-second. The day had been jam-packed with motions, but Ashley had withdrawn all those to make room in the court's calendar for Vivian's hearing.

"I'll read you the headline, and you tell me."

"Then do it," Katie said, dropping her legs to the floor so she was sitting properly in the seat, her attention focused on Ashley.

"This is what it says," Ashley's gaze shifted to her computer screen, 'Mother released, father investigated.'"

Katie bit her lip, looking up at the ceiling. "I have no idea. It makes me want to read more. I guess that's the whole point of a headline."

"True." Ashley turned back to the article and continued reading. "Vivian Ross, the mother who was arrested for child endangerment causing death after giving birth at the local hospital was released from the Brine County Jail on August eighth after an intense court hearing resulting in Judge Steinkamp ordering Ms. Ross's release. The father, Bruce Ross, was present at the hearing. The couple have one older child, age five, who wasn't present at the hearing. On August ninth, a complaint was filed by Deputy George Thomanson, alleging the five-year-old had been subjected to physical abuse while the parents were both at Vivian's August eighth hearing. The alleged perpetrator of the child abuse was Miranda Birch, a longtime friend and confidant to Bruce Ross. Ms. Birch was arrested and charged with child endangerment, no injury, an aggravated misdemeanor. Sources say that Bruce is still under investigation for allegedly orchestrating the child abuse."

Ashley finished reading and turned back to Katie. "What do you think?"

"Good. Definitely good."

"I thought so, too. I just wanted to make sure."

"How are Penny and Vivian doing?"

"They are settling in," Ashley said.

The mother and daughter were reunited shortly after Vivian's release from custody, but they hadn't gone back to the Ross home. Bruce had access, and there was no telling what he would do when they returned home. Sure, he was under investigation for child abuse, but no charges had been issued against him yet, and there would not be a protective order in place until after his charge and arrest. That left Vivian and Penny exposed and unsafe.

That's why Ashley had offered for them to stay at her home out in the country. Bruce wouldn't know where to look for them. Of course, Bruce had known that Ashley harbored Penny the last time and he would come looking for her again, but he'd probably look for her at Ashley's office. It wasn't a large leap to get to Ashley's home, but there wasn't much choice in the matter. It wasn't a perfect plan, but it was better than the alternative.

"Has Vivian heard anything from Bruce?"

Ashley shook her head. "Not that I know of."

It was deeply troubling to Ashley, Bruce's radio silence, but she hadn't uttered her concerns aloud. He was unraveling. The once polished businessman had grown desperate. He'd always been violent, Ashley knew that now that Vivian had finally opened up about her marriage, but he'd also never been sloppy. He'd terrorized and abused his wife for years and was never caught. The incident with Penny proved that was changing. That was concerning, especially with Bruce's silence. The phrase *no news is good news* did not apply to the emotionally unstable.

"Has anyone heard from him?"

Ashley's phone started ringing. It was her direct line, a number few people knew. She lifted a finger in a *one-minute* gesture and picked up. "This is Ashley Montgomery."

"Where are they? I know you have them."

Ashley lowered the receiver and mouthed, "Speak of the devil." Then she clicked the speaker phone button and cradled the receiver.

"Why, hello, there Bruce. Lovely to speak with you, too."

"Stop with your bullshit, Ashley. I want to know where *my* wife and child are." His voice sounded rough, like he'd been up all night. "Miranda is in jail, and it's your fault."

"Seems like it's more *your* fault than it is mine. Since it was you who told Miranda to lock Penny up."

"I only did that because of *my* wife's actions at her hearing."

Ashley cocked her head to the side. "You punished Penny because of Vivian? How very domestic-abuse-like of you."

"My family is none of your business. I know what's good for them. I was the only reason my baby boy was born alive. Then she killed him. That snake. The horrible, horrible woman. And now she's out of jail."

"I didn't realize you'd found a way to carry a baby as a man."

"Shut up," Bruce hissed. "That's not what I mean. I meant she was going to have an abortion. That slut Bambi was getting her the abortion pill. Bet you didn't know that."

Ashley had known that. Vivian had told her, but she wasn't about to relay that tidbit of knowledge to him. "Okay. How is that supposed to matter to me?"

"Because I stopped Bambi."

Ashley raised her eyebrows. "I don't know what you mean."

"Bambi and her boyfriend both used Miranda and Oliver's services."

This was code for *they bought drugs from them*, but Ashley didn't clarify because she wanted to keep him talking. This was the connection she needed to know.

"Bambi's boyfriend told Miranda about Vivian and Bambi's plan. He let it slip when he was high one day. Then Oliver took care of the little problem for me."

"By hitting Bambi with a car," Ashley said, her tone blunt. "Wasn't there some easier way to do it? Like asking her to give the pill to you. Or asking her to throw the pills away?"

"No, she'd just get more. That's how those druggies work. They have no loyalty. Even if I paid her to flush it, she'd go back to Vivian and ask for more money, and Vivian would have given the addict more of *my* money."

"Let me get this straight," Ashley said, rubbing her temples, "you chose to kill Bambi, a grown woman—"

"A drug addicted slut," Bruce interjected.

"Who also happened to be pregnant, so that you could prevent your wife from taking an abortion pill. Do I have that right?"

"Yeah."

Ashley blinked, at a loss for words for a moment. Bruce had completely lost his mind. No sane attorney would make an admission like that. Unless, of course, he was arrogant enough to think that nobody would believe her over him.

"You understand that Bambi's baby was just as much a baby as yours had been at that time."

"Maybe, but that baby would have grown up to be just like her mother. A meth whore. I did society a favor by getting rid of both of them."

Ashley looked at Katie and mouthed, *this guy is a psychopath*.

Katie nodded. *Off his rocker*, she mouthed back.

Bruce's thought process wasn't completely without logic, but it was self-serving and warped. He obviously blamed Bambi for using drugs, but he didn't extend that blame to Miranda, who had been supplying the drugs.

"Alright Bruce, I'm not sure what you want me to do with that information, but duly noted."

"I want you to know that I'm not messing around. That's what I want you to do with the information. You have one day to deliver my wife and child to me, or there will be major repercussions."

"That's sounds like a threat, Bruce."

"It is. You now know that I can carry out my threats, so you should take this one seriously."

"Oh, I do, Bruce. I do."

"And don't go reporting it to that bitch investigator of yours."

Ashley's gaze shifted to Katie. *Too late.*

"She'll tell her deputy boyfriend and he'll go arresting me. And that is not a good plan, by the way. You do not want to know what will happen to you if things go that way."

"I don't?"

"No. You don't."

"Alright, well it was lovely talking to you, Bruce, but I really must be going."

"One day. You have one day to deliver them to me."

"Got it."

"I'm not kidding."

"Also got it."

"Good. See that you get it done."

"Goodbye," Ashley said, lifting and hanging up the receiver. Then she turned to Katie. "What. The. Actual. Fuck."

"That was messed up."

"I wish I would have thought to record it."

A smile spread across Katie's lips. She lifted her phone, pressed a couple buttons, then Bruce's voice rang out, loud and clear, *Oliver took care of the little problem for me.*

"Did you record everything?"

"From the moment he said," she pressed another few buttons, then Bruce's voice came again, *Stop with your bullshit, Ashley. I want to know where my wife and child are.* "I figured it could only go downhill from there. I was right."

"That's why you're the best," Ashley said. "Now, call your boyfriend. We've got a crime to report."

"Gladly."

As Katie called George, Ashley turned back to her computer, drafting a motion she'd suspected she'd need to create for quite some time. With Bruce's arrest, Vivian would be a witness against him. That also made him a co-defendant to Oliver, which meant she could withdraw from Oliver's case. It was a conflict to have one client testifying against another. Ashley could choose which client she wanted to keep, and without a doubt, she was choosing Vivian.

It seemed like everything was headed in the right direction, but Ashley knew better than to believe that they were in the clear. Even if Bruce was arrested—and he probably would be considering the recording—that didn't mean he'd remain in jail. Bond would be set, and he could post it. He'd posted Oliver's bond, so he'd surely be able to post his own. That would place Vivian, Penny, and Ashley in even further danger. She hoped Bruce wouldn't make good on his threats, but he had sounded serious.

It was a risk, but it was one that she was going to have to take.

37

VIVIAN

Saturday, August 13

The day had started out the same as any day in the middle of August, except everything was different. It was nearing seven o'clock when Vivian's eyelids fluttered open. At first, she didn't recognize her surroundings. Not the old dresser in the corner or the cheap, scratchy sheets of the bed. Then her gaze fell upon the little figure lying next to her, and it all clicked into place. She was at Ashley's house, and Penny was right there beside her. No jail cell. No Bruce. For the first time since she met Bruce, she was free.

She had been tied to Bruce Ross for as long as she could remember. He had owned her, and to be honest, he still did in some ways. Getting away physically was not the same as finding emotional safety. It would be a long, arduous process, filled with therapists, domestic advocates, and antidepressants, but she'd do anything for Penny. Her happiness was paramount, and Penny would never be happy living with that man in her life. She'd never be safe with him. Not after what he'd done to her.

"Mommy," Penny murmured, snuggling closer into Vivian's side. Her eyes were not open yet, but she was stirring.

Vivian ran her fingers through her daughter's copper colored hair, studying every freckle on her little face. She'd lost the baby, and that left its mark on her, despite her refusal to bond with him. That was a true loss, a fresh wound, one she would probably forever feel, especially since she had a hand in his demise. But her connection with her little girl, it was something entirely different. It was a love that almost ached. Unshakable. Unbendable. Complete.

They laid like that for what seemed like an eternity and no time at all, then Penny's eyes fluttered open, her long eyelashes flashing like the wings of a butterfly.

"Hi, Mommy," Penny said, gazing up at Vivian with wide, trusting eyes.

"Good morning, sweetheart," Vivian said, placing a soft kiss on Penny's forehead.

"Morning."

They'd never slept together, not until now. Bruce refused to allow it. Even when he had moved out to the garage, he'd insisted that they each sleep in their own rooms. He didn't have cameras in their rooms, not like he had throughout the rest of the house, but he could come back any time. Vivian had always been too scared to risk it. Not even when Penny came in during the night with tears streaming down her cheeks, complaining of nightmares. Nightmares were bad, but Bruce was always worse.

"We should get up," Vivian said, "the day has already begun."

"Is Ashley still here?"

"Oh no, she left hours ago." Vivian had heard her moving around, presumably getting ready for work. It had been sometime around four o'clock in the morning. Vivian heard the noises and started, afraid it was Bruce coming for her. But it wasn't. It was only Ashley. It was the middle of the night to most of the world, but not to Ashley. It added to Vivian's newfound respect for her attorney, something that had continued to grow with each passing day.

"What are we going to do today?"

"We have that funeral," Vivian said. Her voice caught and she couldn't say more.

Sometimes, she didn't know why the loss of the baby even bothered her. She hadn't wanted him. He was an additional tie to Bruce that she couldn't bear. If he had lived, she would have never gotten away from Bruce. Yet, here she was, barely able to speak about the baby. It was another topic she surely would need to broach with a therapist. The list was long. As soon as she had some money of her own, she'd start seeing someone.

Penny sat up. "But Bruce will be there."

"We'll be fine, honey. There will be lots of people there, including Ashley, Katie, and Katie's boyfriend, George. George is a deputy sheriff, you know. He'll keep us safe."

"I remember George. He helped Katie save me."

"Exactly."

"Okay," Penny said, but she didn't look convinced.

"Let's get moving," Vivian said, standing up.

She went to the closet and removed a lightweight pant suit for herself, all black, and a black, shift-style dress for Penny. Before leaving Vivian's house with Penny, Katie had gone through both of their closets and grabbed as many pieces of clothing as she carry. Vivian was grateful for this because she had no money to buy new items. Bruce had control of all the accounts.

Vivian laid the clothes out on the end of the bed and studied them for a long moment, wondering if they were sufficient. People would be judging her today. She needed to make a positive impression. A grieving mother was tasteful, but not attractive. Professional, but not cold. The Brine locals would be judging her until the end of time. Even if the judge dismissed her charges, half of Brine would still have their opinions.

"It will be okay," Penny said, placing a little hand on top of Vivian's, pulling her out of her thoughts.

"Thank you," Vivian said, and she meant it. She needed Penny's little reminders that she was still a good person.

Vivian showered in the guest bathroom and got herself ready, minimal makeup, hair pulled back into an elegant chignon. She styled Penny's hair in the same way, and they descended the stairs toward the kitchen. A pot of coffee sat warming on the counter with a box of doughnuts beside it. There was a note from Ashley right next to the doughnuts. Vivian's heart fluttered at the sight of the note. It was an automatic response. Most of her notes over the years had been from Bruce, all of which contained threats. She knew this letter would be different, but the response was so engrained in her.

Penny approached it first, picking it up and bringing it to Vivian. "What does it say?"

Vivian looked down and read to herself.

Coffee is fresh. I set it to turn on at eight o'clock.

Vivian glanced at the clock. It was ten minutes after eight o'clock.

Donuts are less fresh, but I picked them up at Casey's on my way home from work yesterday. I know you plan to go to the funeral today. I wish you wouldn't. But since I know you will, I'll meet you there. Stay in the car until we come to you. Keys are hanging beside the front door. See you at ten o'clock.

"What does it say?" Penny asked again.

Vivian forced a smile. "Just that coffee is fresh, and you can have as many doughnuts as you want."

"Oh good," Penny said. She was already eating a chocolate one with chocolate frosting.

Ashley was allowing Vivian to borrow one of her trucks. It was old and clunky. It had belonged to Ashley's mother and had been stored in one of the back barns for years now. Looking at it, it was surprising that it even ran.

Vivian drank a cup of coffee and watched Penny devour two more doughnuts. Normally, she'd slow her down, issuing warnings of sugar rushes and worrying about Bruce's wrath if he found out his daughter had downed so much sugar in the morning. She knew what he'd say. *That girl is going to get fat. She already has red hair, that's bad enough. Now, you want to make her fat.* Vivian shook the thought from her head. She had to get him out of her mind.

"Ready to go?" Vivian asked.

Penny nodded and wiped her mouth with a napkin. They hopped in Ashley's old truck and began making their way toward town. It was a thirty-minute drive, and Vivian drove slowly. Ashley was allowing her to use her car, but she had no car seat, and an accident would be extra dangerous for Penny.

They arrived at the church a few moments before ten o'clock. The place was packed. She could see two news vans and two large groups of protesters facing off across the street. One pro-life with signs saying *Life Starts at Conception* and *Save the Babies*. The other group was pro-choice, raising signs that said things like *My Body, My Choice*. Vivian closed her eyes and looked away. She didn't want to think about any of that right now.

A knock at the window drew her attention. Ashley waved to her and mimed shutting off the engine and getting out. Katie was already at the passenger door, opening it and ushering Penny out.

"Where is George?" Vivian said. "I thought he would be here."

"He is, but he's stuck in crowd control," Katie said nodding toward the large group of protesters.

There were three officers with their backs to Vivian, all standing with their hands behind their backs, watching the group for signs of violence. The protestors easily outnumbered the officers ten to one, and the groups were growing in size. It wasn't a good omen.

"Don't worry. He's going to come inside with us," Katie said.

"Are you ready?" Ashley asked.

Vivian gripped her daughter's hand and looked up at the giant Catholic church looming over her. Taking one deep breath and releasing it slowly, she said, "Ready as I'll ever be."

They made their way toward a side door, Ashley leading the way. The whole incident felt surreal. Like a dream rather than reality. The shouting of the crowd pressed against Vivian's ears, growing louder. They paused at the side of the building while Katie texted George. He appeared a few minutes later, and they entered through the side door. With a whoosh of the door closing behind them, all the sounds were gone, replaced with the reverent silence characteristic of churches.

Vivian should have felt relieved. But the only emotion she could muster was dread.

38

KATIE

Katie didn't like crowds. They were unpredictable, especially when emotions were involved. Few things were more emotional than a funeral.

The church was crowded. Katie's gaze darted from left to right, surveying the building, noting the exits. Every pew was full. Individuals were packed in shoulder to shoulder in every open space, except for one. The pew designated for family. It was front and center, directly across from the altar. Only one person occupied that pew, and it was Bruce Ross. Ashley started in that direction, but Vivian didn't follow. She froze, staring, clutching Penny's hand like it was the only thing tethering her to reality.

Ashley glanced back and saw they weren't following and returned. "It's the only open place," Ashley whispered. "And you are family."

Vivian shook her head. "I can't. Penny can't. That man..." She was terrified. Her pale skin had grown paler, and a light sheen of sweat was forming on her brow.

"Then what do you want to do? Leave?"

"I don't know. Maybe." Penny tugged at her mother's hand, and Vivian looked down. "What is it, honey?"

"You can do this, Mommy," Penny said. "We can do it together."

Tears sprang to Vivian's eyes, and she blinked several times to keep them from falling.

"I'll sit next to Bruce," George offered. "I've got some business with him, but I've been instructed to wait until the funeral is over before taking care of it."

Vivian cocked her head to the side, confused. Katie and Ashley hadn't told her about the threatening phone call from Bruce. She had plenty on her plate already, she didn't need to worry about threats to Ashley and Katie. They could take care of themselves.

"And I'll sit by George," Katie added. "You can sit by me, Vivian. Penny will be beside you, and Ashley can sit on the end. How does that sound?"

Vivian didn't look convinced, but she did agree to the plan, and she allowed George to lead them down the aisle, toward the front of the church and the reserved pew. Every eye seemed to watch them as they made their progression. Murmurs followed the stares, the sounds of the whispering voices reverberating off the high ceilings and echoing back down to the crowd, enhancing the sound. They probably thought George was there because of Vivian—a deputy sent to supervise the criminal in their midst—but Katie knew they would soon find out the truth.

Bruce was at one end of the pew, the left side facing the altar, so George led them to enter on the right side. Shimmying past Bruce would have been a complete disaster. Bruce didn't notice them at first. He was facing forward, like he was studying the altar, but his eyes were unfocused. Tears tracked down his cheeks and he didn't bother to wipe them away. He seemed frozen, but that only lasted until George sat down next to him.

"This is my spot," Bruce growled, his head snapping toward George. "You cannot sit here."

"I'm with the family," George whispered, a smirk forming on his lips.

"The fam..." Bruce's voice trailed off when his gaze settled on Vivian. He was silent for a long moment, then he shot to his feet. "Look at that, my bitch wife is here. And her little welp, I mean, bitch-in-training is right next to her, holding her hand. Aren't you two something special."

The whispers of the crowd had died down. Bruce hadn't noticed, but everyone was listening to the conversation. Thanks to the high ceilings of the church, everyone could hear it echoing around them, too.

Ashley leaned forward, drawing Bruce's attention, a sly smile spreading across her features. "I told you I'd bring them to you. Here they are. You're the one that demanded their presence and placed a time limit for me to comply."

Vivian's eyes grew wide. Katie leaned into her and whispered, "Don't worry. It's sarcasm. I'll explain it all to you after mass."

"So, you can drop the threats now," Ashley said.

"Speaking of that call," George said, "we need to have a little chat about it once this whole thing is over."

Bruce ignored Ashley and George, his gaze locked on Vivian, his eyes aflame, then he shifted to Penny. "Locking you in a closet wasn't enough, was it? That didn't teach either of you a lesson. You don't defy me. *You don't do it!*"

He had shouted the last few words, and their echo all around him seemed to bring him back to reality. He saw then that all eyes were on him, and everyone could hear him. That his words, especially those directed at the small five-year-old child clinging to mother while tears tracked down her cheeks, could have dire consequences. This was not a good look for Bruce, and even he seemed to realize he'd gone too far, because he nodded and dropped back into his seat.

There was silence in the church through the remainder of the funeral. Vivian cried, Bruce stared straight ahead, running a hand through his thick hair every few minutes. The family was irreparably broken. That, Katie felt, was certain. Sitting between them felt like standing in no man's land during a tenuous cease fire. It was barely stable. Sooner or later, someone was going to get shot.

The moment the funeral was over, Bruce rose to his feet, intent on leaving.

"Hold on there," George said, placing a hand on Bruce's arm.

Bruce yanked his arm away. "Don't touch me."

"I need to talk to you."

"About what?"

Katie remained seated as she watched the discussion unfold, turning her body so she could shield Vivian and Penny if things went sideways. And an arrest at Bruce's son's funeral could easily go that way.

"Your involvement in the death of Bambi Clark."

Bruce's gaze cut to Ashley and then to Katie, his lip curling into a snarl. "I don't know what you are talking about."

"There's a recording that says otherwise. Do you want to tell me about that?"

"No."

"Then, I'm afraid I'm going to have to arrest you for conspiracy to commit murder."

"*Murder*," Bruce shouted. "I'm not a murderer, she is." He pointed an accusatory finger at Vivian. "Arrest her."

"We already did, and the justice system is currently dealing with her."

"That's bullshit and you know it."

Again, the church had fallen completely silent, the onlookers watching the scene with interest.

"They are going to let her off," Bruce shouted, a wild gleam in his eyes. "You heard the judge at her bond hearing. He's going to dismiss the charges."

"You don't know that," George said.

"Don't lie to me. I *fucking hate it* when people lie."

"Cuff him already, George," Katie said through gritted teeth. The guy was coming unglued. He was starting to make Katie nervous, and she was not easily spooked. She knew a murderous expression when she saw one. If Bruce had a gun, he would have shot all of them right then and there. Witnesses be damned.

"Turn around," George said.

When Bruce didn't move, George grabbed him by the shoulders and forced him to comply. He snapped the cuffs around Bruce's wrists, then led him into the aisle. The church remained silent, and Katie, Ashley, Vivian, and Penny stayed in their seats right up until the moment George and Bruce had exited through the back door of the church.

"Let's go," Katie said when Bruce was gone and the murmurs of the crowd started picking up.

As they made their way toward the side door, Katie could still feel eyes upon them, but this time they didn't feel quite so intense. They didn't hold the same judgment, the condemnation. This time, they seemed more curious than anything. And that felt like a win for Vivian.

Bruce's awful display and his recent arrest would do wonders for Vivian's reputation. That shouldn't have a bearing on how the judge viewed Ashley's motion to dismiss, but it couldn't hurt. It was Bruce's turn to face public scrutiny. The problem with Bruce was his mental state—especially if he bonded out of jail, which was a likely scenario since he had control of all the family accounts. Once released, there was no telling what he'd do to retaliate. Katie hoped it was nothing, but her instinct told her otherwise.

39

ASHLEY

August 18

Bruce posted bond. It wasn't ideal, not by any stretch of the imagination, but virtually all crimes were bondable, and he had the money. There was nothing Ashley could do to stop it. That was the way of the court system, and she'd always trusted it. Vivian and Penny were not safe. Ashley knew it without a doubt, she could feel it in her bones and sensed it in that way only those who have spent years working in the criminal justice system could.

As a result, Ashley was doing all she could to keep Bruce from finding the mother and daughter duo. Few people knew where Ashley lived out in the country, and that had helped, but eventually, Bruce would discover their location. He was a smart man and a lawyer. Ashley was living out on her mother's old acreage property, and it wouldn't take much digging into property records to realize that Ashley was living there. But what other option did they have? Vivian and Penny couldn't stay with Katie. She lived in town. Bruce would track them down in a heartbeat.

The screen to Ashley's phone lit up, catching her attention, buzzing against the kitchen table. She looked at it. A smile spread across her face as she read the name of the caller, *Rachel Arkman.*

"Well, well, well, look what the cat dragged in," Ashley said as she picked up the phone.

"I'm sorry it's been so long," Rachel said, her voice sheepish.

Rachel had once been Ashley's client. She'd been barely eighteen at the time, accused of murdering her stillborn baby. Her case had similarities to Vivian's, but they weren't the same. Rachel and Ashley had grown close through their attorney/client relationship. After Rachel's acquittal and release from jail, she had nowhere to go, so she'd gone to live with Ashley. In that time, Rachel had become more like a daughter to Ashley. One who had grown up, flown the nest, and recently started law school at Drake University.

"Don't apologize. I'm just kidding," Ashley said. "I know it's been a long time, but I remember what it was like in law school. You don't have time for anything."

"Still..."

"None of that," Ashley said, taking a sip of her lukewarm coffee. "What's going on? Do you need help with something?" It was a work day, but she hadn't gone into the office. She had brought her laptop and a stack of files home the night before and was now working from her kitchen table.

"No, umm, I wanted to call you to tell you good luck today."

Today was her interview with the Governor for the judgeship. That was why she'd elected to work from home. Her interview wasn't until two o'clock, but she would have to drive to Des Moines for the interview, which was an hour's drive. Ashley had a way of losing herself in her work while at the office, and she needed to watch the clock.

"Oh, you didn't need to do that, but thank you." The words felt awkward coming from Ashley's mouth. She didn't often have cause to thank others. She was out of practice.

"Are you going to behave yourself?"

"Meaning..." Ashley knew exactly what Rachel meant, but she wanted to make her say it.

"Don't intentionally sabotage yourself. I know you don't like the Governor, but please try to keep from saying anything too offensive."

"I'm making no promises."

"Ashley…" Rachel sighed in a *what are we going to do with you* sort of way.

"Alright, alright, I'll behave myself."

"Unless. There is an unless in there somewhere."

Rachel knew her too well. "Unless, of course, she says something that pisses me off first. Then, I promise nothing."

"I wouldn't expect anything else."

"Good."

They were silent for a moment, then Rachel said, "I had one other reason for calling." Her voice had grown more tentative, and she sounded nervous.

Ashley was immediately alarmed. Rachel had a difficult childhood. She'd adjusted well after her acquittal, but Ashley still worried about her mental health. "What is it? Are you okay?"

"Oh, I'm fine. I actually wanted to talk to you about Vivian."

"Vivian," Ashley repeated. "What about her?"

"I know she's staying with you."

"How do you know that?"

"Because I stayed with you, and I know you. You wouldn't abandon her. There's a lot of media coverage. I remember how that can lead to death threats and danger. You would never force Vivian to confront that on her own."

Again, Rachel knew her too well. "I'll concede that point."

"I know you and Aunt Stephanie don't get along…"

Rachel's *Aunt Stephanie* was Stephanie Arkman. She was one of the richest women in Iowa. Stephanie was born with a silver spoon in her mouth, and she'd taken that silver and turned it into gold. She was influential, and she knew it. She was exactly the type of person who rubbed Ashley the wrong way. Ashley and Stephanie had had their fair share of spats over the years, especially when it came to Rachel's wellbeing.

"What about Stephanie?"

"She wants to offer Vivian a place to stay. You know the family has several homes out in the country, all gated, and a private security staff."

Ashley didn't say anything at first, she didn't have the words.

"She'll be safe there. It's not personal. I just worry that you are endangering yourself too, and—"

"Rachel," Ashley said, interrupting her. She had misinterpreted Ashley's silence for anger, and she was scrambling to explain herself. Ashley stopped her before she babbled on for too long. "That's an excellent idea."

"It is?"

"Yes. It solves a lot of problems."

"Oh, good. I'll call her and tell her to send a car." Stephanie was that kind of rich. The send-a-car kind of rich.

"Great. I'll let Vivian know the news."

They exchanged a few more minutes of conversation and then ended the call, both eager to facilitate Vivian and Penny's transition to safety. It was approaching noon, so Ashley didn't have a lot of time before she needed to head to Des Moines for her interview. She explained the situation to Vivian, who was more trusting than Ashley would have thought, and she graciously accepted the new arrangement. Ashley said her goodbyes to Penny, then hopped in her car and started the long drive to Des Moines.

She drove in silence, an effort to keep her mind focused on the interview. If she turned on the radio, she would risk hearing what the news had to say about Vivian's case. In the public eye, there were two clear camps, those who saw Vivian as a murderer, and those who thought Vivian had the freedom to do whatever she wanted with her body. Both were hyperfocused on the wrong thing, at least in Ashley's opinion, but that was politics. It boiled down to talking points. Whether those talking points made sense in criminal justice system terms didn't really matter.

It was one-thirty when she finally found a parking garage close enough to the Governor's office to walk. Security at the state capitol building was similar to TSA airport security. She had to take off her shoes, send her laptop bag through a scanner, and allow a large man with acne scars on his cheeks to run a wand over her body. It was invasive, but still probably inadequate to stop someone who was truly dedicated to causing mayhem.

"Ms. Montgomery," a soft voice said just as the security guy finished his final sweep of the wand.

"That's me," Ashley said, looking up to meet the gaze of a young, blond woman with bright blue eyes and a tentative smile.

"I'm Elsa Bowman," the girl said, extending her hand.

Ashley accepted it and shook. Elsa's grip was weak, and Ashley wanted to say *put some power behind it,* but she didn't. It wasn't her place.

"I'm here to take you to Governor Ingram."

"Wonderful. Lead the way."

That's exactly what Elsa did. She led Ashley through a labyrinth of hallways and locked doors accessible only with a keycard, making twists and turns that had Ashley so directionally confused that she doubted she'd ever make it out of there without help. With each passing turn, she grew more and more anxious. She was out of her world, her comfort zone, and she knew, without a doubt, that she wasn't entering a friendly zone. Governor Ingram was not going to like anything Ashley had done over the past month, and she felt sure the Governor would make her opinions known.

What Ashley didn't know was whether she would be able to hold her tongue in the face of that kind of confrontation. She almost wished she had made that promise to Rachel to behave herself. At least then, she'd have that agreement as motivation. As it stood, this interview was likely to dissolve into a disaster.

40

KATIE

"Do you know Stephanie Arkman?" Katie asked.

"A little," Vivian answered.

They were standing outside Ashley's house, waiting for Stephanie's driver to arrive. Ashley had asked Katie to come and wait with Vivian and Penny while she interviewed with the governor. Vivian and Katie were on the porch, seated in two old rockers while Penny was in the yard playing with Ashley's dogs, a border collie named Finn, and an Australian shepherd called Princess. They were outdoor dogs that spent their days patrolling Ashley's acreage, but they were sticking close by today to play with Penny. She was running in large, looping circles and the dogs chased after her, barking and yipping with excitement.

"She looks so innocent out there, doesn't she?" Katie said.

Vivian didn't answer at first. Katie looked over to see Vivian watching her daughter through tired, bloodshot eyes. The past few weeks had been grueling on her body and her soul.

"She does. Watching her out there," Vivian sighed, "It's hard to believe she's lost so much. Her brother. Her home. Most of her things..."

Katie's gaze shifted to the two small duffle bags beside Vivian's feet. It contained all the items Katie and George were able to remove from the home. It wasn't much. "She has lost quite a lot, but circumstances are starting to look up. You are out of jail now, and your case seems to be headed in the right direction. As for your things and the house, they still exist. You'll have them back sooner than you think. Especially if Bruce goes to prison for his involvement in Bambi's hit and run and his role in locking Penny in the closet."

Vivian stopped rocking and turned her knees toward Katie. "You think he'll go to prison?"

Katie shrugged. "It's possible."

Vivian shifted her weight and began rocking again. "Then I'm in more trouble than I thought."

"What do you mean by that?"

"He'll be desperate."

"Most people are once they are caught."

"He'll want revenge."

"That'll be hard to do," Katie felt less confident in her words than she sounded.

"What happens if he doesn't go to prison?"

"He'll be on probation."

"What does that entail?"

"Meeting with a probation officer once a month."

"What then? Even if he goes to prison, what about before then? You mentioned my house and my things would still be there. No, they won't. I know Bruce. He's destroyed my clothes, and he'd rather burn the house to the ground than allow me to have it. He'd fill it with carbon monoxide or let loose a poisonous snake at the very least."

Katie nodded as though she understood, but she didn't. Vivian was under a lot of stress, and she was exaggerating. The criminal justice system was not perfect, but Vivian had a doomsday outlook on life. Katie didn't blame her for that, considering all the horrible things she'd gone through, so she chose not to respond. There was no point in upsetting Vivian.

A black sports utility vehicle turned onto the drive. The dogs saw it first, freezing in their game of chase-the-five-year-old, and bolted toward the property line, heading straight for the vehicle.

"That must be Stephanie's driver," Vivian said, rising to her feet.

"His name is Bryce," Katie said, standing and picking up Penny's bag. "He's a strange guy, but he means well."

Katie knew Bryce from the time when Rachel Arkman had lived with her Aunt Stephanie. He rubbed everyone the wrong way, and that made him a suspect in another case. However, Stephanie had always trusted him, and she'd been right. Bryce was harmless.

"I've had just about all the strangeness I can take."

"Will you be comfortable at Stephanie's house?" Katie asked.

"I don't know. I've never been to Stephanie's house. She's attended some of the same events as me over the years, but she wasn't hosting any of them."

"She likes her privacy."

"I guess I should be grateful for that," Vivian said with a sigh.

The SUV pulled forward at a low speed, the dogs running beside it. It came to rest at the front of the residence, the tires crunching against the gravel. The driver, Bryce, hopped out of the vehicle. He wore a black suit, tailored to fit his lean physique. Ashley's dogs sniffed his feet, but he ignored them, turning his attention to Vivian and Katie.

"Vivian Ross, I presume?"

Vivian nodded.

"And Nancy Ross," Penny said, running up onto the porch to stand next to her mother.

"Are you ready to go?"

"As I'll ever be," Vivian said with a sigh.

Katie carried Penny's bag and placed it in the trunk. Bryce carried Vivian's bag and did the same. He opened the side door for them. A large car seat occupied the spot behind the driver. "Sorry," he said. "You will probably need to get in on the other side. Ms. Arkman suggested that I provide proper restraints for the little one. I hope that's not presumptuous."

"Not at all." Vivian looked relieved as she walked around to the other side of the vehicle.

Katie helped Penny into her seat. Then she stared at the buckle. It was a contraption with several buckles and looping belts. Penny climbed into the seat and threaded her arms through two of the buckles.

"This one attaches to this one," Penny said, clicking two of the restraints together. "And these two attach down here." She picked up the remaining two belts and indicated the base of the contraption.

It took Katie a moment, but she clicked the last two buckles into place and stepped back. The vehicle started up, and she waved as the vehicle backed out, made a three-point turn, and headed up the driveway. The back windows were so dark that Katie couldn't see inside, but she imagined that Penny was returning her wave. The dogs chased the vehicle up to the property line, stopping at the very edge of the driveway. Katie and the dogs watched the vehicle turn onto the highway and disappear down the road.

Katie wondered when she'd see them again. She hoped it would be soon. She was growing attached to the little girl and her quiet, but intense mother. She didn't have long to dwell on the thought, because her phone started buzzing in her pocket. She removed it, reading the screen. It said *George* and displayed a photo of George in his deputy outfit, holding a doughnut and giving her the thumbs up sign.

"Hello."

"Sheriff St. James wants to talk to you. Can you come to the law enforcement center?"

"Why?"

"You know why."

She still hadn't given the sheriff her answer on his job proposal. She'd been avoiding him. That was probably why he'd asked George to call her instead of making the call himself. One call she'd answer, the other she wouldn't.

"I suppose I can't put it off any longer."

"Suppose not."

Katie glanced at her watch. It was a quarter past two o'clock in the afternoon. Ashley would be at the Governor's office. Katie assumed she'd be there for a while, so she did have some free time. "I'll be there in thirty minutes. I'm out at Ashley's place." It would take her close to thirty minutes to get back into town.

"Alright. See you then."

Katie hung up and got into her old Impala, started the engine, and headed toward town. She needed a new car, but her finances weren't in the best shape. Taking the job with the Sheriff would solve that problem, at least.

Once in town, she parked in her usual spot behind the Public Defender's Office. The law enforcement center was down the street, so she opted to walk rather than feed quarters into a parking meter and hope the clock wouldn't count down to zero before the meeting was over.

Katie walked across the street and entered the law enforcement center with a heavy sense of trepidation. Sheriff St. James wanted an answer, but she had none to give. She hadn't spoken to her father about potentially leaving the fledgling family business, and she had no idea how Ashley's meeting had gone with the governor.

"Howdy, ho," George said, tipping an imaginary cap at her. He was standing at the glass partition separating the Sheriff's Department from the main hallway.

"Cute," Katie said.

"You're grumpy." George pressed a button and motioned for Katie to enter.

A lock clicked, sliding out of place, and Katie pulled the door open. "I'm not grumpy. I'm just..." She didn't know what she was; her emotions were all twisted.

"Agitated?"

"No."

"Aggravated."

"No."

"Frustrated."

"I will be if you don't stop," Katie growled.

"Like I said, grumpy," George said as he turned and started down the hallway that led to Sheriff St. James's office. After a few steps, he stopped, turned back to her, and motioned for her to follow.

They stopped a few feet before they reached the Sheriff's open door.

"Are you ready?" George asked.

Katie's hands grew slick with sweat.

"Do you know what you will say?"

Katie shook her head.

That was the problem. She had no idea what to say or do. She wanted this job, but she didn't want it. She missed the uniform, but she also liked the freedom she had while working with Ashley. She wanted to spend more time with George, but she didn't want that to lead to problems in their relationship.

"Don't just stand out there," Sheriff St. James's voice came from the inside of his office. "Come in."

She was out of time. Katie would have to give him an answer. She hoped it would be the right one.

41

ASHLEY

August 22

It was ten o'clock and the courtroom was packed for the hearing on Vivian's motion to dismiss. Several deputies were interspersed throughout the crowd, ready to react if one of the two clear camps for or against Vivian caused problems during the hearing. George Thomanson was among them. Some were in full uniform, and others were in plain clothes.

Ashley sat at defense table at the front area of courtroom, the area reserved for counsel. Vivian was next to her. Katie was not there. Or at least Ashley hadn't seen her yet. Katie had been exceptionally busy with other things that didn't involve Ashley over the past week, which was fine. She didn't work *for* Ashley anymore, but it was odd. It was almost as though she was avoiding Ashley.

Charles Hanson was at the prosecution table, and Bruce was in the gallery, seated directly behind Charles. Ashley saw Bruce when she and Vivian had walked in, and she could still feel his penetrating glares running along the back of her neck. Ashely did the only thing she could; she ignored him.

"How are things going at the new residence?" Ashley said to Vivian.

These few moments before a hearing started were always awkward. She and Vivian had already discussed how the hearing would progress in detail, so all they were left with now was small talk, something Ashley despised. She was an intense person by nature, and small talk was meant to be light. It was a little easier with Vivian, now that they'd spent some time living beneath the same roof.

"It's peaceful. Stephanie has been a gracious host. She's given us an entire wing of her spacious home, far more than Penny and I need. Especially since Penny is still sleeping in my bed."

"Is she still having nightmares?" Ashley asked.

"Every night."

Ashley nodded, unsurprised. The little girl had been tied up and locked in a dark closet. That would make anyone afraid of the dark. "Where is Penny now?"

A content smile spread across Vivian's lips. "Probably following the gardening staff around, pestering them."

"The gardening staff?"

Vivian smiled. "Penny has taken an interest in plants. Stephanie has a large vegetable garden at the edge of her property and many, many flower gardens. At first Penny was interested in the thought of growing her own vegetables. Now she's gotten a bit obsessed. She wants to know everything there is to know about every vegetable."

Ashley studied Vivian as she spoke. It was almost shocking to see the changes in her since she'd gotten away from Bruce. Her pale skin had color. She'd gained some weight. Her cheeks were no longer concave. She still sat up straight, but she held herself in a more relaxed manner, more like a ballerina off the stage rather than one poised and ready to start a show.

"She feels safe," Ashley said. "You both do."

"I wouldn't have left Penny alone if I didn't. Stephanie is staying with her just in case, but Penny has already forged many friendships with the employees and children of employees who live on the property. She's just that kind of kid."

"She is that kind of kid."

They fell into a short silence, then Vivian turned to Ashley and said, "How did your interview with the Governor go?"

Ashley blew out a long breath. "As expected."

The past week had been a long one. She'd heard no news one way or another. She and the Governor had both behaved themselves, but the sense of dislike had flowed evenly in both directions, an ever-present undercurrent just below the surface of polite conversation. Every word exchanged had a passive aggressive edge.

"Is that a bad thing?"

"I think it went as smoothly as possible, which is a good thing. It would still be a minor miracle if she chose me."

Overall, the meeting was uneventful. The Governor asked a bunch of random questions about Ashley's background and her upbringing. She didn't query on anything of substance. They didn't argue, but Ashley left with the feeling that the Governor had already made her choice, and it wasn't her.

"When will you know something?"

Ashley shrugged. She was trying to be nonchalant about it, but that was getting harder with each passing day. Even her steady nerves had their fraying point. "Hopefully soon."

The las thing the Governor had said was that someone would be "in touch." Ashley hadn't yet received her rejection call, but she fully expected it any day now. Until then, she'd remain on edge. Not because she expected anything in her life to change, but there was still a chance, however minute.

"All rise," Judge Steinkamp's court reporter said as she hurried into the courtroom.

Ashley and Vivian rose to their feet as did everyone else in the courtroom. The bench seats creaked and moaned with the movement of bodies. The judge entered a few moments behind his reporter, strutting in and smiling at the crowd. Darren Steinkamp never was lacking in the confidence department. Not even when they were lowly law students. Ashley supposed that hadn't changed since he'd taken the bench.

"The honorable Judge Steinkamp presiding," the court reporter said as she sat in front of her steno machine.

"Hello, everyone," Judge Steinkamp said. "Please take your seats." He lowered himself onto the bench as the remainder of the crowd reclaimed their places and positioned themselves as comfortably as they could in the stuffy courtroom. "We are convened today in State of Iowa versus Vivian Ross, Brine County case number FECR100201. Today, I am hearing the Defendant's motion to dismiss."

"That's bullshit and you know it. You better not rule for her." It was Bruce's voice, Ashley easily recognized it now, but there was a strain to it that she'd never noticed before.

Judge Steinkamp frowned, his gaze frosting over and settling on Bruce. "If you interrupt this proceeding one more time, sir, I'll hold you in contempt of Court and have you escorted out of here in chains. Do you understand?"

There was no response.

"Do you understand?"

Ashley had never heard the Judge, her former law-school boyfriend, get angry. Obviously, she knew he was capable of it, everyone was capable of anger, but she'd never heard it. There was a dangerousness to his voice that said this was no bluff. Another outburst from Bruce would result in incarceration. Contempt held a maximum of six months in the county jail. Ashley hoped that Bruce would interrupt again.

"I understand."

"Are the parties ready to proceed?"

"Yes," Charles said.

"Yes, your honor," Ashley said.

"It's the Defendant's motion, so go ahead and proceed Ms. Montgomery."

Ashley stood, wiping her sweaty palms on her pants. "Thank you, your honor." She had a microphone in front of her, but she didn't need it. The courtroom was completely silent, everyone straining to hear what she would say next.

"My client, Vivian Ross, has been charged with child endangerment causing death. In order to convict my client, the State must prove all elements of the offense beyond a reasonable doubt. One of those elements is that a *child* died."

She paused, taking a slow, steadying breath, then continued. "The Iowa Code defines a child as 'any person under the age of fourteen years.' The word 'person' is not defined in the code. I would urge the court to define a 'person' as someone that is identifiable. Someone who has a birth certificate. If born here in the United States, that person would have a Social Security Card. Corporations can be 'people' for the purpose of the law, but they too have unique identities and are given entity identification numbers and are not 'persons' until they are registered and receive their EIN number."

A throat cleared loudly. The sound came behind Ashley and to her right, behind the prosecution table. Ashley didn't need to turn around to see who had made the noise. Without a doubt, it was Bruce.

"Crimes are prosecuted based on the date that they were allegedly committed. The Statute of Limitations is calculated from that date as well. Here, the State alleges that Vivian Ross committed child endangerment upon her son, Ronald Reagan Ross, between June twenty-fourth, and July thirty-first. However, Ronald Reagan Ross was not born, and therefore not a 'person' until August first."

Another grunt from the right side of the gallery, earning a sharp look from the judge.

"All elements of every offense must be present on the date of the offense. Not the day before, not the hour before. Ronald Reagan Ross's birth certificate states that he was born on August first. Therefore, the State is missing the element of 'child' in child endangerment, and the defense moves to dismiss the charge against Vivian Ross."

Ashley lowered herself into her seat, folding her hands together in front of her.

"I'll hear the State's position now," Judge Steinkamp said, turning his gaze upon Charles Hanson.

Charles lumbered to his feet, stood there for a moment, the room in complete silence, then cleared his throat and began speaking. "Ms. Montgomery is correct that the Iowa Code defines a child as any 'person' under the age of fourteen. She is incorrect on her definition of a 'person.' The State's position is that a 'person' is anyone, including unborn children."

"From what point?" Judge Steinkamp said. He was leaning on the bench with his head propped on one hand, studying Charles with interest.

"From what point?"

"Yes. In your view, at what point does an 'unborn child' become a person?"

"At conception," Charles said. His response was automatic, and expected, but it also felt like a trap to Ashley. The judge was backing him into a corner.

"By your definition, you could be prosecuting a lot of potential mothers who have no idea they are even pregnant yet. How is a woman supposed to know she is pregnant before she's missed her period?"

Charles's round face flushed red. "Well, umm, they should take tests."

Judge Steinkamp smiled, but it had no mirth. "When should they take these tests? Daily? Or perhaps they should refrain from intercourse completely."

Charles's face darkened to a nearly crimson shade.

"And what about the men in their lives? Should they be charged with aiding and abetting child endangerment for pouring their wife a glass of wine?"

"Well, no, but—"

"Doesn't the father have the same obligation to ensure the safety of that child?" He used air quotes around the word "child."

"Not exactly."

"So, then, children belong to their mothers. Why do courts provide shared care to so many couples in child custody matters, then?"

"I, umm," Charles tugged at his collar.

"And I've yet to see a father bring a pregnant mother into court, demanding custody. How, on earth, could he have custody?"

"Well, your honor—"

Judge Steinkamp put up a hand, silencing Charles. "I've heard enough. I'm prepared to rule. The State is missing a primary element in this offense. The Defendant's motion is granted. The case against Vivian Ross is dismissed with court costs assessed to the State."

"*What?*"

This time Ashley did turn to see Bruce Ross, standing up at the partition separating the gallery from the front of the courtroom, his nostrils flaring.

"You will take your seat, sir," Judge Steinkamp said, his tone even, but low.

"I will not. This is preposterous. That woman. *That woman,*" he pointed an accusatory finger at Vivian, "murdered my son. And you are simply dismissing her charges? What kind of kangaroo court is this?"

"One that will be holding you in contempt if you don't shut your mouth and do as you are told."

Bruce ignored the warning. "That woman should go to prison for the rest of her life!"

"Deputy," the judge said, his gaze focusing on Bruce. "Cuff him and bring him up here."

This was not good for Bruce.

George Thomanson sprang up, grabbed Bruce's wrists, and handcuffed him. He was smiling as he hauled Bruce up to the front of the courtroom. He looked like he was enjoying it as much as Ashley.

"I find you in contempt of Court, Mr. Ross," Judge Steinkamp said. "You have violated a lawful Court order on multiple occasions, despite my reminders to control your outbursts. I sentence you to six days in jail."

"But I—"

"You can start serving your sentence immediately." Judge Steinkamp stood and left the courtroom through the back door.

The gallery remained silent despite the Judge's departure. George hauled Bruce down the aisle toward the back door and the jail. Bruce resisted the entire time, but George was far stronger.

"It's kinda nice watching someone manhandle him," Vivian said.

"Yes, it is."

"Thank you for this," Vivian nodded toward the empty Judge's bench. "I never gave you the respect you deserved before I ended up needing you."

"Nobody ever does," Ashley rose to her feet.

"I'm sorry—"

"No apologies. I get it. I'm a public defender. It goes with the territory. I kinda like being the underdog." Ashley stood and motioned for Vivian to do the same. "Let's get out of here, shall we? Before news stations catch wind of what just happened and descend upon us like a bunch of vultures."

"Nice visual."

"Thanks."

Ashley led Vivian through the crowd and out the back of the court-room. They exited the courthouse through a side door rarely used by others. There would be press out front. This was the best way to avoid them. The less time Vivian spent in front of cameras, the better. Her ordeal was over, and it was time for her to start a new life, not dwell on the past one.

42

KATIE

August 29

Katie was taking the job with the Sheriff's Department. She was rushed when making the decision, but now that she had more time to reflect, she knew it was the right choice. She belonged in law enforcement. It was in her nature. Now that she'd taken the new position, she'd spent the last week doing her part to wind down the business, and her father would take it from there.

Katie's father had taken the news of her departure surprisingly well. He was a businessman, not an investigator, and they weren't making money. He was ready to pivot, and so was she, but they'd stayed quiet, barely treading water, both afraid to raise the topic with one another. They'd both learned something in that moment. Communication was important. In the end, the dissolution of their business would ultimately make their father-daughter relationship stronger.

Ashley had also been surprisingly receptive of the news. All she'd said was, *I get it. But don't turn into an asshole again.* Katie had hated Ashley back when she was a police officer, but that was because she didn't understand Ashley's job. Now she did, and she would never treat Ashley poorly again. It was easy for Katie to make that promise.

Today was her first day in the brown uniform of a deputy sheriff. She was on her way to the law enforcement center to get things set up in her office, her actual office. As a police officer she'd always been stuck in a flimsy cubicle. As a member of the sheriff's department, she had four solid walls and a door with a placard hanging outside that read *Katie Mickey, Sergeant.*

Katie's new career would come with different routines, odd hours, and unexpected deadlines. To maintain her friendship with Ashley, she needed to create a routine that included her. That's why she decided to stop by the public defender's office before heading to her new office. It was eight o'clock, and Ashley's car was parked in the back parking lot, as always. Katie parked next to it and used her key to come through the back door. Ashley was at her desk, flipping through some documents in a file. Katie rapped her knuckles on the open doorframe, and Ashley gasped, her gaze darting to Katie.

"Jesus, Katie," Ashley said, releasing a heavy breath. "You scared the crap out of me."

"Sorry."

Ashley's gaze darted to her cradled phone. "Elena didn't say you were here."

"I came through the back." Katie held up her keys and entered the office, dropping into one of the chairs across from Ashley's desk. "I suppose I should be returning these now."

"You'd better," Ashley said with a mischievous smile. "You work for the enemy now."

"I thought we weren't doing that me versus you thing again."

"We aren't."

"Good. Because I'd like to start stopping by here in the morning. I know we can't talk shop anymore, but we'll find something to argue about, I'm sure."

"Obviously." Ashley said. "There's no one in the world I'd rather spend my time fighting with."

"Good." They were silent for a moment, then Katie said, "So, how was Vivian's hearing last week?"

Katie had missed Vivian's hearing. She'd been stuck in a private job, her last one ever. The rest of the week had flown by with both Ashley and Katie busier than ever, Ashley with news stations wanting to interview her about Vivian's case, and Katie with winding down her business.

"I heard Bruce lost his shit and the Judge sentenced him to serve six days in jail." Katie wasn't there, but gossip in Brine spread like wildfire and she had seen the news reports.

Ashley nodded. "That definitely happened."

"Speaking of judges, have you heard from the Governor?"

"No. And I'm starting to get irritated. Tomorrow is the last day for her to announce her decision, and she still hasn't called me to say I didn't get it."

"Why are you so certain that she didn't choose you?"

"Because I am." Ashley said with a huff.

Just then, Ashley's phone starting ringing. She picked it up. "Hi, Elena," she said into the receiver. She paused for a minute then said, "Who is it? Katie's here." There was another pause, then she said, "Alright. Patch them through." She turned to Katie and said, "Speak of the devil. Every time you stop and mention someone's name, they call. Why is that?"

Katie shrugged. She'd obviously done nothing, but that was how it had worked with Bruce as well. They'd been discussing him, and he called to threaten Ashley. Katie had been there and able to record it, which led to some of his charges now pending. The guy was looking at spending the rest of his life in prison.

"This is Ashley Montgomery," Ashley said. A moment passed and she pressed the speaker phone button, cradling the receiver and pressing her finger to her lips to indicate that Katie should stay silent.

"Yes, Ashley, this is Beatrice at Governor Ingram's office."

"Yes, hello Beatrice, so lovely to *finally* hear from you again." Ashley wasn't even attempting to hide her sarcasm.

"Yes, well, we've had some hiccups on our end."

"Oh?" Ashley leaned forward. "Do tell."

"That's not important," Beatrice said.

"Right."

"I'm calling to tell you that the Governor has selected you for the position."

Ashley was taking a sip of coffee at the time, and she choked, spitting it back into the cup.

"Hello?" Beatrice said. "Did you hear me?"

"I heard you. But I don't think I heard you right. Did you say the Governor chose me?"

"Yes."

"Why?"

"That's a good question," Beatrice said dryly. "The truth is that she didn't have a choice. Your competitor, Magistrate Makala Mirko withdrew her name, leaving Governor Ingram no choice. You were the only option."

"Wow, okay," Ashley said, her expression stunned.

"Congratulations," Beatrice said with no excitement.

"Umm, yeah. Thanks."

"Court administration will be in touch about scheduling your investiture. Have a good day."

"Yeah," Ashley said, slowly leaning forward, raising, and lowering the phone receiver to hang up.

An investiture would be Ashley's swearing in ceremony. After that, she would officially don the black robe and become a judge. She was dumbstruck. She'd applied for the position, but only at Judge Ahrenson's urging. She had never truly believed she'd be selected.

"You got it!" Katie said, a surge of excitement bursting within her.

Now, more than ever, she was thankful she'd taken the position with the Sheriff's Office. Ashley would not be a public defender for much longer, which would have placed the private investigations firm in more financial trouble. They wouldn't have survived. Without that concern, Katie could be properly happy for her friend.

"I guess I did."

"You did!"

"I wonder why Makala withdrew her name."

"What does it matter? You got it!"

Ashley still seemed too stunned to talk and they fell into silence.

The screech of Katie's new deputy radio cut through the quiet, a frantic dispatcher's voice filling the room. "*All cars. Calling all cars.*" It was alarming in the silence, and more so because of the desperation coming from the dispatcher. Dispatchers were professionals. Their job was to remain calm. This was completely out of the ordinary.

Katie reached to her shoulder and pressed the buttons to respond. "This is Katie Mickey. What's going on?"

"We have an active shooter situation."

"Where?"

"At the elementary school."

43

ASHLEY

Penny. That was Ashley's first thought. She'd started kindergarten the week earlier. Ashley's gaze shifted to the clock at the bottom corner of her computer screen, hoping it was too early for children to be there. No such luck. It was nine o'clock in the morning. School would have already started.

"I'm on my way," Katie said into the radio as she shot to her feet and headed toward the door.

Ashley followed close behind, frantically dialing Vivian's number. She'd barely brought the phone to her ear when Vivian picked up.

"Hello."

"Where are you?" Ashley demanded.

"I'm at Stephanie's house," Vivian said. There was a short hesitation and then she said, "Why? Has something happened?"

"Is Penny with you?"

Ashley's mind told her that, no, there was no way Penny would have skipped school, but her heart hoped that Penny had caught a cold that prevented her from attending.

"No. She started school last week. Why?"

"There's an active shooter. At the school."

Vivian gasped.

"I'm on my way there now. Katie is, too."

"Bruce," Vivian groaned. "He got out of jail yesterday…"

She didn't need to say more. He would be desperate for revenge. They'd defeated him—his wife and a lowly public defender—and he wanted to even the score. He believed that Vivian killed his child. He was probably at the elementary school to return the favor.

"I'll be there as soon as I can," Vivian said. "Please, do anything you can."

"I will," Ashley promised.

She jumped in her car and followed Katie down the street to the elementary school. The entire area was lit up with red and blue flashing lights. Deputies surrounded the scene, trying to determine a way to gain access. Katie jumped out of her car and raced toward the line of deputies. Sheriff St. James was beside his vehicle talking to the prosecutor, Charles Hanson. That's where Ashley headed.

"It's Bruce Ross, isn't it?" Ashley said when she reached the prosecutor and the Sheriff.

"You're a defense attorney, Ashley, we can't tell you that kind of stuff."

"Not for long," Ashley growled. "You'll be calling me 'your honor' here pretty soon, so shut the fuck up with all that red tape bullshit and tell me what is happening here."

Sheriff St. James and Charles exchanged a look, then Charles turned to her and issued an awkward, "Congratulations." He, too, had gone for that position, but he didn't make it through committee.

"Shut up with that and tell me what I want to know." It was asinine that anyone would bother wasting words with congratulations at a time like this.

"Most of the children are out," the Sheriff said after releasing a heavy breath. "It seems that the shooter was looking for one child in particular."

"Penny."

"Umm, no. A child by the name Nancy Ross."

"That's Penny," Ashley said, the air whooshing out of her as though she'd been struck in the stomach. "Her friends call her that."

"The shooter has released all the children and the teachers except for the kindergarten class."

"The shooter is Bruce Ross," Ashley said. This time she had no doubt.

She didn't need verification. He was the only person who would single Penny out amongst a crowd of kids.

Sheriff St. James nodded.

"Get a search warrant," Ashley said.

"A what?"

"Get a search warrant for that damn garage," Ashley said. "The one on Bruce Ross's property. Send two deputies out there to search the place."

"Why?"

"Because we need to know what kind of arsenal he has. Does he have explosives or is it only firearms? What kind of firearms? How long has he been planning this assault? Did he leave any clue as to his end game? If the answers to any of those questions exist, they will be in that garage."

Sheriff St. James nodded.

"I'm going in there," Ashley said, her gaze settling on the front door to the school.

"Oh, no you're not," the Sheriff said. "You're going to get yourself shot."

"If it stops him from shooting Penny or some other child, that's a risk I'm willing to take."

Ashley took off running toward the building before the Sheriff could say anything more. Katie tried to stop her as she ran past, grabbing her by the arm, but she shook herself free, intent on getting inside. When Katie couldn't stop Ashley, she started following.

"What do you think you are going to do?" Katie said just before they pushed the front doors open and entered the eerily silent building.

"I don't know," Ashley whispered, "but we aren't going to stand around and wait for Bruce to put a bullet in Penny's head."

"Let me go first," Katie whispered back, unholstering her service pistol and dropping into a crouch.

Ashley mimicked her movements—minus the gun—and followed close behind.

They made their way down the hall, following colorful signs with dancing zoo animals and arrows indicating the direction of the kindergarten room. When they reached the door to the room, they found that it was still ajar, and they could see inside. The children were hiding beneath their desks, and Bruce Ross was circling the room, looking under each desk, looking for his daughter.

"Come out, come out wherever you are," Bruce said through gritted teeth. He had an assault rifle in one hand and extra magazines in a pouch around his waist. He was dressed in full camouflage, like a military man ready for battle. His chest was larger, more pronounced, a bulletproof vest, no doubt. Bruce had come prepared.

Where did he get all this stuff? Ashley wondered. She felt sure the answer would be discovered through the search warrant.

"We need a distraction," Katie whispered. "Before he gets to Penny."

"Are you sure?" Ashley whispered back.

"He wants Penny, that's all. He won't hurt these other kids."

Ashley nodded. She could provide a distraction. Easy enough. She'd probably get shot in the process, but Bruce was a lawyer, not a soldier. He had to be a terrible shot, right? She hoped so, because that was the only way she would going to live through what she was about to do.

44

ASHLEY

Ashley nodded, her expression forming into one of grim determination. Then she straightened and leaned forward, ready to take a step into the doorframe.

"What are you doing," Katie whispered. "I meant a distraction from outside. Not us."

Ashley lifted a foot to step forward.

"Do not do that. It's suicide. It's stupid."

"We're way past that, Katie. Penny needs us, and stupid is our only option." Ashley took a step forward, exposing half of her body in the open doorway. Then she kicked the doorframe.

Bruce's head jerked up, taking his attention, at least momentarily, away from the kids. His gaze fell on Ashley, and a small smile flicked into the corners of his mouth. "Ashley Montgomery. What a surprise."

"Two lawyers enter a school...," Ashley said, taking another step forward, exposing herself further. "It sounds like the start to a bad lawyer joke, doesn't it?"

He raised the barrel of the gun, "And only one came out."

Panic rose inside Ashley's chest, but she tamped it down. If this was where she died, so be it. Everyone died. It was part of living. "That doesn't sound very funny. Which one of us comes out?"

"I think you know the answer to that."

"Do I? I mean, what's your end game here? Murder suicide?"

"Suicide? Why would I do that?"

"You can't possibly think you are walking out of here with your reputation intact. You have enough problems with the charges stemming from Oliver hitting Bambi with your car, but at least you had the staunch pro-life people that might have your back on that one. But nobody, and I mean nobody, supports a school shooting. It's senseless."

"I don't care about my reputation."

"What do you care about?"

"Revenge."

"And then what? I mean, really, think about it. If you shoot Penny now, if you shoot me, then you have your revenge, but what next? Is this vengeful moment the highlight of your life? If so, you might as well kill yourself afterwards since things will only go downhill from there."

Bruce lowered the gun and pressed a hand to his forehead, he shook his head several times, pressed his eyes closed, then reopened them slowly. Watching him felt like watching a tense scene in a horror movie. He was the definition of unhinged, barely hanging on to some version of reality.

"What are you doing here?" Bruce said after a long silence.

"What are you doing here, Bruce? What are any of us doing here?"

"You know why I'm here. She killed my child; you destroyed the punishment. I can't let Vivian go on thinking she didn't do anything wrong. I'm getting even."

"Okay," Ashley lifted her arms. "Then shoot me instead."

45

KATIE

What the hell is she doing? Katie thought, frantically trying to assess the situation. Bruce didn't shoot Ashley at that moment, but he didn't need an invitation. One wrong move here and they were all dead. Ashley needed to be more careful with her words, but there was no way for Katie to communicate with her.

"So, what happens next?" Ashley asked, her gaze focused on Bruce rather than the gun. Thankfully, it was still at his side, pointed toward the floor.

Bruce cocked an eyebrow. "What, you don't have a plan?"

Katie crouched down, counting the students under the desks. She counted twenty and one teacher. It didn't feel like there was any way Katie could get everyone out alive. Not while Bruce was still breathing. She could try and shoot him, but that plan was problematic. Bruce wore a bulletproof vest. That meant the only shots that Katie had were to the head, arms, and legs. These were not easy targets even if Bruce stood perfectly still. Katie was trained with firearms, but it had been a while since she'd used one. Her skills were rusty.

All she could do was watch and wait. To shoot would be to risk missing and that would only anger Bruce, making him more likely to kill everyone in the room. So, she watched the conversation from the doorway, a sense of helplessness hanging over her. Then she noticed something. Ashley was slowly inching farther into the room as they spoke, pulling Bruce's attention away from the doorway.

There were several desks near the door. Katie could see little bodies crouched beneath them. She lowered down so she was eye level with the nearest child. It was a little girl with wide, dark eyes, chestnut brown skin, and tight, curly hair. She was visibly shaking. Katie caught her attention, then motioned for her to crawl toward the doorway. At first, the girl seemed too frightened to move, but then she took a deep breath, released it, then began moving toward the door. It was only a few feet and Katie nervously watched Bruce the entire time, but he was too engrossed in his conversation with Ashley to notice the fleeing girl.

When the little girl reached Katie, she pulled her out of the doorway and dropped to her knees to look her over.

"Are you hurt?"

"N...n...no. I don't think so," the girl whispered back.

"Do you know your way out?"

The child nodded.

"Go outside. There are deputies there who will protect you. But don't make any noise as you leave. Okay?"

The little girl nodded, then silently began sprinting toward the front door, her tiny feet barely touching the tiles.

Katie turned her attention back to the room, focusing on the next desk. There was a little boy under that one. He had brown hair and deep, baleful eyes. His knees were pulled tightly to his chest.

"Can you crawl to me?" She whispered to the boy.

A cheer rang out from the crowd outside. The little girl had made it out, and the onlookers were celebrating.

Shit. Shit. Shit, Katie thought. It was not time for celebration. One child saved left twenty others at risk. Katie could not lose twenty people. Not on her first day as a deputy. Not ever.

"What was that?" Bruce said, moving toward the side window to look out.

The blinds were closed. Bruce didn't fully open them; he used his fingers to make a hole in them so he could peek out. Katie assumed he was paranoid someone outside would try to shoot him through the window. That was an impossible shot, considering his bulletproof vest, but he didn't seem to know that, and that was just fine with Katie. It meant his attention was away from Ashley and the children. If Katie could get a couple of the closer kids to come to her, she could—

"Run!" Ashley suddenly shouted.

The room erupted into noise, chairs moving, desks dumping over, people, children sprinting toward the door. Katie jumped inside before they clogged the doorway. She ran toward Ashley, toward Bruce, dodging people as she moved. There was no gunfire yet, and Katie discovered the reason when she made it to the spot where Bruce and Ashley had been standing near the window. Ashley was on top of him, wrestling him for the gun. He wasn't in good shape, but he was stronger than Ashley. It was only a matter of time before he regained control of the weapon.

Katie dashed to their side. Bruce had no idea that she was there. His singular focus was on Ashley. She had to end this dangerous wrestling match, and quickly. Katie flipped her service pistol around and brought the butt of it down hard on Bruce's face. There was a sickening *crunch*, and Bruce's body went still.

Ashley wrenched the gun out of Bruce's hands, rolled back and hopped to her feet, panting hard. "Took you long enough," she said after a few breaths.

"You're a psychopath, you know that, right?"

"Yeah."

"You could have gotten everyone, including yourself, killed."

"But I didn't."

Katie sighed heavily and shook her head. Her gaze settled on Bruce's crumpled form. He looked so small and frail like that, unconscious and unable to speak. "I hope he's not dead."

"We can agree to disagree on that one."

Bruce's eyes fluttered and he groaned, reaching a hand toward his head. Blood ran steadily from a wound in his skull. It was hard to tell if the injury was serious. Head wounds always bled so much, no matter the severity.

A loud cheering came from the crowd outside. The group of students and their teacher had made it out.

Katie's phone buzzed in her pocket. It was an unknown number, but she answered anyway.

"You turned off your radio," Sheriff St. James said.

"It's hard to sneak up on someone with a radio squawking."

"That was dangerous."

"I know."

"What's going on in there?"

"The shooter is down."

"I didn't hear any shots."

"I didn't shoot him. I hit him. We need medical in here. He doesn't look good."

"Is the scene clear?"

"Yeah."

"Sending in the Calvary."

"Thanks," Katie said, hanging up the phone.

"The others are on their way inside," Katie said, turning her attention to Ashley. "Give me that gun before someone comes in here and shoots you."

Ashley handed her the gun. She seemed relieved to have it out of her hands. A moment later, deputies and emergency medical technicians streamed into the room.

"Well, should we go check on Penny?" Katie asked Ashley. Bruce wasn't their problem anymore. The other deputies had him covered.

"I thought you'd never ask."

They made their way outside, side by side. They pushed the doors open in tandem. The sudden burst of bright sunlight assaulted Katie's eyes, causing her to shield them. A second later, a cheer rang out. It was a roaring sound, like cheers at a sporting event or a concert. Katie looked around; her eyes were now adjusted to the light. Hundreds of people were huddled around the parking lot, all cheering for Katie and Ashley. Somehow, against all odds, they had become the heroes of the day.

There, at the center of the crowd, was Vivian and Penny. Vivian clung to her little girl like a life preserver. Tears stained Penny's cheeks, but she was safe and she was whole. She would be okay. They would all be okay.

46

KATIE

Next comes the good part, Katie thought. Now that she was in the brown uniform of a deputy, she would interview Bruce Ross in the school shooting investigation. The stakes weren't high, they had plenty of evidence to convict Bruce without a confession, and that made the job even sweeter. No matter how she approached it, she couldn't go wrong.

"Do you want to go in alone?" Sheriff St. James asked.

Katie, George, and Sheriff St. James stood outside the interview room, watching Bruce fidget with his wrist restraints. He was in one of the flimsy, blue plastic chairs. The deputy that had placed him in the room had switched his restraints, so his arms were now cuffed in front. It allowed him to sit more comfortably, but still told him *you are ours now*.

"No," Katie said. The answer came automatically, without much thought.

"No?" The sheriff lifted an eyebrow.

"I want George with me."

"I figured you'd want to take this one on your own. It was your arrest," the Sheriff had said. "You should have all the glory."

She hadn't intended to share in the glory either, but now that the words were out there, she knew it was the right approach. "This isn't about me. It's about those kids. We don't need a confession, but every little bit helps."

"But why George?" The sheriff's gaze shifted to George beside him, "No offense."

"None taken," George said. And he really didn't sound offended. He seemed surprised by Katie's response as well.

"We work well together. We always have. At least up until he turned into an asshole when he was selected as detective. But that was a long time ago, and this time I'm his superior. I *know* I won't let the rank difference go to my head."

"Now, that, I take offense to," George said, but his smile didn't falter.

"Alright, you two love birds get in there and get a confession," Sheriff St. James said.

Katie took a deep breath, exchanged one last look with George, then pulled the door open and entered the room.

"Oh, good, someone's here, these handcuffs are digging into my wrists..." Bruce's voice trailed off as his gaze fell upon Katie. Several emotions flitted across his features, there one moment, then gone the next. The relief melted into surprise, then twisted into rage. "What the hell? *You* don't work for the Sheriff's Department."

"I didn't," Katie said. She smiled in a sardonic way that would have made Ashley proud. "But I do now. You don't know this, but I was the one who hit you on the head inside the school."

"My head hurts. I need to see a medic."

"You've seen a medic," George said. "They cleared you. You had a little bump on your head, but you'll be just fine."

"I want to see a doctor, not some stupid, uneducated EMT."

"Education isn't everything," Katie said, dropping into the chair across from Bruce. "Look at you. You are one of the most educated people in this county, and you're in chains."

"I'm thirsty," Bruce said.

"We're going to chat for a minute, and then I'll get you some water. How's that?" George said.

Katie would have preferred to let the guy suffer, but George had always been a softer soul than her. That was one of the reasons they worked so well together. He was the good guy, she the bad bitch.

"I had a look around your garage," George said.

"You can't go in there without a search warrant."

"Oh, we had a warrant." He slid a document across the table. It was a copy of the search warrant. "Do you know what we found in there?"

"No."

George slid a second document across the table. It was the list of property seized. Bruce didn't even look at it.

"You had quite the operation going with Oliver Banks and Miranda Birch."

"I don't know what you are talking about." Bruce's words broke at the end, indicating the opposite.

Katie was the only person in the room who didn't know, and she was interested to find out. She hadn't been part of the execution of the search warrant. She'd been inside the elementary school, trying to save the children and keep Ashley from getting herself killed.

"Well, drugs to start. You had quite the pharmacy going there. Cocaine, meth, mushrooms," he ticked the items off, raising a finger and holding it up with each new substance. "Ecstasy, Propofol, and many, many other prescription painkillers."

Bruce grunted, but he didn't deny the accusation.

"And that's not all. I wish it was all. Do you know what else we found?"

"No."

Katie leaned forward in her seat.

"Guns. Lots and lots of guns. Sawed off shotguns, illegal silencers, armor piercing ammunition, assault rifles, ghost guns, and much, much more."

"I don't know anything about that."

"Well, see, here's the problem with that," George said. "Oliver and Miranda were there when we executed the search warrant. Caught red handed, so to say." He turned to Katie. "Where does that phrase come from? Caught red handed?"

Katie shrugged. "Maybe it comes from someone caught with blood on their hands after a murder?"

"That's plausible," George said with a nod. "Remind me to look that up when we are done with him," he nodded toward Bruce.

"Sure thing."

"Anyway, where were we?" George tapped a finger against his chin. "Oh, yeah. Your little buddies, Miranda and Oliver. They knew they were caught, and you know what they did?"

"No."

"They did the only thing they could to save their skins. They ratted you out."

"They are liars."

"I thought you might say that. Except, you see, you're a lawyer. An educated sort of person. Someone used to keeping ledgers and logs, tracking profits and losses."

Georges eyes widened.

"That wasn't kept in the garage, I know, but Miranda told us it was at her place. She took us right to it. Want to see it?"

"No."

George produced a clear evidence bag. Inside, was a composite notebook. The bag was large enough for George to open the notebook and display the pages without taking it out of the bag. "See here," he pointed to a page. "This is your handwriting. I'm sure we can find plenty of writing samples to compare it to at that law office of yours. Or should I say your former law office? I hear your partners have pushed you out. Damage control or something. It might be a little late to completely save their reputations, but better late than never."

Bruce glared at him.

"You've got state charges, but guns and drugs," George shook his head, "that's federal stuff. If you don't do the rest of your life in prison on our charges, the feds will pick up from there."

Bruce's face reddened, and his expression grew mutinous, but that only lasted a moment. All the fight seemed to leak out of him a moment later. "I wasn't making any money practicing law."

"That tends to happen when you don't go to the office," Katie said.

Bruce ignored her. "Miranda and Oliver approached me with a proposition. I already had a setup that would work out there at the garage, and a reason people would come and go regularly. I could say they were coming for legal consultations. We set thirty-minute meetings and sent people on their way. It worked well."

"Until you lost your mind," Katie grumbled. "Or maybe it was gone before then."

Bruce shrugged. He didn't seem remorseful for any of his actions, only that he'd been caught.

"I don't care why you did it, why you sold the guns, drugs, or even why you invaded a school and emotionally scarred those children for life. The *why* doesn't matter to me. What I want to know is *how*. How did you get into the school? It should have been locked."

"Oliver."

"What?"

"The school janitor is one of our clients. We gave him a good deal on a bunch of stuff. In exchange, he gave me a copy of the key. He gave it to me before Vivian killed my baby, but I had already known I might need some leverage. Vivian had already tried to kill Ronald, so I prepared my revenge in case she succeeded."

Katie thought back to all those weeks ago when she witnessed Oliver handing Bruce something small. It was the same day she'd taken the pictures of Vivian running on the treadmill. That felt like a lifetime ago, but it was only a matter of weeks.

"Well, thank you for that," Katie said, rising to her feet. "That's all the information I need."

"Wait, that's it? Aren't you going to let me out or give me house arrest or something?"

Katie was already walking toward the door, George following at her heels. She stopped and turned back to Bruce, another sarcastic smile tugging at the corners of her mouth. "Now, why would we do that?"

Then she turned and left the room, George following behind her. Bruce was shouting something, but she paid him no attention. She had everything she needed. Their case against Bruce was airtight. He would never harm anyone ever again.

EPILOGUE

ASHLEY

September 29

The day had come for Ashley's swearing in ceremony. It was held at the courthouse. Everyone who mattered was there. Katie and George sat together. They were now openly and officially a couple. Katie's father, Michael Michello, a felon and a good man sat on Katie's other side.

Rachel Arkman, Ashley's once client turned roommate turned daughter that she never had, sat next to her aunt, Stephanie, a person Ashley had once hated, but had now learned to begrudgingly respect. Tom Archie, Ashley's former boyfriend, was beside Rachel. They'd formed a relationship working together on the mental health response team, back before Rachel left the job to enter law school.

Ashley's gaze snagged on Tom, and he gave her a tentative smile. She returned the gesture with a broad smile of her own. He'd once broken her heart, but that was in the past. Time truly did heal all wounds, but it hadn't stifled the flame she'd been carrying for him. Even after all these years, she could feel it burning within her chest. Judging by the widening of his smile, he felt it, too.

Elena, Ashley's office manager, sat next to Tom. She was still young, but no longer a girl. She'd grown into a beautiful, strong woman. Now that

Ashley was becoming a judge, she didn't know what would happen with the public defender's office in Brine. That would be up to the main office in Des Moines. They could try and replace Ashley, but the more likely outcome was that they would close the office entirely. Elena knew the risk to her job, but still she beamed with joy for Ashley. She'd always been such a selfless person.

Sitting front row and center were two of Ashley's new favorite people, Vivian and Penny Ross. Ashley had seen them several times since the school shooting, and the two had been more inseparable than ever. Today was no different. They were pressed together, every part of their bodies touching from their shoulders to the tip of Penny's toes. One day they would loosen their hold on one another and experience a little independence, but for now, they were working through the trauma together.

Judge Ahrenson stood next to Ashley at the front of the courtroom. He had taken senior status, so he remained on the bench. She'd chosen him as the judge to preside over the ceremony. He was the one who had encouraged her to take this leap and apply for the position. It was only fitting that he be the one to place the black robe in her hands.

"Is everyone ready to proceed?" Judge Ahrenson said, his voice clear and concise.

The room full of people dropped into a reverent silence.

"Bring the judges in," Judge Ahrenson said.

A procession of judges then entered the courtroom through the door leading to judge's chambers. It included every district court, district associate court, and magistrate court judge in the district, including Judge Steinkamp, Ashley's law school ex-boyfriend. He winked at her as he entered the courtroom, and she fought the urge to roll her eyes. He was married. She'd heard he wasn't happily married, but that didn't matter to her. There was no chance they'd ever get back together. There was no spark between them, not like there was with Tom.

Judge Ahrenson started the proceeding, giving a long speech about Ashley's accomplishments. She tried not to blush, but she was unsuccessful. When he finished speaking, he handed her the black robe and she slipped it over her shoulders. It was a perfect fit, as expected. Court administration had taken her exact measurements. The robe was meant to be perfect, and it was exactly that.

"Is there anything you want to say, Ashley?"

Ashley had thought about what she might say for days now, and words always seemed to escape her. But she couldn't just say "thank you," and then sit down. That wouldn't do the situation justice.

She took the microphone from Judge Ahrenson and sighed heavily. "I have no idea what to say, so I'll have to wing it."

Several people smiled, and Ashley was encouraged.

"Everyone here has been a part of my journey to this position. I want to thank you. Even those of you who were real assholes to me at the start."

Everyone laughed.

"I'm talking to you, George and Katie."

The laughter grew louder.

"But here we are. All friends. You showed up for me, even though I only marginally deserve it. I don't take this position lightly. I'll do my best to get things right every time on the first try. Thank you."

She handed the microphone back to Judge Ahrenson, covertly wiping away a tear before sitting down in the front row next to Penny. Ashley had always hated being the center of attention, but she supposed she was going to have to get over that.

Judge Ahrenson brought the proceeding to a close, and he formally invited everyone to celebrate Ashley's ascension to the bench at Mikey's Tavern, a small hole-in-the-wall bar in downtown Brine, but still the best in town. As everyone got up to leave, Ashley approached the one person she had been meaning to speak to for over a month.

"Magistrate Mirko," Ashley said as the magistrate passed her. "Can I have a word with you?"

"Call me Makala," the magistrate said, a smile spreading across her features, "your honor."

"Call me Ashley." She could feel her cheeks flushing red. It would take a while to get used to the new title. She didn't feel any more honorable than she had the day before or the year before.

"Okay, Ashley."

"Why did you withdraw your name? The governor was going to choose you."

"I did it because it was the right thing. I knew she was going to choose me, and you deserved it more."

"She'll never pick you for the district court bench. Never. She's pissed you stole her ability to choose."

Mikala shrugged. "I know. And that's fine. I never wanted that position. I like my job as a part-time magistrate. I can maintain my private practice. I only applied because Judge Ahrenson told me to."

"What?" Ashley raised an eyebrow, her gaze cutting to the old judge. He was talking to Judge Steinkamp and laughing heartily.

"He knew you'd do something to screw up your chances. So, we devised this plan. I'd try to get through committee then withdraw my name."

"That's devious."

"Maybe," Mikala said, her eyes twinkling with delight, "but the Governor isn't the only one who can play politics. If she thinks she can control the judicial system, she's got another thing coming."

"Well, I'll make sure she's disappointed in me every day," Ashley said with a laugh.

Makala patted her on the shoulder. "I wouldn't expect anything less."

Ashley's gaze traveled across the courtroom. This place had been her home for so many years. She'd defined herself at that defense table, built a career as a defense attorney. That was all changing now. She hadn't realized she needed something different, but now that she was here, she knew that it was right. She was ready for this next step in her career. She'd impacted lives as a defense attorney, and she could do so much more as a judge.

MOLLY SAND MUST DIE

Molly Sand must die..
And someone will make it happen.

Trapped in a suffocating marriage, Molly Sand's life is spiraling into chaos. With her controlling husband's grip tightening, she is desperate to break free and escape with her children. But beneath her fragile facade, a fire burns, fueling her overwhelming urge to shed the realities of her current life...even if it means descending into the darkest recesses of her psyche.

Angel Malone, a skilled attorney, finds herself caught in the vortex of her own imploding marriage. Weary of shouldering the financial burden and enduring her husband's increasing instability, she's pushed to confront her own vulnerabilities. As Angel struggles to safeguard herself and her children, a fateful meeting binds her path with Molly's...hurtling both women down a collision course with fate.

Prepare to be immersed in the heart-stopping tale of infidelity and danger crafted by attorney Laura Snider. In this gripping thriller, the boundaries blur between right and wrong, and the pursuit of justice takes an unpredictable twist.

ABOUT THE AUTHOR

Laura Snider is a practicing lawyer in Iowa. She graduated from Drake Law School in 2009 and spent most of her career as a Public Defender. Throughout her legal career she has been involved in all levels of crimes from petty thefts to murders. These days she is working part-time as a pros-ecutor and spends the remainder of her time writing stories and creating characters.

Laura lives in Iowa with her husband, three children, two dogs, and two very mischievous cats.

Sign up for Laura Snider's newsletter at
severnriverbooks.com/authors/laura-snider